SHE MAKES IT LOOK EASY

— A NOVEL —

MARYBETH WHALEN

David C Cook®

transforming lives together

SHE MAKES IT LOOK EASY
Published by David C Cook
4050 Lee Vance View
Colorado Springs, CO 80918 U.S.A.

David C Cook Distribution Canada
55 Woodslee Avenue, Paris, Ontario, Canada N3L 3E5

David C Cook U.K., Kingsway Communications
Eastbourne, East Sussex BN23 6NT, England

David C Cook and the graphic circle C logo
are registered trademarks of Cook Communications Ministries.

The website addresses recommended throughout this book are offered as a
resource to you. These websites are not intended in any way to be or imply an
endorsement on the part of David C Cook, nor do we vouch for their content.

This story is a work of fiction. All characters and events are the product of the author's
imagination. Any resemblance to any person, living or dead, is coincidental.

LCCN 2011924092
ISBN 978-0-7814-0370-2
eISBN 978-1-4347-0389-7

© 2011 Marybeth Whalen
Published in association with the Wheelhouse Literary
Group, PO Box 110909, Nashville, TN 37222.

The Team: Terry Behimer, Nicci Jordan Hubert,
Sarah Schultz, Jack Campbell, Karen Athen
Cover Design: Amy Kiechlin Konyndyk
Cover Photos: iStockphoto; Veer

Printed in the United States of America
First Edition 2011

1 2 3 4 5 6 7 8 9 10

032911

What people are saying about …

SHE MAKES IT LOOK EASY

"Oh how subtly sin can tangle its way into lives. A masterfully written story with a warning every woman should read and heed."

Lysa TerKeurst, New York Times
best-selling author of *Made to Crave*

"I sit here with tears in my eyes having just reread the last chapter featuring Marybeth Whalen's character Justine, and I wonder how many women will read this novel and decide to make different choices because Whalen was brave enough to put into words what so many women deal with in their lives, even if it just plays out in their heads. Although this book definitely brought out the nosy neighbor in me, it also made me seriously examine my own life to determine which character I had more in common with. And sometimes, that's a hard place to go. I simply loved this novel and think every woman should read it!"

Shari Braendel, America's foremost
Christian modesty expert and author of
Good Girls Don't Have to Dress Bad

"Marybeth Whalen knows Southern! *She Makes It Look Easy* is as lovely and delightful as iced tea and lemon meringue pie, and Ms. Whalen makes it look easy as she dishes up a charming and emotional story."

Leanna Ellis, award-winning author of *Forsaken*

"Skillfully written, compelling, and honest, Whalen's heartfelt story takes a revealing look at the price of perfection, the weight of secrets, and the blessing of those who love us just as we are."

Lisa Wingate, national best-selling author
of *Larkspur Cove* and *Dandelion Summer*

"Who hasn't had a friend with an enviable life? With her typical Southern charm, Marybeth Whalen has penned a novel about friendship, love, and the power of true happiness."

Jenny B. Jones, four-time Carol
Award–winning author of *Save the Date*
and the YA series A Charmed Life

"If you've ever wanted to walk in someone else's shoes—without actually stepping in their messes—you'll enjoy this novel, which lets you see a situation from two points of view. One is that of 'perfect' Justine and the other is of Ariel who is trying to live up to Justine's standards—and they both find out they are wrong, wrong, wrong. But which one is eternally wrong?"

Latayne C. Scott, author of *Latter-Day Cipher*
and fiction blogger on NovelMatters.blogspot.com

"In *She Makes It Look Easy,* author Marybeth Whalen creates authentic characters that could easily be your neighbors or mine. With each decision, I asked myself what I would do in the face of temptation and disappointment. Mixed with interludes of humor that any mom can relate to, this thought-provoking novel is a must-read!"

Cindy Thomson, author of *Brigid of Ireland* and *Celtic Wisdom*

"Marybeth Whalen writes with a strong, insightful voice that pulls you into her stories. In this wry, compelling story, she dissects the inner workings of the lives of wives and mothers with engaging characters and fascinating twists. A terrific story!"

Judy Christie, author of the critically acclaimed Green series, including *The Glory of Green*

"In this novel, the author addresses head-on the way we as women compare ourselves, leaving us feeling empty and unfulfilled. Read this engaging novel and you'll enter a neighborhood of women living lives eerily like your own, from the overworked mom with a life of chaos to the mom who's created the image of a perfect, yet loveless world. Join Ariel on a journey toward freedom from comparison, inspiring us to live our lives as God has called us and to develop deep friendships with other women."

Cara C. Putman, author of *Stars in the Night*

"Marybeth Whalen possesses a remarkably keen understanding of the inner workings of a woman's heart, and in her new and timely novel, *She Makes It Look Easy,* she takes an unflinching look at the lives of two upper-middle-class women in search of meaning and purpose beyond their seemingly picture-perfect existences.

This novel will remind you of what is most important, and it will certainly stir your soul."

Beth Webb Hart, best-selling author of
The Wedding Machine and *Love, Charleston*

"Marybeth Whalen's *She Makes It Look Easy* is a riveting story that proves, once again, the grass is never greener."

Sharon K. Souza, author of *Lying on Sunday* and *Every Good and Perfect Gift*

"*She Makes It Look Easy* is poignant and insightful, dramatic and challenging. Whalen details the inner struggle of two ordinary women with grace and wisdom, women who could easily be our friends, our neighbors, our family. This is a great read."

Rachel Hauck, award-winning author of *Dining with Joy*

SHE MAKES IT LOOK EASY

For the real Ariel and the real Erica ...

Ariel, of course I had to name the character
after you. All of my writing somehow
involves you ... why not this, too?

Erica, you have been and will continue
to be one of my heroes. Keep getting up
and fighting, because I am confident one
way or another, you'll win this battle.

ACKNOWLEDGMENTS

You might want to sit down ... this is going to take awhile. A mom of six doesn't see a novel all the way through to publication without a lot of help.

A big thank-you goes out ...

To the Word, for supplying my words.

To my family, for supporting me like you do.

To Jack, Ashleigh, Matthew, Rebekah, Bradley, and Annaliese ... I am blessed six times over. You inspire me, each one of you in your own unique way.

And to Curt, so many thanks. You make countless sacrifices and never waver in your support of this crazy dream I have of writing novels. What a gift you've given me.

To my mom, who really is my biggest fan and cheerleader. I was so fortunate to have been raised by you. You made me who I am, and I love you.

To Becky Sykes and Nancy Scott Malcor, you are friends and family, both.

To the folks at Cook: I have thoroughly enjoyed working with each one of you. You all are total professionals with hearts of gold. Special thanks to Terry, Don, Amy, Karen, Jack, Ingrid, and Michelle.

To Jeane Wynn: You and I clicked the moment we started talking about the subject matter of this book. Thanks for helping spread the word about it.

To Nicci Jordan Hubert: You didn't give up on this book even though most likely you wanted to at times. Thanks for dragging a great story out of me. Again.

To the Writers and Sisters in Christ: Cara Putman, Kim Cash Tate, Jenny B. Jones, Cindy Thomson, Nicole O'Dell, and Kit Wilkinson. I love how we pray for each other, cheer for each other, and spur each other on to bigger things. I love crazy believing with you girls!

To the Southern BelleView girls: Lisa Wingate (who totally thought of the idea for our group blog—genius that she is), Jenny B. Jones, Rachel Hauck, and Beth Webb Hart. You girls gave me a seat on the porch when really I should still be in the yard. I am blessed to be a Belle.

To the Proverbs 31 Ministries team: There are too many names to list individually, but I have to say, I love what we do as a team. Thanks for the chance to share great fiction through She Reads and to share truth through the devotions. It is an honor to serve women through this ministry and to witness firsthand all the ways it touches so many lives. A special shout-out to Rachel Olsen, Lysa TerKeurst, Karen Ehman, and Shari Braendel for always making me laugh.

To fellow writers who have turned into friends: Mary DeMuth, Susan Meissner, Alice Wisler, Judy Christie, Carla Stewart, Christa Allan, and Leanna Ellis. Love our writing and life conversations.

To Tonia Bendickson: You push me, encourage me, challenge me, and listen to me. Thanks for listening in the middle of the night when I know you'd much rather have been sleeping!

To Lisa Shea, Tamery Stafford, Christy Baca, Melissa Milbourn, Dawn Massey, and Debra Zantman: Thank you for always praying for me.

To Jonathan Clements: Thanks for serving as my agent, talking music with me, and politely laughing at my dumb jokes.

To Kathy Patrick: Thanks for making me an official Pulpwood Queen and for including me in Girlfriends Weekend. You are an inspiration!

To the employees of Caribou Coffee, Panera Bread, and Barnes and Noble. Thanks for always having coffee, food, and a place away from the chaos that is my home.

To the young women who care for my kids when I can't be there: Kara Simpson, Bradelyn Levi, and Laura Mullen. Your presence is an assurance to this mom.

To my blog readers, Facebook friends, and Twitter followers. You guys are amazing people who encourage me so much. Thank you.

And a special thanks to Mandie Cipcic, who took my youngest for playdates and freed me up to make my deadline in the process. You didn't even know what a big deal that was for me. Perhaps now you do.

She is dancing away from you now
She was just a wish, she was just a wish.

Fleetwood Mac, "Gypsy"

PROLOGUE

⁓

Ariel

I saw her years later in the grocery store near my house. I had to look twice to be sure it was her. She had lost weight, a lot of weight. Her collarbones jutted out from the neckline of her shirt like the framework of a building. When she spoke to the young woman accompanying her, her neck muscles pushed against her skin as though they were straining to break free. I thought of all our morning walks together and had to stop myself from approaching to congratulate her. She always did want to be thinner.

Her hair wasn't blonde anymore. It was the exact color of my second son's hair, a mahogany red that I clearly remembered her exclaiming over as she stood in my kitchen shortly after we met. "I love this hair," she had said, wrapping a single curl around her finger as my son squirmed and grimaced. "Do you know how much I'd have to pay to get hair this color?" she had said.

"But your hair's a beautiful blonde," I had offered. My own hair was auburn. I'd always wanted to be blonde.

She had shrugged, rolled her eyes. "Do you know how much I had to pay for hair this color?" she had said, laughing. And I, as always, had laughed with her.

Now, standing at a distance, it took me a moment to determine that the young woman with her was actually her older daughter. It appeared that the weight she had lost, her daughter had found. She slouched along beside her mom, a permanent sulk on her face, wearing skinny jeans that were not made for her figure and a T-shirt that read "I Didn't Do It." An unappealing white roll of flesh poked out between the jeans and the shirt. Her hair was no longer the blonde airy curls I remembered from back then, perennially clipped into ponytails with matching ribbons. Instead it was a dishwater blonde I imagined closely matched her mother's real color, hanging dank and stringy around her acne-spotted face. I closed my eyes to block the longing I felt at the image of her at eight years old, radiating light and happiness. The girl I was looking at was not the same person. Yet she was.

I found myself tailing the two of them, watching her just like I used to when she was my neighbor, and I was fascinated—too fascinated—by her. Once, I had wanted to be just like her. Once, I would've done anything to be like her. As she pulled microwave popcorn and diet sodas from the shelf, I thought about the time when I knew her. Or, when I thought I knew her. There was still a part of me that wanted to talk to her, to ask the questions I never could get her to answer, just in case I might finally understand what drove her to do what she did. I wondered if I looked into her eyes if

I would see a flicker of the person I once knew, or if I would just see blankness. I imagined a gaping absence that was always there, even when I chose not to see it.

CHAPTER 1

Ariel

I pulled the photo proofs out of the envelope, fanning them out on the granite countertop in my client's McMansion with a flourish. I loved how the word *client* sounded, and I threw it around whenever I could.

"I have a meeting with a client."

"My clients are so demanding. They all want their proofs back yesterday."

"This client had some very particular ideas about what she wants."

After years of snapping candids of my own children, I took my photography professional after someone with connections noticed that I was good at catching the little moments of life that most of us walk right by—the furrow of a tiny brow, the contentment of one lone spit bubble on a sleeping baby's pursed bow of a mouth, even the personality of a flailing, screaming two-year-old. "Someday," went my pitch, "you'll appreciate the reality of the photos. Not just the posed smiles but the whole package. The mess and the mess-ups. You'll look back and see pictures that reflect your life as it really was." If they wanted Sears Portrait Studio, they were welcome to go to Sears Portrait Studio. But if they wanted art, that's what I created. Few things pleased me more than seeing a portrait I shot gracing one of my clients' walls, surrounded by a heavy, impressive mat and frame. I aimed to create pictures that caused others to stop and stare, frozen in the awe of how something so simple could be so beautiful. Sometimes I found myself staring too.

I leaned over the proofs on the black and gray flecked counter, watching Candace Nelson's face as she looked at the photos we'd taken just a week before. I suppressed the urge to talk to her about them, to point out my favorites or ask her what she thought. I had learned the value in waiting quietly. It was as true in art as it was in marriage: The compliments meant more when they were unsolicited.

She looked up at me, her eyes misty with tears. "You totally got it," she said, pulling me into a hug. Candace Nelson and I had never met before I came to her house to photograph her children, one of whom was born prematurely and had defied the odds, home just a few days from the hospital. Candace had cried happy tears the whole time I snapped, the rhythmic clicking of my camera at times the only sound in the room. Her older two children, I noticed, had a kind of reverence for the baby. It was in the way they had held him and talked to him and even looked at him. Their reverence had hung in the air around them, an invisible force that transferred through the lens onto paper.

"These are just lovely," Candace went on. "They're … priceless."

I nodded my assent, honored to have been a part of remembering the early days of her new son's life. I had been inspired to start my business when I found old 8x10s of my sister shoved into a faded envelope with the words "Your Priceless Memories" stamped in tacky green and gold on the outside. My mother had apparently stuck the envelope in a trunk and forgotten all about it. I unearthed the photos like a time capsule, Ginny in her patchwork dress and me in a pea green turtleneck that clashed with her dress. My hair needed brushing, and neither of us was smiling. So much for priceless. So much for memories. I longed to give my kids—and other families—so much more.

Candace held up the price sheet I had handed her with the proofs. "Can I keep this?" she asked. "Talk over the order with my husband?" She giggled like a teenager ogling her prom pictures. "I know he's going to want them all." She paused, a somber expression washing over her face. "There was a time when we didn't think we'd even get to take him home, much less take snapshots." She pressed her palms onto the counter on either side of the spread of photos. "I can't thank you enough."

I thought, but did not say, *A big fat order would be plenty thanks.*

My cell phone buzzed in my pocket. I looked down at it briefly but didn't reach for it. "Oh, you can get it," Candace said, dismissing me with a wave as she buried her nose back in the photos.

"Yes?" I asked hesitantly into the phone, not sure if I wanted to know. I had left David and the boys supposedly packing up our house for our impending move to the home of our dreams. Three more days and we'd be movin' on up. It didn't take much for me to break into the theme song from *The Jeffersons* in those days before the move, the boys clapping their hands over their ears whenever I did.

"Uh, honey?" David asked. "A guy just called and said he's got the moving van you rented ready and they're about to close? He said one of us needs to come pick it up ASAP."

My heart began to pound in that way it does when I've screwed up. I vaguely remembered the conversation from a few days earlier. The man had said if we wanted to go ahead and start packing the van, we'd better get it sooner rather than later. I told him we'd be there by Saturday at noon. I looked at my watch. It was Saturday at 11:45. I backed away a few steps from Candace and smiled as she looked up at me. "Okay," I said sweetly. "I'll be there right away. I'm just finishing up here."

David started to argue about how there was no way we'd make it, but I hung up before he could say more. Another lecture from David about organization was the last thing I needed. Candace looked at me again. "Everything okay?" she asked.

"Oh sure," I said, gathering up my things. "We're moving and there's just some stuff I need to go take care of. You know how it is."

She nodded as the corners of her mouth turned down. "We moved here five years ago," she said, gesturing to the palatial digs she called home sweet home. "And I never intend to leave. I told people, 'Write this address down in ink, because we are staying put.'" The corners of her mouth turned up again.

I offered a polite laugh and began backing toward the door, wondering how I could possibly get to the van on time. I slung my backpack over my shoulder and nodded without really listening as she threw different dates out that we could get together to place the order. "How about I just call you?" I asked. I gave her another hug and backed out the door and across her front porch. I almost backed right down the imposing set of front steps, but Candace reached out and grabbed me.

"We don't want you hurting yourself," she said, pretending not to be dismayed at my less-than-graceful exit.

"Just what I need, a broken leg," I said with a rueful chuckle. I looked away, toward my car parked in her driveway, a minivan with more mileage than I thought possible. *"It still runs,"* David always said when I complained.

"Where did you say you're moving to?" Candace asked.

My eyes shone a bit brighter as I answered. Thanks to my photography business picking up and my husband's new job, we were moving to an address I could finally be proud of. "Essex Falls," I told her. It wasn't as upscale as her neighborhood, but it was nice.

"Oh, I love Essex Falls!" she exclaimed. "I've got tons of friends there. I'll tell them all to call you for appointments." Clearly resigned to my hurry, she waved the folder with the proofs in it for emphasis. If I'd had more time, I would've dug into my backpack and given her a stack of business cards. All the business books I read said not to let a chance to market yourself pass by. But the business-book authors didn't have miffed husbands at home waiting for them to not come through. Once again I wished that David had just let us hire movers instead of doing it all ourselves.

"That would be fabulous!" I replied. *Fabulous* was not a word I usually threw around. "Tell your friends I'm already booking for fall. The outdoor leaf shots are to die for." Another phrase I didn't typically use.

I held on to the wrought-iron railing, descended the steps, said good-bye, and boarded my van. David was waiting for me, and while I might be good at taking pictures, I wasn't so hot at keeping up with the needs of my home and family. I drove away thinking that after the move, I would buy a new calendar or read a book on time management or ... something. I would figure out a way to get on top of things. Especially if Candace Nelson was going to be telling all her friends about me. It sounded like I was going to be busier than ever.

I pulled into the driveway of our home to find the moving van parked there and a little pickup truck idling by the curb. A skinny little man sat in the truck with his hand out the window, smoke curling from a cigarette clamped between his fingers. I wrinkled my nose at the smell. The boys were outside playing in the backyard. "Hey, Mom," I heard. I blew quick kisses to my sons before ducking into the kitchen. I heard voices coming from the den and followed the sound, stopping just short of the doorway so I could listen without being detected, curious as to what might be said.

"Thanks a lot for this. You really saved the day," I heard David say.

A gruff voice answered. "Eh, no problem." The accent was distinctly Northeastern, which stuck out in our North Carolina suburb. I remembered it from the other day on the phone. The man laughed. "I got a wife, kids. I know how crazy it can get."

"Yeah," David said with a chuckle, using his polite voice, the one he reserved for strangers. "And my wife is … exceptional." He exhaled loudly. He was being sarcastic.

The other man laughed, and I could hear him patting David on the back. "We all think that. That's why we marry 'em."

"Exactly," David said in a near groan. "She's this really talented photographer. And now she's building an incredible business. Which is great, right?" He paused. "I mean … she sees things no one else would notice but walks right by things no one else would miss. Like this. She knows we're moving in three days, knows she reserved the truck, but … forgets."

I heard the man offer something between a grunt and an affirmation. Why was my husband practically pouring out his heart to the moving-van guy? The answer came to me in an instant: because he couldn't say it to me.

David went on. "The thing is, I took this new job and she's going to be doing a lot of stuff on her own. Because I'm going to be traveling. I just worry about her." Another pause. I could almost hear the moving-van guy shifting uncomfortably. "I mean, what if I wasn't here to bail her out? I'm not always going to be there like she's used to."

I didn't stay to hear the man's answer. Instead I slipped away, heart pounding, back toward the kitchen where I came from. I collected myself and then made a show of opening the door loudly, calling out, "I'm home," so that he would never know I heard him trash me to a stranger with a Brooklyn accent. The moving-van guy came into the kitchen first and avoided looking me in the eyes as he shook hands with David and slipped out the door.

"I see you got the moving van," I said after the door closed.

Did David look guilty? "Yeah, he offered to bring it over. Said he was closed Monday and knew we'd be behind the eight ball if we didn't get it today."

"Well, I'm glad he saved the day." I wanted to tell him about the big order I felt certain Candace Nelson was going to place, to somehow justify my gaffe, but I was too thrown off by his secret confessions. Instead I said no more. A few seconds of silence passed between us before David began packing up a kitchen box.

I turned to look out the large picture window just above the kitchen sink, watching the boys chase each other around, intent on injuring each other in some new way. We had brought each one of them home from the hospital to this house, my arms filled with their little bundled-up selves. A wave of nostalgia rolled over me. I looked over to David, who was concentrating a little too hard on wrapping glasses in hand towels. Now wasn't the time to share my reflections with him. I looked out the window again and smiled at the boys. It was at this sink that I had once scrubbed my hands with antibacterial soap, scared to death of passing on harmful germs. I remembered feeding the boys strained squash in this small kitchen and making bottles at this kitchen counter. I was not sad to be moving, but I also had to admit what we were leaving behind.

The unlikely spring heat radiated off the glass as I pressed my fingers to it. Knowing my housekeeping ability, the fingerprint whorls would still be on the window when we left, a piece of me lingering even as the new owners—a sweet young couple who would someday bring their children home here—unpacked their wedding gifts from the boxes they came wrapped in just as David and I had done years ago.

I turned away from the window and poured water for the boys so they didn't get dehydrated. It was just my luck we were moving as record temperatures were making headlines. I didn't relish the thought of doing the work ourselves, but I wasn't going to win that tired argument. My husband valued saving a buck more than making me happy sometimes. David turned and left the room without another word. I heard him open the attic, the creaking hinges loudly pronouncing that our move was under way.

Once we were settled into the new home, I planned to create a different kind of life for us, one where I kept up with things better, made better decisions, and disappointed David less. I couldn't afford to disappoint him. Only negative things could come of that. I sighed deeply and went to see what David thought I should do first.

⁓

"Boys. Look over here," I repeated on our last day in the house. "Please. Just one more time." My oldest son, Donovan, rolled his eyes. He looked exactly like David when he did that. He looked exactly like David, period: the same thick ebony hair, same green eyes, same self-possessed demeanor. He came out of the womb looking at me with an expression that was so David I laughed out loud. From that moment to this, I marveled at how little of me was in the child. I was just the incubator.

Donovan and Dylan, my second son, looked over at me, while Duncan continued playing with the bubble wrap, trying hard to pop the bubbles like his brothers had taught him. He grew frustrated and started to cry. Donovan and Dylan looked back at Duncan, their faces concerned over their baby brother's tears. I started snapping more shots as they bent their heads toward him, a study in genetics—black, red, and blonde hair all touching. Duncan forgot his tears as Donovan and Dylan began jumping on the bubble wrap, the bubbles popping in rapid-fire stereo. I was grateful we had crated our dog, Lucky, outside or he would've joined in by barking. As it was, the noise was so deafening David came running into the room. His shirt was soaked with sweat from moving heavy furniture. He glanced over at me with my camera and shook his head.

"I see you're getting a lot of packing done here." He and some friends were taking down the beds and loading them in our rented van piece by piece. His lips were pressed into a thin, patient smile.

I held up the camera. "Just taking some shots of the boys playing in the box. It was too cute," I said. "I thought I'd send it out with our moving announcement. You know, write something like 'We're all packed up and ready to go.'"

He crossed his arms across his chest. "You know I love your photos, but I really need your help."

I smiled at him. "Let me just finish first."

He laughed in spite of himself, never one to curtail my photography hobby. "Boys," he said, turning his attention to them. None of them looked at him. "No more jumping on that bubble wrap. You just about gave me a heart attack."

Duncan, age four, looked at him wide-eyed. "What's a heart attack?"

"Ask your mother," he said as he began to walk away. "Apparently she's got all the time in the world."

I was about to make a crack about how we should've hired a mover when I heard the front door open and went to see who it was instead. Arguing any further about the moving situation wasn't going to get us anywhere except into a fight. I rounded the corner to see Kristy, my across-the-street neighbor, standing there with a mopey look on her face. I smiled at her and held out my arms. "It's not that far," I said.

She walked into my embrace. "I've always hated good-byes," she said. We hugged for a minute, and I tried hard to feel the same amount of sadness she did. I think the person getting left behind always feels worse than the person doing the leaving.

"Just remember," I said into her hair. "I'll be twenty minutes away. And always just a phone call."

She pulled her head back to look me in the eyes. "But who will I go to when I can't get Kailey to stop crying? Who will I come ask for random stuff I need to borrow? Who will I complain to when Josh is being a jerk?"

I shook my head. I didn't have an easy answer for her. "I'm not leaving town, just the neighborhood."

She sniffed and looked away. "I just don't know if I can do this without you." She seemed more emotional than normal. I didn't know how to react to her tears.

I took her hand and squeezed lightly. "You can," I said, willing my voice to sound reassuring and comforting. The truth was I knew Kristy depended on me a lot. I had even talked to David about how responsible for her I had come to feel.

"She's going to eventually figure this all out for herself," he had said. "Maybe moving away is ultimately good for her." As I hugged Kristy, I let myself believe that. I had come to care deeply for her, but my gorgeous new house had more pull.

The boys climbed out of the box and started wandering in the direction of where David and his friends were dismantling furniture. My eyes darted after them and back to Kristy looking mournful. "I hate to do this, but I've—"

"I know, I know," she said, waving me away. "Go do what you need to do. I knew you'd be busy, but I just had to come say good-bye one last time." She paused, and I could hear the boys' excited shouts and demands to "help" the men. I expected to hear David yell my name at any moment. "I just …," she went on, "I just wanted to thank you. You've been such a great friend, and you've inspired me to be a good mom to Kailey and a good wife to Josh."

I didn't feel deserving of such effusive praise—especially considering how being a good wife and mom was hardly my territory—but I stepped into her open arms and let the sounds of my boys and the noises of moving day fall away. If I could have, I would've snapped a photo of the two of us in that moment. And on the back of the photo I would've scribbled down the words Kristy said to me so I could go back and read them whenever I needed to. Somebody thought I had it together. That was something to hold on to.

CHAPTER 2

Justine

The ringing phone was, frankly, a relief. I had dropped off the girls at day camp, their matching pink quilted bags (even the monograms were the same: CAM) packed with the required labeled towel, the required one-piece bathing suit, and the required nutritious lunch with the required extra bottle of water, labeled of course. I had dropped off the dry cleaning, set out the chicken to thaw, and mixed up a batch of cookies to bake when the girls got home later. I had returned the library books at the library down the street, stopped by the church to pick up some casserole containers I said I would take, and juiced the overripe lemons that really weren't fit for anything else but lemonade, Cameron's favorite. I had folded the laundry and swished out the toilets and dust mopped our hardwood floors because it was a Tuesday and those were the chores I did on Tuesday. I had done everything but exercise, and had the phone not rung when it did, well, it was the only thing left.

I answered sweetly, like I was excited to hear from the person on the other end just like my mother taught me. It is funny how much you will still do just because your mother told you to. I wondered what I told the girls that they would carry stalwartly into adulthood, my voice resounding in their heads even when they wanted to silence it.

"Justine?" the caller said. "It's Liza."

"Yes, Liza, good to hear from you. I know you're probably calling because you need my column." Liza was the editor of our neighborhood newsletter. I wrote a column on organizational tips that I'd been told was the most popular feature, which warmed my heart.

"Well, yes, I do need your column for the summer edition, but it's not due till next week. I never worry about you turning things in on time. I wish I could say that about all my writers. But I actually called about something different." She paused, and in that moment—that gap between when she drew a breath and when she started to speak—I knew that what she was about to say was not good. In fact, it sounds dramatic, but I knew that what she was going to say was going to change everything. "Rumor has it that someone else auditioned for your part in the Patriotic Pageant up at the church. And she's good."

Liza did not say, "She's better than you," but, of course, that's what I heard.

I had just been at the church, yet no one said a word about it to me. Surely Liza had been given some misinformation. My mind scanned backward over my quick trip into the church kitchen to get the disposable casserole containers we used to bring meals to people in need. I oversaw the church's Helping Hands ministry, coordinating meals for people who were sick or had lost a family member or had a baby. Had I seen anyone associated with the choir as I darted in and out, intent on accomplishing my task? And if I had, would they have said anything, or would they have avoided me altogether?

"I really hate to hear that, Liza." I fumbled for the right words to say, words that didn't sound too pitiful or too hopeless. Just because someone else dared to audition for a part that I sang every year—that everyone knew was mine—well, that didn't mean she would get the part.

Liza read my mind. "Now, I don't think that this means anything, but I did want to warn you, just so you could be mentally prepared." She clucked her tongue sympathetically. "I mean, I'd want to know if I were you."

"Well, yes, yes, of course," I said, even as my mind scanned through the women in the church who might possibly try to take my part from me. I always sang the closing solo as the church overflowed with every child from the children's program, waving little flags. It was the high point of the whole service. Everyone cried as I filled that entire sanctuary with my voice, feeling about as good as I thought possible as I sang "God Bless America." When it was over, I always got a standing ovation. People spent the rest of the year telling me how touched they were by my singing and those little children all blending together in one spectacular display. There was rarely a dry eye in the house. One thing I knew: There would be many disappointed people if someone else sang that part. It had become part of people's Fourth of July tradition. I could think of no one who would attempt such a thing. Not even Geraldine Cleavis, who sang the solo in the Christmas program every year. Christmas, it was understood, was her turf. Fourth of July was mine.

"Do you know who it was?" I asked Liza. "Who auditioned?"

"Well, that's the funny thing. It's some new woman, new to the church. I mean, it would have to be someone new. Someone who doesn't know who you are. I mean, you're the next Dorothy Rea."

Being compared to Dorothy Rea was the ultimate compliment in our church. Too old to do much of anything now, Dorothy walked slowly into every event to a standing ovation. There was a new wing and a women's event named after her. She was once the leader of everything at the church and the epitome of a godly woman. Everyone in our church wanted to be the Dorothy Rea of our generation. Liza had paid me quite a compliment and I stammered out my thanks. I had always secretly hoped that was how people saw me.

Liza went on talking while I reassured myself that my part was sewn up and no newcomer could take it from me. "You don't think it's the people who bought Laura's house, do you?" Liza asked. "Wouldn't that be so weird?" She almost sounded happy as she asked, as though the irony was delicious and she wanted to enjoy the flavor, roll it around on her tongue.

I strode over to the window and pushed the plantation shutters back to look at the empty house that sat exactly behind mine. There was no sign of life there yet. The house had that soulless quality that overtakes all empty houses. I noticed a lone plant, grown spindly and dry from lack of care, on the empty deck. "No, no, it couldn't be her. No one's moved in over there yet."

I had already decided not to like whoever moved in, even though Laura assured me it was a nice family. No one could take my best friend's place. In fact, as soon as Liza and I hung up, I was going to call her. We hadn't talked in a week. She was busy getting her new life set up in Chicago, trying to fit in with a bunch of Yankees, and I was here, still avoiding looking at her house because it was too painful to see the shell of a place I had once spent half my time in. I kept the shutters closed along the back of the house and hoped Mark didn't complain. He never did. Mark wasn't one to complain about much.

"Well, I'll let you get back to whatever it was you were doing before I interrupted you," Liza said. "I don't know how you do all you do with those little girls and your work at the church and the school and the neighborhood. Whoever does move in is going to be very lucky to have you for a neighbor."

I thanked Liza and said good-bye. I dialed Laura's number and hoped I'd catch her at a good time. Lately she'd been too busy to talk. We'd promised that the distance wasn't going to cause a chasm in our friendship, but I was starting to doubt it. Yet she was the only person I felt I could be even halfway honest with. I wanted to tell Laura about the person who was after my part, about how things were bad for Mark at work and that he was getting on my nerves with his down-in-the-mouth attitude. Before we hung up, Liza had told me she'd pray for me. I told her I could always use prayers. But if someone else got my part, I was going to need a lot more than prayers. I was going to need a restraining order.

⁓

A week later, I had the table set beautifully and the food all finished at precisely the same time—one of the signs of an accomplished cook, if you asked me. I stepped back and inhaled deeply. A perfect summer meal sat waiting. But Mark was late and the food was cooling. "Girls, dinner," I called. "Cameron. Caroline."

I heard a flurry of motion upstairs as they flung down whatever it was they were playing with and came down the stairs. Caroline, my younger daughter, twirled and jetéed down the stairs. Cameron pretended she was riding a horse. "Can I take horseback this year, Mom? Can I please?" she asked as soon as she trotted into the room. "Jillian's taking horseback, and she said I totally should too." At eight, she was already talking like a teenager.

A thought skittered across my mind: If things kept going the way they had been, we wouldn't be able to keep paying for ballet, much less add horseback. Financial problems used to be something that happened to other people. "We'll see," I said to Cameron. I pointed her toward the table. "Did you wash your hands?" I asked before she could land in the seat. She beamed at me and nodded.

I took my place at the table and commenced with serving their plates. Caroline looked toward Mark's empty place. "Where's Daddy? Why aren't we waiting on him?" she asked.

I didn't look over at her, just kept dishing out the grilled chicken, the twice-baked potatoes, and the salad, with the homemade yeast rolls. It was too bad I wasn't hungry. I cut up Caroline's meat and started in on Cameron's before she protested that she could do it herself, so I gave it back.

"Mommy? Where's Daddy?" Caroline asked again, accepting her plate complete with bite-size pieces of chicken courtesy of me. "We should wait for him." She looked down at her plate. "I don't like salad."

"Eat three bites," I responded automatically. She had to know by this time I would respond that way, that I always told her to eat three bites. Sometimes I felt that motherhood was nothing more than automatic pilot, repeating the same words over and over like a robot. No one said anything while we ate our food. Hours of work that disappeared in ten minutes, fifteen if you threw in some family conversation. Lately I wondered why I tried so hard.

We heard the sound of the garage door going up and a car pulling in. The girls' eyes widened, and their forks clattered to the plates as they bolted for the door, calling, "Daddy! Daddy!" I stayed at the table, focusing on the centerpiece I had created the week before: sand and shells in a hurricane vase, two open clam shells with white votives tucked inside on either side of the vase. I had forgotten to light the candles.

"Hi," Mark said.

I looked up at him, remembering my mother's advice to always greet my husband like a conquering hero when he returned home from work, to stand, to hug, to smile. I stood and went to the cupboard to retrieve a lighter. "Hi," I said. I forced myself to go over to him, to wrap my arms around him like a robot. All these years and I was still hoping the love would come with the action.

The girls took their seats, and Mark laid down his briefcase and suit jacket just inside the doorway where it didn't belong. Later I would have to move it. He took his seat at the table as I lit the votives and smiled. Our eyes locked, and my smile disappeared like a flame being extinguished. Every day I said I would do better, would fake it to the point that he believed it, that I believed it. And every day by the time he came in the door, I just didn't have the energy to play pretend. We both looked down at our plates. The food had become cold, but I didn't offer to heat his up. He didn't say a word about it, but for some reason I wanted him to.

Cameron had opened the kitchen shutters that afternoon when she was coloring, and I could see Laura's house from where I sat. A man was on the deck fiddling with the umbrella on a dilapidated table that had seen better days. The man was handsome—good build, a strong jaw, a thick shock of black hair. I wondered if his eyes were brown or green or blue. A little boy with red hair ran up and down the stairs while the man worked. He stopped working to speak to the boy. A woman came out the door that led from the den to the deck. I looked away before my mind could register what she looked like.

"So, Caroline, tell Daddy that story about what Ellie did at camp today," I said. I looked over at Mark. "Ellie is the Stewart girl," I explained. He nodded and put on his interested face as he turned to listen to Caroline animatedly tell the long and involved story I'd already listened to that day. My mind wandered back to my conversation with Laura. I'd finally gotten to talk to her after a week of trying. I felt a momentary pang for what had floated through the phone lines as I told her about my troubles.

"I feel like you left me," I said before we had hung up.

She sighed, as though my admission exhausted her. "You know I wouldn't have left you …," she said, "if I didn't have to."

"I feel like everything's changed since you left," I said. "I need you to be right where you were."

"No one ever stays right where you need them to be," Laura said.

My eyes flickered back to her house. The people were gone, but signs of life were there. Outdoor furniture, though ugly, now filled the deck. The dead plant had been removed, replaced by a fern. I always thought that a house without a family was like a body without a soul. Would it be better for Laura's house to be filled rather than empty? Would I rather hold vigil over a soulless house, some kind of memorial to a lost friendship? Caroline finished her story, and I turned to Mark.

"So, I heard from the church," I said. I had to tell him, and it would be easier since I'd told Laura earlier.

He looked at me, his eyebrows raised. "And?" He still had his interested face on.

I looked down at my plate, moved around my untouched food. "They gave the part to that other person." I hadn't even bothered to learn her name. What did her identity matter?

I felt his hand on my shoulder. He squeezed gently. "I'm sorry," he said.

I sat that way for a long time, letting him massage my shoulder, willing his touch to break through the steel I felt sheathed in. When it didn't work, I stood up and went to the sink with my plate, washing the uneaten food down the garbage disposal and watching it disappear.

In my dream I heard a dog barking. I looked from room to room in our house for the dog but couldn't find it. I racked my brain to remember when we had gotten a dog, wondering how the girls had talked me into it. I had never wanted the mess, the hair, the added responsibility. Even in the dream I was questioning myself, wondering what emotionally weak moment had ushered a dog into my home. I opened the door to my bedroom to discover the dog sitting in my bed, his mouth stretched into what could only be described as a grin.

Before my eyes he changed into a lion and roared, a sound that woke me with a start, looking around to discover that I had fallen asleep in the middle of the day on my living-room couch. I lay there blinking and looking around for a moment, trying to remember what I was doing before I had fallen asleep. I came home from dropping off the girls at day camp. I was going to mix up some bread dough and do my exercise DVD. Fatigue had settled over me so powerfully I had staggered to the couch to lie down, the last thing I remembered.

Then I heard a dog barking just like in my dream and sat up. Was I going crazy? Was I sick? I wasn't the type to sleep during the day. Nor was I the type to hear things. I stood and went toward the direction of the barking. It was coming from the garage. I opened the door to the garage and peered into the darkness. I sighed with relief when I saw that the garage door was closed—that I hadn't forgotten to close it. I was about to go back inside when I heard the jingle of a dog collar and the clicks of dog toenails hitting the cement floor. Before I could close the door, a big black Lab stepped into the light from the doorway looking awfully happy to see me. I stooped down, and he walked slowly toward me, stretching and shaking out his four legs as he did. He had no collar on but looked well fed. Someone in our neighborhood—some irresponsible pet owner—had lost their dog, and he had somehow gotten into my garage.

Because I couldn't think of what else to do, I swung the door open and invited my guest in. Laura had a dog, a blonde cocker spaniel she had named Mopsy. Mopsy had been a guest at my house so many times I started keeping little dog biscuits for her. I was glad I hadn't had the heart to throw them out yet. I motioned for the dog to follow me into the kitchen where I kept them. He did, his eyes looking at me with trust and warmth. Maybe I'd been wrong telling the girls no about a dog. Maybe I needed the companionship. I imagined calling Laura to tell her that, in her absence, I'd decided to get a dog. And not just any dog, but a big black Lab. "So let me get this straight," I imagined her saying, "I've been replaced by a canine." I smiled at the image as I opened the canister and threw two biscuits toward the dog. He caught them in midair and swallowed them without chewing, that doggy smile on his face. Then he ambled over and sat at my feet, pushing his head into my knees.

I bent down and scratched his ears, soft as peach fuzz, wondering what to do. He looked up at me, opened his mouth, and panted. "Oh, boy, you must be thirsty," I said, and he kept staring at me like I was on the right track. I put water in a bowl and set it before him, then took a seat at the kitchen table to watch him drink it. Without the frenzy of getting ready for the Patriotic Pageant at church, I had less to keep me busy. I needed a purpose to distract me from the two losses I had just stomached. It felt like emotional indigestion.

The dog finished the water and came to rest by my feet, his big body splayed out on the cool kitchen floor. For a moment I let myself think about Laura really being gone, about my part really being sung by another woman. I thought about how last year I had sung in the pageant with Laura in the audience, never realizing that just one year later she'd be gone and so would my part. A single tear slipped down my face and I let it fall into the dog's fur. He didn't even look up as I slunk down on the floor beside him and wrapped my arms around his big furry body—not even caring that he smelled like he'd spent the morning trapped in my garage. I buried my face in his neck and let a few more tears fall, grateful I wasn't alone.

CHAPTER 3

———

Ariel

The music wasn't doing the trick. I couldn't hear it over the din of the boys' thundering feet, riotous squeals, and intermittent bouts of crying. I looked mournfully at the bank of boxes waiting to be unpacked along the den wall and strained to hear the music coming from the portable CD player David had set up for me before he left. Shaking my head, I turned it off, sat down in the middle of the floor, and put my head in my hands. I figured maybe I could shed a few tears and relieve some of the stress that way. As I held my hands over my eyes, one of the boys zipped by me. "Sorry, Mom," he yelled as his makeshift sword clunked against the back of my head. Duncan.

I grew up believing that if you put a little music on, every job got easier. When I was in middle school and my mom assigned me the arduous task of cleaning my room, I cranked up DeBarge and danced around to "Rhythm of the Night" while I sorted the stuffed animals I couldn't bear to part with (which seemed to multiply in the recesses of my room) and tried to organize my closet into submission. When I moved into my dorm at college, my roommate, Karen, and I bobbed our heads along with Bob Marley's *Legend* album while we turned the tiny space into what we thought was a place of beauty. Now we joke that it looked like Laura Ashley threw up peach and blue. Later, when David and I were newly married and worked together to strip the heinous wallpaper in our first house, I put on U2 and we both sang along to "Beautiful Day," working side by side, just like I had always imagined married life would be—a series of beautiful days unspooling like ribbon.

But this? This was not anything like what I had imagined all those years ago as David and I balanced on our stools and talked of the future. For one thing, I pictured David *around,* not off earning a living and traveling constantly for his job, leaving me to fend for myself and care for the wild hooligans we had created. I don't know why it never entered my mind that if David worked, someone else (me) would have to stay home and actually take care of the children we had imagined. Feed them. Hold them. Take them to places like the library and the doctor's office and the grocery store. Wipe their faces. Clean up their messes.

"Mama?"

Duncan, my youngest's, voice. I looked up.

"Yes, baby?"

"You crying?" The look of concern on his face was unbearably sweet.

"Trying to," I said as I rose from my place on the floor. I had hunkered down in the only spot that wasn't covered by boxes. I dusted off the jeans I was wearing, David's jeans, the ones with the hole in the knee that he tried to donate and I rescued for such occasions as this.

"You miss our old house, Mama? That why you're crying?" Duncan continued. Somehow he'd gotten strawberry blonde hair in spite of my auburn hair and David's black hair; found it in the depths of our gene pool, making him look part baby, part angel with the wisps flying around his head like an orb of light. At four he was losing his baby look, but his hair still reminded me of an angel's.

"No, honey. Mommy doesn't miss our old house."

"I do, Mommy."

"I know, sweetie. But you'll get used to it."

So many times I had circled this neighborhood—a prime location near Charlotte, North Carolina—the boys dozing in their car seats in the backseat as I eyed the latest listings and pulled sale flyers from the little boxes in the front yards like a stalker. David got tired of me leaving the flyers in strategic places to inspire him to sell our old house.

Our old house had once been a perfect fit. When Donovan joined our little family, it still wasn't bad. I wasn't even upset when we added Dylan. I remained stoic as David showed me his spreadsheets of projections about the money we were saving by staying put while all our friends sold their starter homes and moved into more advanced accommodations. After Duncan was born, I stopped being stoic and started bargaining. Eventually, my campaign paid off, and here I was, surrounded by boxes I needed to unpack while my children complained they wanted to go back where we came from.

I loved the way the name of our neighborhood sounded. *I'm meeting a client in Essex Falls.* It rolled off the tongue.

The master-planned community featured homes with big square footages and price tags to match. Each home boasted a spa bath, master suite with sitting room, gourmet kitchen, and spacious recreation room. The neighborhood amenities included a beautifully decorated community clubhouse with an Olympic-size pool plus a kids' pool, nature trails, a playground, dog park, and a social committee that hosted parties and events throughout the year. I could hardly wait to be invited to serve on the social committee.

"I miss our old house," Duncan repeated, apparently still standing at my side. He looked around. "This house is too messy." Our other house, I didn't remind him, was also messy because we were crammed in it and there was no room for all of our stuff.

I smoothed down his flyaway hair and noted that he needed a haircut, but refused to add that to my mental to-do list just then. "Well, it won't be messy for long," I told him. Wishful talking. I sighed as I surveyed the boxes again. The number of them had not diminished while I was trying to have my breakdown, I was sad to note. "Mommy's going to unpack all these boxes and make it feel like home," I said with more resolve than I felt. "Only a bigger home, with more room to run and play, and a nicer neighborhood with better schools."

Duncan shook his head. "I don't want to go to school," he said, popping his index finger into his mouth, a habit I had yet to break him of. He took the truck he was carrying in his free hand and began to drive it up the back of the couch and down the arm.

"Well, you've got awhile before you go to school," I said, pulling him onto my lap as I sank into the couch, a purchase I convinced David was in honor of our new house. *"New house, new furniture,"*

I had reasoned with a smile while he rolled his eyes. Our other furniture consisted of donated items from family members and pieces found in secondhand stores. I wanted all new stuff, but all I had been able to talk him into was the couch. Duncan kept running his truck across the fabric. I heard the truck catch, followed by a small tearing sound. I looked down to see a thread pulled, the large loop sticking out from my pristine, perfect couch like white pants after Labor Day.

"Duncan!" I yelled. "Look what you did."

He shrank away from me, his liquid chocolate eyes filling with tears as he pulled his finger from his mouth. "Sorry, Mama," he said. I tried in vain to push the thread back into the couch so it didn't show as much.

Ignoring Duncan's tears, I launched into rant mode, the yelling a substitute for the tears I had tried to muster earlier. "Why can't just one thing in this house stay nice for longer than five minutes?"

After a brief moment I felt guilty so I stood up and kissed Duncan, then sent him away to escape Momzilla. I pushed past the boxes to the kitchen, which was at least somewhat unpacked. David had insisted we set up the kitchen before he left on his business trip. I still couldn't forgive him for leaving me home alone with the boys four days after we moved in. "I'm sorry," he had said, his suitcase in hand, not looking sorry to me but instead relieved to be escaping the chaos. "You knew it would be like this and you said it would be fine."

"Then go. If it's so important to go, then go." I had stood in front of the sink, dumping the boys' soggy, uneaten cereal down the drain. It was only after he left that I realized he hadn't kissed me good-bye. As I shoved bowls into the dishwasher, I thought of a book I often read to the boys: "Who wants to kiss a cactus? Who wants to hug a porcupine?" No one wants to be around you when you're prickly.

I took a clean glass from the cabinet and ran water from the spigot. As the water ran, I willed again for the tears to come, but all I felt was a burning sensation just behind my eyes. I drank the water and looked up to see that Duncan had reappeared, his truck in his outstretched palm. "Here, Mama," he said. "You can put my truck on restriction since I messed up your pretty new couch." His eyes were still watery.

I smiled down at him. "It's okay," I said, letting my words heal us both. "It was just an accident. Mommy knows you didn't mean to do it." I stooped down to his level, remembering my caveat for buying the nice couch. "You are more important to me than furniture," I whispered to Duncan.

He threw his arms around me, clunking me in the back of the head for the second time as he did. I wondered if a concussion would be a good excuse for not unpacking boxes. "I can help you with the boxes," Duncan said, totally oblivious that he had injured me.

I put my glass into the sink and wandered back toward the den. "No, honey, I'm afraid you can't help me with this," I said. I pictured Tom Sawyer as I spoke, envisioned me sitting on the couch reading a book while I got the boys to unpack for me. Tempting as my fantasy was, I knew better than to put an eight-, six-, and four-year-old in charge of carrying off our belongings to the dark recesses of our house, never to be seen again.

"Hey, Duncan," I called before he could disappear. "Where are your brothers?"

"Playing at the neighbors'," he said matter-of-factly.

"What neighbors?" I asked, an edge of concern in my voice. We hadn't met any of our new neighbors. There was the reclusive man next door who darted inside whenever we waved. David had nicknamed him Silent Joe because he never said a word. He played music from his screened-in porch so loud it could be heard all over our cul-de-sac. In only one week we learned that his tastes ranged from classical to jazz to Sinatra to Springsteen. I swore at one point I heard Christmas music playing.

"They're at the neighbors' behind us that have that huge playset," he answered. He was driving his truck on the boxes now, not the couch.

I dashed out to the back deck that overlooked our small backyard. A fence separated the neighbors' yard from ours, but somewhere in the history of the house, a gate had been installed between the two fences. When I saw it the day we looked at the house, I pictured Lucy and Ethel swapping stories and baking each other pies as they let themselves into each other's yards, houses, lives. I did not see myself as Lucy or Ethel and automatically assumed our new neighbors would not like unauthorized visits from my passel of rowdy boys. To my sons a gate meant access, not exclusion. It would be tough convincing them otherwise.

"Donovan! Dylan!" I yelled from the deck.

Two heads popped up in unison from the top of the tower that rose from the center of the ornate playset. "Hey, Mom!" Dylan said. "Isn't this cool?"

In my sternest mom voice, I said through clenched teeth, "Get down from there and come inside. Now."

They looked at each other, and I imagined one of them saying, *"She's always ruining our fun."* Slowly they climbed down from the tower, crossed the neighbors' yard, opened the gate, and made their way to me. I scanned the windows along the back of the house to see if anyone was watching. No one appeared to be, and I breathed a sigh of relief. Maybe they weren't home and this offense wouldn't be held against me. I didn't want to gain a reputation around the neighborhood as "that mother who doesn't watch her children."

I narrowed my eyes at my wayward sons as they joined me on the deck. "Do you boys know why I called you over here?"

Dylan looked over at his big brother, the one who always seemed to have the answers. Donovan looked back at him with an expression that said, *"I got nothin'."* They both shook their heads.

I put one hand on Dylan's shoulder and one hand on Donovan's, pulling them closer to me and to each other. David called this huddling up. He loved having boys, but I still longed for a daughter, even though he made me promise I would stop mentioning trying for a baby girl when we bought this house. "Besides," David liked to warn me, "it would probably be another boy."

I was determined to keep my promise and be grateful for what I had. At least until the unpacking was done and we got settled. I will admit to thinking that one of the bedrooms in the new house would make the most perfect girl nursery. But to my credit I did not say that to David. It wasn't my fault that I had gotten a bad case of baby-girl fever five minutes after they laid my third son on my chest. In four years it hadn't gone away.

Focusing on the boys, I pointed across the yard. "That playset over there?"

They nodded soberly.

"It's not ours. It belongs to another family."

Donovan, always the spokesperson, argued. "But it's in our yard," he reasoned.

"No, it's not. See that fence?"

They nodded again. "That fence is where our yard ends and that house's yard begins." I pointed at the large white house that sat behind us complete with a beautiful, straight-out-of-*Southern Living* screened-in porch. "We stay in our yard at all times."

Donovan thought for a moment. "But what if they invite us?" he asked. Donovan could always find a loophole. It was a gift.

I looked again at the house. The porch had ferns that swayed when the breeze blew. Delicate, tinkling wind chimes made of breakable materials created a faint melody. A large adjoining deck was handsomely outfitted with expensive-looking deck furniture that was clearly not purchased at Walmart like ours. "Chances are they won't," I said, looking at the crack in our glass-top table that resulted from Dylan smashing a planter into it. I doubted the lady of that house would want her *House Beautiful* furniture to meet a similar fate. I could picture one of my boys batting at the wind chimes with his light saber, the smashed pieces raining down on the floor as she tried in vain to stop what was already done. My boys typically left a wake of disaster wherever they went. I didn't intend for that wake to extend across our shared yard. The fence was more than a barrier between property lines. It appeared to me to be a line marking two entirely different lives.

"Why don't I go inside and make us some lunch?" I offered as I noticed the boys looking longingly at the playset. I made a mental

note to look into a childproof latch for the fence. Of course, knowing my boys, they would have it figured out about a second after I
installed it. Or they would just climb the fence.

"If we can't play on their playset, then do you think Dad will
build us a playset like that?" Dylan piped up.

David worked so much that I knew better. Weekends were left
to playing catch-up with all the things he hadn't done while he was
traveling. Large projects like playsets were an impossibility. So I did
what I had learned to do when I didn't want to tell my children no
but didn't want to make a commitment either. "We'll see," I said and
made my exit.

Just as I opened the door to the house, I heard Donovan educate
his younger brother. "That means no," he said as he followed me into
the house offering a counterbargain. "If we can't have a playset, can
we at least have a Popsicle?"

"Yeah! Popsicles!" Dylan brightened, pumping his fist in the air.

"If you eat a hot dog and some fruit first, I'll let you have a
Popsicle after. But you have to eat it on the deck." It was an easy con-
cession. I could unpack at least one box while they ate their Popsicles.
I would work all afternoon and evening, parking the boys in front
of a video during the hottest part of the day. Perhaps I would make
a significant dent in the work by the time David returned home the
next evening. He would be impressed.

I was halfway through my third box when Donovan came running
into the house, his face covered with red Popsicle juice that had

dripped down his arms, making him look like he was bleeding. I glanced up at him, all too familiar with this scene, before returning to my box. Donovan was panting from his short run, always one to indulge in a bit of drama, as if our lives didn't include enough without creating more. "What's wrong, bud?" I asked.

"Mom," he huffed. "I can't find Lucky."

I groaned. I did not have time to stop the groove I was in to go in search of our escape-artist dog. We had named him Lucky after the old joke about a lost dog with a myriad of problems, the punch line being that the dog answered to the name Lucky. Turns out the name was either prophetic or self-fulfilling. I could never decide which.

I looked out the window into the backyard and our neighbors' yard beyond. Part of the appeal of this house was the fenced yard that, we thought, was high enough to keep the dog contained. I had flashbacks of chasing him through our old neighborhood. Our former neighbors all knew him and brought him back when they would find him wandering. No one knew us—or our dog—here in Essex Falls.

"Did you check under the deck?" I asked, hoping for the easy solution.

"Yes, Mom. He's not under there. Come on!" Donovan yelled, his panic mounting as he waved me toward the deck, where the other two boys were perched like spies on the railings, hoping for a glimpse of Lucky. I heard them taking turns calling his name.

I prayed for the first time in several days as I walked out to the deck. "Lord, please let us find that stupid dog," I whispered. My spiritual life had taken a turn for the worse since the move. It was as if I expected to eventually unpack it from somewhere in the boxes, putting it back in its rightful place in our home.

From my vantage point on the deck, I spotted not the dog but the culprit. The boys had left the back gate open when they had come in, but I had been too focused on the neighbors' playset to notice whether or not they closed it. I pointed to the gate. "I see how he got out," I said. "See why we have to keep that gate shut?" Donovan and Dylan nodded, frowning.

"We've got to find Lucky," Duncan said, his finger in his mouth so his words were garbled.

"Dunc, finger," I said. He pulled it from his mouth and blinked back at me.

"Okay, well, let's find Lucky, boys." I tried to sound more hopeful than I felt as I surveyed the landscape of unfamiliar homes occupied by complete strangers. I missed David.

Donovan was wringing his hands like an anxious old man. "But where could he be?" he said as he paced. "We don't know anyone here."

Dylan chimed in. "Yeah, remember in our old neighborhood we always knew to start at Mrs. Montgomery's house."

"That's 'cause he liked her dog's food," Duncan added.

I raised my hands and sighed. "Okay, all I know to do is get in the van and drive around to see if we find him," I said. "Fair enough?"

"Can we stick our heads out the windows and yell for him?" Dylan asked. By the way he was hopping from one foot to the other, I could tell that this was an adventure to him.

I frowned, picturing an accident in the making and ending up in a worse situation than a lost dog. "No," I said.

The boys followed me to the van and jumped into their respective places. It still felt like a major accomplishment that they could now dress themselves and get into the van on their own. I drove slowly down the street, my eyes trained to discern movement in bushes to spy any 105-pound black animals lolling in the shade in someone else's driveway. It felt like a vain exercise, but what else could I do?

After slowly circling the entire neighborhood three times, I pulled back into our driveway. "Let's see if he's back in the yard," I told the boys, hoping for a miracle. "Some help would be nice," I prayed as I rounded the house and entered the backyard. I looked under the deck, which had quickly become Lucky's favorite place to cool off. No black tail wagging, no sound of panting. I stood up to face my sons' disappointed faces.

"Mom, call Dad," Donovan offered. David was his hero and, by his estimation, could fix anything—even a missing dog from all the way across the country.

"That won't help, dummy," Dylan said, socking Donovan in the arm. "What's Dad gonna do?" Though Dylan was voicing my own thoughts, I still sent him inside for hitting his brother and calling him a dummy.

He stomped up the stairs hollering, "It's not *my* fault that Lucky's missing!" I thought of the gate I found open and wanted to yell back that it *was* his fault, even though I didn't know technically which brother didn't bother to latch the gate. I glanced at the boxes through the window and wanted desperately to get back to work. I had lost valuable time, not to mention motivation, with this latest crisis. And David wondered what I did all day.

I rested my hands on Donovan's and Duncan's shoulders for a moment. "Boys, I'm afraid there's nothing left for us to do except wait for him to come back."

Duncan's lip quivered. "But he doesn't know his way home," he said. "He might not know where to go."

I picked him up and held him close, inhaling the earthy, sweaty little-boy scent I had grown to love over the past eight years. "Lucky knows where to go. He has an incredible ability to smell his way to places. He can smell things human beings can't smell."

Forgetting his trouble for a moment, he giggled. "Like poop?"

I smiled. Leave it to a little boy to go to bathroom humor in the midst of a crisis. "Like lots of things. Like you and me and Donovan and Dylan. He knows each of us by smell, and he can find his way back to us by smelling his way."

I put him down, and he crouched on all fours with a big grin on his face, pretending to sniff the ground. "Hey, Donovan, I'm Lucky. I'm smelling my way home."

Just then I saw Donovan raise a finger and point to our backyard neighbors' house. "I think I see Lucky!"

I tried to follow his line of sight but saw nothing outside, no movement, no black figure. "Honey, I don't see anything." I ruffled his hair and was about to walk back inside to get out of the heat for a moment, but he persisted for me to look again. I wrote it off as his eyes playing tricks on him.

"No, Mom. *Inside* the house," he said, jabbing his finger toward the house.

I looked again, through what I assumed was the kitchen window. Sure enough, I saw a woman petting a large black dog. "Boys," I said cautiously, "that might just be their dog. We don't know that's Lucky."

"It *is* Lucky. It is! I can see him!" Duncan said, jumping up and down with enthusiasm, though I doubted from his height he could see much of anything. He climbed up on the deck railing to get a better view, but I pulled him off before he could fall. I had no choice but to call for Dylan to come with us and, flanked by my band of merry warriors, trek into the neighbors' yard.

The boys clustered behind me, satellites around my orbit, as I pressed the neighbors' doorbell. The dog—who I now knew was Lucky—barked his head off as I heard our neighbor unlocking a series of dead bolts, which incidentally seemed excessive in this safe suburban neighborhood. "I heard Lucky in there!" Duncan smiled around his finger, which had worked its way back into his mouth on our walk. I didn't bother telling him to remove it.

The door opened a crack as the woman checked us out. Apparently assuming a mother and her three little boys were safe enough, she swung the door open with a smile. "Yes?" she asked.

I gestured at the boys, who were all pressed close to me, suddenly shy. "We were looking for our dog and wondered if maybe he wandered over here," I said.

On cue, Lucky pushed his nose through the space between her and the door, shoving her out of the way with his big head as he bounded toward the boys. "Lucky!" they all shouted at once.

"I was just on the phone calling animal control," she said with a look of relief. Her face looked familiar to me, but I couldn't place her. She gestured at the dog. "He wasn't wearing a collar."

I felt oddly scolded. "I know, yes. Well. He has a collar. We just took it off, and I … well, I forgot to put it back on him. We just moved, and everything's been—"

"Are you the new family who moved in behind us?" she asked. Her hand rose to her sleek bob, smoothing down her hair, although it looked perfect to me. She wore lipstick, even though she didn't appear to be going anywhere. I wondered what I looked like in David's baggy, ripped jeans; stained, threadbare T-shirt; and greasy hair desperately in need of shampoo. I wore lipstick only to special events. She smiled at me, displaying perfect straight white teeth and dimples. I imagined she got her teeth bleached at a dentist. I hadn't been in for a cleaning in over a year.

I shoved my hands into my jeans pockets. "Yes, we are. I'm Ariel Baxter, and these are my boys, Donovan, Dylan, and Duncan."

"Oh, you did Ds," she said. "We did Cs."

"Pardon?" I asked.

"Your boys' names. All Ds. My girls are Cameron and Caroline. Cs." She smiled and extended her hand. We shook with the stiff formality of strangers. She then shook each of the boys' hands while they looked at me questioningly but, thankfully, went along with it.

"I'm Justine Miller," she said. "I guess we'll be neighbors now." She laughed. "I apologize for not coming over yet. I saw movement over there and should have been by with some goodies for you." She seemed to be scolding herself. Lucky flopped down by our feet on her front porch. "You guys look thirsty. Would you like to come inside for some lemonade?" she asked.

"Sure," the boys said in unison, never ones to turn down juice or the chance to potentially destroy someone else's house. Before I could protest, Justine waved them all in, including Lucky. "I could go put Lucky back in the fence," I offered.

"Oh no. Lucky's fine." I noticed he walked in like he owned the place, the traitor sticking close to Justine. She giggled. "He knows I have treats for him in here." She ordered him to sit while she opened a canister and threw two dog treats at him, which he greedily swallowed after catching them in midair. I looked around but saw no dog anywhere. I decided not to ask. It was none of my business why this woman kept dog treats in her house but didn't own a dog.

We all stood awkwardly in her kitchen until she commanded we sit down. Each of the boys took a seat at the table, where she placed a plate of sugar cookies. "I just baked these today. I'm so glad I did," she said. The boys snatched the cookies off the plate just as greedily as the dog had gulped down his treats. I didn't say a word but made a mental note to go over manners with them when we got home. I looked up to see Justine studying us, the full lemonade pitcher in her hand, a puzzled look on her face.

"So you said you have two girls?" I asked, to make small talk. Two perfect little girls would explain the perfectly appointed house full of breakable knickknacks, the time to bake homemade cookies, her calm demeanor. I surveyed the large kitchen/eating area/living room. Not a thing was out of place.

"That's right. They just got home from summer camp and are upstairs resting for a bit. They get so tired from a full day of activities," she said, shrugging her shoulders.

My boys never rested. They had two speeds: bouncing off the walls or passed out. She turned to the boys. "I know my girls would love to meet you. You all could play together. We have a lovely playset outside, and you guys are welcome to come play anytime."

Donovan looked over at me with a look that said, *"See, you overreacted earlier."* "That's a nice offer," I said, "but we might want to put some limits on it. Trust me—you don't want my boys constantly in your yard."

"Oh, the more the merrier, I always say," she replied, grinning broadly at the boys. "I noticed you don't have a playset, and my girls don't play on it nearly enough. Might as well get some use out of it."

I felt stung, as if our lack of a playset was some sort of commentary on my ability to provide entertainment for my children. "Well, we have the trampoline," I said. "The boys love that, and it's a great way for them to get some energy out." Why did I feel the need to justify our outdoor play-equipment choices?

"Your girls are welcome to come jump anytime," I added, matching her kind offer with an equally kind one, I thought.

She shook her head gravely. "No, I had a friend whose child was severely injured on a trampoline. Our girls know not to get on one."

"Oh," I said, feeling chided and a little embarrassed. I took a long swallow from my lemonade and calculated how quickly I could get out of there. I looked up to see Dylan and Duncan using Justine's long scrolled candlesticks as guns, pretending to fire them at each other. This, I remembered, was why I didn't have nice decorative touches in my home. I plucked a candlestick from each boy's hand and deposited them back onto the wrought-iron holders in the center of her glass-top table, which, I noted, was strangely devoid of fingerprints, smudges, or smears. Except for the ones my boys had just added.

"Well," I said, draining my glass, "it's really nice to meet you, but we'd better get back home." I eyed Donovan so he would follow my lead. I stood up and hoped the boys would too. Instead all three of them snatched the rest of the cookies off the plate and gulped the lemonade like orphans.

"Oh, I wish you didn't have to rush off so fast," Justine said. She was wearing a perfectly pressed pink polo shirt and white shorts. Maybe they were new. Or she actually ironed. Which meant that we could never be friends.

"Well, I still have quite a bit of unpacking to do," I offered, gesturing at my house, which was clearly visible from the bank of windows in the room we were in. My eyes rested on the framed portrait above her fireplace, a portrait I remembered taking at a charity event. *That* was how I knew her. It had been one of my first real gigs, a nightmare afternoon of families full of fussing children moving on and off the front porch where I was shooting the pictures. One family after another had paid an exorbitant fee for fifteen minutes on a porch swing flanked by ferns.

Justine had picked the one of just the two girls, each dressed in white eyelet dresses, huge bows on top of their blonde heads. I remembered taking some good ones of their whole family and wondered why she hadn't chosen one of those. Her husband, I recalled, had been quiet as Justine told me exactly what shots she wanted done, as if she was the expert and I was just the hired hand. It was all coming back to me the longer I stood there. I pointed at the photo. "I remember taking that," I said and smiled at her.

Her eyes widened as she realized what I was saying. "You? That was you that day?"

I chuckled. "You'll do just about anything when you're first starting out, trying to build a name for yourself."

"Well, you must've really wanted to build a name. It was hot as Hades out there," she said and laughed, fanning herself dramatically to make her point. "I nearly melted." She looked at the photo for a second, as though she had forgotten it was there.

"I remember you have a beautiful family."

She smiled brightly again. "Well, thank you." She pointed at the portrait. "And you do good work, even when it's 112 degrees outside. Wait till I tell everyone that you live here now. You're going to be super busy once everyone finds out that you are here. I get oodles of compliments on that portrait. There are a ton of families in this neighborhood that would love your services. Do you have some cards?"

"Yep." I smiled. I had just received in the mail the new ones with our updated address. "I'll run some over here sometime."

"Or I'll just stop by if that's okay. I am going to personally see to it that you stay busy, just you wait and see."

"That would be fine for you to stop by, but I have to warn you the house is a disaster."

"Oh, girl, you just moved in. It's fine. No one's expecting *House Beautiful.*"

I wondered how to tell her that my house would never—barring a miracle—be *House Beautiful,* that I could already tell that was her area of expertise. Instead I asked, "How long have you lived here?"

"Five years. We love it here," she added quickly.

"We're very happy to be here," I said. "But I'll be happier once I get everything unpacked and organized."

"Well, you might be in luck because organizing's kind of my thing. You know, like photography is your thing. So if you need any help, just say the word." She visibly brightened as she said it. From the looks of her house, I knew she was telling the truth. How organizing could be *anyone's* thing was a mystery to me.

"I just might take you up on that," I said and smiled back at her, though I doubted my smile was as high wattage as her ultrawhite one. "Well, come on, boys, it's back to work." I tried to make my tone match her cheery one. I made my way to the door, the boys and Lucky dragging behind me. As I put my hand on the knob, Justine's voice stopped me.

"Are you coming to the summer-kickoff party?"

I turned to her again. Her smile was still in place and she wore an expectant look. I vaguely remembered a flyer affixed to our mailbox when we moved in. The sun had faded it slightly so that the bright red paper was a pinkish color by the time I brought it in and laid it down on the built-in desk in my kitchen. It had been buried under other papers since then.

"Remind me what it is?" I asked.

"Oh, it's just the hottest thing going in this neighborhood. You just have to come! I've already got the girls' bathing suits picked out. Cutest little matching polka-dot bikinis!"

I thought about my boys' mismatched suits and wondered if I needed to do a quick shopping trip so they, too, would match.

"It's this Saturday," she added. "I hope you'll come. If you do, I'll introduce you around and tell everyone how lucky we are to have you living here. You can become our official neighborhood photographer!" She clapped her hands together.

I found myself nodding along with her. "Sure," I said. "We'll be there."

The truth was David and I had promised each other we'd spend Saturday doing nothing but unpacking. Oh well, the packing could wait a day longer. And we didn't have to go to church on Sunday anyway. That could wait. Making friends in our new neighborhood couldn't.

I reminded the boys, "Say thank you for the cookies."

They all imitated angel children and thanked her. I breathed a sigh of relief that they had complied. We *really* needed to work on their manners. As we tromped back across the yard, stopping to wave to Justine, who was watching us through her kitchen window, I couldn't help thinking that, compared to Justine, I had lots to work on.

CHAPTER 4

Ariel

We made a ragtag crew as we lumbered our way from the parking lot to the neighborhood pool. David carried the cooler, and I held a jumbo-size tote bag full of towels and sunscreen and pool toys— anything I could think of that might be needed for an afternoon by the water. Walking with the boys was like walking with the Three Stooges as they fell into each other and picked at each other every step of the way. David was intent on successfully getting the impossibly heavy cooler past the pool gates without dropping it. I made another mental note to buy a cooler that rolled. I knew there were many other items on that growing list, but I couldn't have named one of them on that bright summer day.

I slipped out of my cover-up self-consciously, tugging at my suit in vain. It was the first time I had been in a bathing suit that summer. I didn't know what was worse, my translucent skin or the way the suit showed my rolls in all the wrong places. David still raised his eyebrows and whistled when I took off my cover-up, but I couldn't discern whether he meant it or was just being kind. He stripped off his shirt and stretched, seeming not to notice or worry that he was as pale as I was.

"Boys, let's go get in the water," he said. "Let Mommy relax for a minute." I mouthed the words *thank you* as he walked off with the boys in tow.

With nothing better to do, I pulled out a parenting magazine that I had stuck in my bag. Articles about potty training, birthday parties, and nutritious snack ideas swam before my eyes, and I longed for a good novel to read instead. I laid the magazine down and rested my eyes.

As I felt my skin warming, I remembered that, though I had slathered the boys with sunscreen, I had forgotten all about myself. I was digging around in my bag for a bottle when I heard someone sit in the empty seat on the other side of me. "I know that look," the woman beside me said. I looked in the direction of her voice. She leaned toward me, extending her hand. "Erica," she said.

"Nice to meet you," I responded, shaking her hand. "Ariel," I added.

"Nice to meet you, Ariel," she said, then paused. "I knew who you were." She smiled with her confession. "Not much happens in this neighborhood that doesn't get spread around. Especially new neighbors."

"Oh," I said. "Okay." I looked over at the boys and back at her.

"I live over on Hastings," she said. Hastings was the main drag of the neighborhood. A large percentage of residents lived on that street.

"I'm on Schuyler," I said.

"Yes. You bought Dan and Laura's house," she said.

"So I've heard."

She smiled at me. Her long dark hair and exotic looks seemed out of place in our vanilla neighborhood. I wondered where she fit in with the other suburban moms. "Dan and Laura were the poster children of the neighborhood," she said with an almost irritated smile. "Laura and Justine used to run the place. I'm sure you've met Justine."

"Yes," I said. "She invited us to this party."

"So tell me about yourself," she said. "Married? Kids? I saw you with those boys. Are they all yours?"

I winced at her use of the word *all*. "Yes," I said, "I have three boys. Donovan's eight, Dylan is six, and Duncan is four. I'm married to David," I added. "He's in sales. He travels," I continued, as if I was completely in support of my husband's travels, the doting wife.

"My husband never traveled," she said. "He was always home every night for dinner." She pulled down the large dark sunglasses she was wearing so I could see her dark eyes. "Not that that helped," she said. She giggled ironically. "We're divorced now. But at least I got the house." She rolled her eyes and pushed the sunglasses back up to the bridge of her nose, hiding her eyes once again. "That's what all the women around here say to me. They can't think of anything else to say because they are too afraid to talk about it. Talking about it makes it real. If you talk about it, it might happen to you." She smiled without showing any teeth and smoothed out nonexistent wrinkles in her towel.

A teenage girl came running up, wearing the regulation swim-team bathing suit I had seen some other children wearing, black with green racing stripes. She shook her head violently, sending water spraying everywhere like a dog. "Heather!" Erica shrieked. "Must you do that?"

Heather, undeniably Erica's daughter, grinned at her mother and then over at me. "Sorry, Mom," she said. "Who's your friend?"

"This is Ariel Baxter. She just moved in. She has three little boys."

Heather waved shyly. "Hi," she said, showing a mouthful of braces as she grinned.

"Heather loves kids," Erica explained.

I waved back. "Hi." As if on cue, the boys ran up, dripping water and energy. Duncan snuggled his wet body up next to mine, and I moved away slightly. "Dunc, you're wet," I said. He giggled and tried to scoot up next to me again. I gestured to the boys. "These are my boys," I said to Erica, who nodded.

"Cute," she said.

"They're wild as bucks," I said.

"I just have the one, which is a blessing now that I am doing it alone. We wanted a whole houseful once upon a time, but it never happened. Now I see it was God's plan. He knew what I needed even when I didn't."

I looked at her and smiled. "God's plan is hard to accept sometimes, though. I mean, when you're going through it." I thought of how plans—whether they were our own or God's—were slippery and exhausting to try to hold on to.

She shook her head. "You have no idea. Oh well, we live and learn, right?"

I nodded. I liked her blunt way of speaking. I felt like I could ask her anything and she would tell me the truth. It was refreshing to find, unusual. "But enough about me," she said. "Are you guys all settled? Unpacked? Are you new to the area?"

"Umm. Sort of settled. The boxes are getting unpacked slowly but surely. It's starting to feel like home. And no, we're not new to the area. We lived across town, but I dreamed of moving here for a long time."

"And is it living up to your dreams?" she asked, cutting to the quick of my own thoughts of life in the stress of the move.

I thought of David being gone all the time with his new job, of Lucky disappearing and knowing no one to help find him, of how much I missed the casual, easy friendship I shared with Kristy when she was just across the street. I wanted to lie to Erica—but something wouldn't let me. Maybe because she had been so honest with me. "Not really," I admitted for the first time.

"Not much in life does, I'm finding," she said. She reached down and took another long sip of water. "Want some?" she asked, extending the water to me. I smiled and lifted my own bottle from the large tote bag that held everything but the kitchen sink.

"Thanks," I said. I meant thanks for the offer, but really I was thanking her for being so honest. I hoped she knew it.

———

A song from the '70s came on the loudspeakers. "How long has this been going on?" the music blared.

Justine giggled from beside me. Erica had politely left when she showed up, but I sensed that there was no love lost between the two women. As the newbie on the block, I didn't dare ask either of them, but I knew there had to be a backstory.

"I love that song. They always play great oldies here at the pool," Justine said. She wiggled in her chaise longue, moving her shoulders from side to side, her breasts in her push-up bikini top attracting the attention of more than one male in the vicinity. I sensed she not only knew it; she liked it. Expected it. I thought of my own tank suit, covering all the parts I didn't want exposed, my pasty white skin, the flesh that had never quite recovered from three pregnancies. With her tan skin, toned body, and confidence, Justine and I were opposites in more ways than one.

The two of us passed the time fielding children and making small talk. I kept an eye on David, who was playing volleyball with some of the other men. Justine's husband, Mark, wasn't there—she said he'd been called out of town on business, which I thought was too bad. It was a bit premature, but I held out hope that our families would become good friends and pictured our children growing up together, maybe even dating, family barbecues in our shared back-yards, a lifetime of history forming on one early June afternoon. I felt happy, peaceful. I wanted nothing more than to be right where I was.

"Justine," I heard someone call over the music, the loud voice shattering my reverie. The Eagles were singing, "You can't hide your lyin' eyes, and your smile is a thin disguise." I looked up to see a large woman blocking our sun, her shadow looming. I shielded my eyes so I could see her better with the sun behind her. She was her own eclipse.

"Hi, Liza," Justine said. "Good to see you."

Liza nodded. "How ya doin'?" she asked Justine with a sympa-thetic look I didn't understand.

"Girl, I am doing just fine." She pointed at me. "Have you met my new neighbor, Ariel?" Justine turned to look at me. She was, I realized for the first time, in full makeup. She hadn't come to the pool to swim; she had come to the pool to be seen.

"Ariel bought Dan and Laura's house. She's a fabulous photographer. She did that beautiful portrait of the girls that's over my mantel? You've got to book an appointment with her!" She caught my eye and winked. "Ariel, this is Liza Blair. She lives over on Hastings Lane."

"Nice to meet you," Liza said. She paused in thought. "Wait a minute! My friend Candace Nelson told me about you! She called me and told me what great work you do and that I should look you up now that you live here!" She extended her hand to me, and I leaned forward to take it, smiling at the compliment. She pumped it up and down vigorously, a handshake I could respect.

Liza turned to Justine. "Thanks for introducing us and helping me make that connection. Have you met the other new neighbors?" she asked her. "They bought that spec that's been sitting empty for so long. Remember we thought it'd never sell?"

"Oh!" Justine exclaimed. "It's got that terrible backyard." She looked over at me, and I nodded. We had looked at it and stayed less than three minutes.

Liza looked around the pool. "The people are around here somewhere. I just saw them. Nice folks. Hang on and I will find them." She made a visor of her hands and looked until she spotted the other new neighbors. She waved them over to what was becoming a growing party, one I was invited to just by sheer proximity to Justine. I wished David were with me so he could meet some new neighbors. But from the looks of things in the pool, he was making new friends courtesy of his competitive streak.

"Tom, Betsy, come meet some neighbors," Liza said as the couple walked closer with smiles pasted on their red, overheated faces. The wife ducked her head and raised her eyes to glance at us before dropping them again. She studied the concrete patio, then scanned the pool as if she would like to be standing anywhere else. The man grinned at all of us, his face changing as he saw Justine. I imagined she had that effect on a lot of men. "Tom and Betsy Dean, meet Justine and—" she paused at me—"Sorry?"

"Ariel," I said, reaching for the wife's hand as she raised her eyes to me and smiled. "Ariel Baxter." I saw David get out of the pool and make his way over to our little crowd. He smiled at me and detoured by the boys to check on them.

"Dean?" Justine asked, eyeing the man. "Like James?"

Tom took her hand and smiled at her. "Exactly," he replied, pumping her hand three times before taking mine and doing the same. "Nice to meet you," he said to me and turned his attention back to Justine. I noticed her face redden and wondered if he was embarrassing her with his attention. Surely she had faced unwarranted attention from men before. I felt sorry for Betsy and tried to diffuse the situation by talking to her.

"So, Betsy, Tom, do you guys have kids?" I asked.

Betsy nodded and returned my smile. She was what I would classify as cute but not gorgeous. She had probably been called cute her whole life, and hated it. I imagined if I got to know her, I would like her a lot. "We have a boy and a girl," she said. "Tyler's nine and Tessa's six." She seemed unassuming and a little overwhelmed by the neighborhood as a whole. I could sympathize.

"Oh, I have two girls who would probably love to play with

your children," Justine said enthusiastically. I felt the smallest sting of jealousy that I wasn't the only one with whom she wanted to arrange playdates. "My girls are right near your kids' ages," Justine said. "We will have to have you guys over for dinner sometime and get the girls together for a playdate."

Tom gestured to our group of children, which now had two more children playing. "Are those your girls?" he asked. "The two blondes?"

"Yes," Justine said.

"And my boys are with them," I added.

He ignored me. "Well, it looks like they've found each other," he said and grinned at Justine. "They're beautiful," he continued. She returned his smile and looked away just as David joined us. Liza, still serving as social coordinator, introduced David to everyone while I sat quietly.

More chairs were pulled up, and we formed a semicircle. We laughed and talked and got to know each other better. Kids came and went. Food was served and eaten. And before we knew it, the day was slipping into night. I pretended not to notice how Tom's eyes kept wandering back to Justine in her revealing bikini. I did notice that David seemed to avert his eyes from looking directly at her, and I wanted to kiss him for it.

As our wiggly, sun-kissed boys climbed into our laps to wind down the evening, I sighed contentedly. This was what I had pictured when I imagined living here: neighbors and children and laughter and community. Perfection was finally within my grasp, and Justine was helping me find it.

CHAPTER 5

———

Justine

No one would've known by looking at me that inside I was hyper-ventilating, that Tom Dean himself had just walked up to me on a sunny day at my pool and smiled like he was just asking what time it was or commenting on the weather, like it was all normal when it was anything but. Our lives had just changed dramatically, but there was no tremor, not even a shift in the wind.

Even more significant than Tom was his wife, the infamous Betsy. All these years I'd wondered what she looked like, who the temptress was who took him away from me. I'd pictured a gorgeous natural blonde with a great figure. Instead she was … cute. Cute in an undeniable and endearing way, but still just cute. Cute enough, I will admit, that I didn't really dislike her. Not until she started talking about visiting my church.

And stealing my part.

It was Tom who told Liza about it right in front of me. "Oh, Liza," he said, his eyes wandering back to my bikini, grazing over me so fast no one noticed but me. "Did Betsy tell you about her good news?"

"Good news?" Liza asked, perking up. Liza liked news of any sort, especially when she was the first to know it. "Let's hear it."

Tom put his arm around Betsy. "She got the part in the Patriotic Pageant at the church."

"She did?" Liza cast a nervous glance in my direction. The chaise longue she was sitting on groaned as she shifted her weight. I could tell she was thrilled to be hearing this right in front of me. For all Liza thought she knew, she didn't know the half of it. "Well," she said, "that's just wonderful, Betsy. Congratulations!" She started to change the subject, but I stopped her.

"What made you try out for that part?" I asked, unable to stop myself. I glanced around at the group of us who had gathered, but no one was listening except Tom, Betsy, and, of course, Liza.

Betsy was caught off guard by my question. Tom, who was making circular rubbing motions on her back, stopped. "What do you mean?" she asked.

"I mean," I said, "you come to a new town, new neighborhood, new church. And right off the bat you audition for the starring role in the upcoming musical. It just seems a bit industrious. You know, all at once like that."

Liza looked at me with her brows knit together. Tom and Betsy just looked confused. "Well," Betsy said, "I really like to sing."

"And she's got a great voice," Tom added.

"Oh, well, obviously, if you got that part. You must have an amazing voice," I said.

"Well ... thanks," Betsy said, her face even redder. She had taken my part. So everything else from then on was fair game.

CHAPTER 6

———

Ariel

On Monday morning I woke up with a fresh resolve to unpack more boxes before nightfall to make up for our lost time at the pool over the weekend. I pulled on a pair of gray knit shorts and an old fraternity T-shirt of David's and set to work.

The boys busied themselves outside, happily playing, and staying away from Justine's yard too, I noted. Perhaps this wouldn't be as hard as I had feared. They seemed content to play in our garage and on our driveway. I supplied them with a large bucket of sidewalk chalk and encouraged them to use their imaginations. Other than the occasional trip inside, I hadn't heard much from them. I unloaded three boxes before the trouble started, as Dylan came inside to report that I should buy some more rockets.

I was hardly paying attention as I held up a vase we had received as a wedding gift and never had an occasion to use, trying not to make it a commentary on my marriage. I would find a spot for it on a high, unreachable shelf. "Why didn't you tell us you had those rockets, Mom? They're cool," Dylan added, climbing inside one of the empty boxes and closing the lid on himself. His voice was muffled as he held the lid down, the tips of his fingers showing.

I had no idea what he was talking about. "Dyl, what rockets?" Even as the words left my mouth, my blood ran cold. I remembered the boys stealing quietly upstairs and coming down with a bag full of stuff. I had assumed it was toys, but what if … "Dylan?"

No answer came from inside the box. "Dylan?" I said, louder.

There was silence for a moment, and then he exploded from the box. "Surprise!" he said. "It's a Dylan-in-the-box!" He grinned at me. He had lost his first tooth the week before. I noticed the missing tooth with the pang of a mom who knows that time is flying faster than she can catch it. "Get it, Mom? A Dylan-in-a-box?"

"Yes, I get it." I set down the vase in a group of things that needed to be put up. "What rockets are you talking about?" I pressed. "Where did you find them?"

"In your bathroom," he said matter-of-factly as he climbed back into the box. "Under your sink."

"Dylan. Get out of that box and come with me right now," I said.

Resolutely he followed me out of the room as I headed for the garage. My heart was racing in rhythm with my steps as I ran out to face whatever it was my boys had done this time. I opened the garage door to find the carnage I had known was inevitable. Applicators, wrappers, and white super and regular "rockets" were strewn all over the garage, the driveway, and our front yard. I found Duncan peeling open the small box of lites with a grin. "We still have these," he was saying to Donovan.

"They're not as good," Donovan replied as if I wasn't there. "They won't fly as far." I just stood there with my mouth hanging open. What a great first impression we were making on Essex Falls. Hey, new neighbors! Welcome to the insanity!

Muffling the half laugh, half cry that threatened to escape, I put on my best scolding face. "Boys, I want you to pick up every single piece of paper and every single—" my mind fumbled for their terminology—"*rocket* you shot off. Put them in the trash. Now."

Donovan just shrugged and began picking up the pieces. He twirled one around by its string. "Hey, Mom, what are these things for anyway?"

I ducked my head down and pretended not to hear him as I joined the boys in the cleanup. I'll bet Justine's nice, quiet, napping girls would never launch their mother's tampons all over her front yard. In that moment I was thankful she lived behind us and was less likely to see what my uncouth boys had done.

"Well, Mom?" Donovan repeated. "What are these for? Can you light them on fire?" Usually I applauded my eldest's curiosity, helping him search out answers on the Internet and taking him to the library to get books on everything from how hot air balloons work to how Saint Nicholas became known as Santa Claus. Of course, this time I told him we'd talk about it later and gave him a look that silenced him quickly.

It was about that time that I heard someone knocking on our back door and, fainter, a voice calling out, "Hellooo? Ariel?" I recognized the voice as Justine's. Her timing was impeccable.

"We're out here!" Dylan piped up before I could muffle him, his fists full of white.

I glared at him.

"What?" he asked.

I wanted to run in and shut the garage door behind me, keep her away from the scene. Although I knew that if the neighborhood gossip was any good, she'd hear about it anyway. Not that I saw anyone watching us, but a few cars had driven by in the minutes that had passed. I was mentally preparing myself for the label "the mother who doesn't watch her kids" when Justine stepped down into our garage with her eyebrows raised and the beginnings of a smile on her face.

"Hi," Donovan greeted her. "We've been playing rockets."

She nodded, her eyes wide. "I see that," she said. She shot me a look that was, thankfully, full of amusement and no trace of judgment. "Used them all up, did you?"

Donovan nodded, his grin widening. "Do you have any we could use?"

She looked back at me, her face a question. Was this normal behavior? Should she say yes and run home for a box? I shook my head vigorously, my eyes as wide as hers. She smiled back at me. "No, I'm sorry. I don't have any."

"Man!" Donovan said and skulked off to the edges of the lawn to gather the last remains of the destruction.

I gestured for Justine to follow me to the kitchen and told the boys to finish their cleanup. Justine waited until we got inside and I shut the garage door to start laughing.

"What—" she began. She tried again, "What were they—"

I held up my hand, barely able to breathe from the rising laughter. "Don't ask. Seriously," I said, my eyes leaking tears from the corners. It occurred to me that with the stress of the move, I hadn't really laughed in days.

"They wanted more. They wanted me to bring them a box!" she said. She wiped at her eyes. "I mean, what was I supposed to say, 'Which size?'" She bent over and put her head down, her whole body shaking with laughter.

"Well, apparently, the lites don't fly very far," I deadpanned. "They need the big guns."

She looked up with tears in her eyes, waving them away, probably to keep her mascara in place. "Well, I will be sure to remember that in the future. You really do learn something new every day." She took a deep breath. "And I thought my girls getting into my lip gloss was bad," she said.

"Stick around," I said. "A friend of mine once told me, 'Boys are like dogs. They do things in packs they would never do on their own.'"

She nodded, her smile lighting up her face again. "And from the looks of things, you've got a pack of your own."

I wondered if she knew how beautiful she was. It was my observation that most women didn't. Sometimes when I met a truly beautiful woman, I just wanted to tell her, in case she didn't know. I took in her appearance: denim capris and a white cap-sleeve blouse that had been crisply ironed. My suspicions were increasing that Justine and her iron were on very good terms. She had tied a hot-pink scarf through the belt loops, which added a perfect burst of unexpected color and style. I remembered my own haphazard ponytail and old clothing and suddenly wanted to melt through the floor.

"I brought you all a loaf of blueberry lemon bread," she said, now that the laughter had died down. "It's my girls' favorite so I baked an extra loaf this morning. I thought it would be something you could snack on while you unpack." She gestured to the slowly decreasing wall of boxes in the adjoining den.

"Yes, well, at this rate I will still be unpacking next year. With interruptions like lost dogs, pool parties, and rocket launching, I can't seem to get anything done." I shrugged my shoulders, once again deflated by the sight of the boxes. "I feel like I will never get caught up on my life again," I admitted, then silently scolded myself. This person was not my friend. She was barely an acquaintance. I had no business telling her my problems.

She looked unfazed. "I meant it about helping. I love to help people get organized."

I looked at her and narrowed my eyes. She laughed and waved her hand at me. "I do! I even give little talks about it. Oh—" she threw her arms up in the air. "I'm giving one tomorrow to the mothers' group at my church. Would you like to come? It's about how to use the summer to get a jump on projects around your house."

"I'd love to, but I have the boys."

"Oh no, we offer babysitting. It's a nice break. Oh, and it's a great place to spread the word about your business."

I envisioned sinking into a chair and having at least one hour away from my boys. "Sure," I said. "That would be nice. I could use some advice on organization." And on discipline and parenting and marriage and time management and meal preparation and …

I remembered my fantasy about having everything in order before David came home from work. Maybe Justine was my answer.

I smiled at Justine, and she smiled back. For just a moment, I wondered if this picture of perfection and I could actually be friends, ironing issues not withstanding. That day in my kitchen, I believed it was possible, even probable.

She looked around. "Do you think you'll change anything in here?" she asked.

I followed her gaze. "David and I talked about it. He says he'd like to paint it a more neutral color. But I told him I liked the yellow. It feels … I don't know … happy?"

She nodded. "That's exactly what Laura said when she painted it."

"So you knew the people who lived here?" I asked. I had already heard a bit from Erica but played dumb. I had met the former owners only once, days before they moved away. They weren't at the closing. The wife, Laura, a pretty blonde who looked remarkably like Justine, didn't say much to me in the short time we spent together.

She answered me quietly. "She was my best friend."

"Oh," I said. Suddenly I knew why Justine hadn't come over those first few days to welcome us to the neighborhood. She wasn't too busy. She just didn't want to see other people in her best friend's house. "I'm sure it was hard to see her go." The gate between the two houses, I now understood, had been installed for them to have access to each other.

She nodded, swallowed. "You have no idea." She forced a smile for my benefit, I was sure. "But I'm glad such nice people bought the house," she offered.

"Well, the jury's still out on how nice we are. I mean, you did witness the rocket incident," I quipped.

She smiled as an awkward silence fell between us. I went to the refrigerator and began pulling out fruit for the boys. I would feed them sliced fruit and Justine's bread for lunch. I had already forgotten what kind she said it was. I held up the loaf she had left on my counter and grinned. "Lunch," I said.

"Well, when you're in survival mode," she said, running her french-manicured fingernails along the granite countertops. I imagined her and Laura choosing the counters together, their blonde heads bent over the samples. She and Laura probably both loved organizing, both dressed impeccably, both had it together. They probably got mistaken for sisters. And here I was in her friend's space. How did I tell her that survival mode was our standard?

The phone rang, and I grabbed it when I saw David's cell number on the caller ID. "Hey, what's up?" I asked. I smiled at Justine over the receiver, and she smiled back.

"I'm going to have to be gone tonight," David said. "I'm sorry. It can't be helped."

I wanted to hang up on him, but since Justine was watching, I played nice. "Oh well, if it can't be helped, it can't be helped." I knew he could read beyond what I said and hear the clipped tone of my voice.

"I'm really sorry about this, babe."

"Okay, well, bye," I said, seething inside. He had promised he'd be home tonight, that we'd have dinner as a family. I hung up and looked back at Justine, wondering why I felt embarrassed, as though his call was some form of rejection.

Justine looked at her watch, hopefully oblivious to what I was feeling. "Well, I need to get going. I have to pick up the girls at camp. It's really too bad you didn't move in earlier. You could have signed the boys up for the camp at the neighborhood club. It's heavenly," she said and giggled.

"Yes, well, it sure beats the alternative activity they found for themselves," I said as I cut into an apple.

"Oh," she added, "and please do give me some of your business cards to start passing out." I looked around for a moment, trying to remember which box they were in. She waved her hand. "I've already been telling people how blessed we are to have you living so close by."

"Thanks, Justine. Nice to see you again." I opened the box and grabbed a stack of business cards to hand her.

She smiled back at me as I pressed the cards into her hand, trying not to give away how grateful I was for her help. "So, I'll see you tomorrow? It's at Church of the Redeemer at nine a.m.," she said.

I tried to picture getting the boys and myself up and ready and where we needed to be by nine on a summer morning in the midst of the boxes that still needed unpacking. But I wasn't going to bring that up. "I'll be there," I said. When she opened the door, I heard a snatch of my neighbor's music: George Winston, or a pianist who sounded very much like him.

After Justine was gone, I called the boys in for lunch. The bread she baked was the best I had ever tasted. I ate it while reading the Bible, bread and Bread, both filling up empty places within me.

That afternoon while the boys lay on the couch to watch a movie, their limbs tangled together so that it was hard to tell which boy was which, I heard a knock on the door. I answered it to find Erica, the woman from the pool, standing on my doorstep, a bag of Oreos in her hand. She waved it back and forth. "I know lots of people will bring you homemade stuff, but I let go of that Suzy Homemaker stuff a long time ago. I don't even pretend to bake anymore."

I smiled at her and opened the door wider. "Come in," I said. "At your own risk."

She waved the bag of Oreos again. "Remember? Nondomestic diva? No judgment over here. But if you have any milk, these are a great afternoon snack. That much I do know."

We sat down at the table, and though I saw the crumbs from lunch, I didn't feel compelled to jump up and sweep them away. Erica unscrewed the top of an Oreo and licked out the filling, grinning at me. "I never can eat them like a grown-up," she offered. I poured us each a glass of milk, and we ate in silence, neither of us feeling particularly compelled to keep up unnecessary conversation.

"This is nice. Thanks," I said.

"I figured you were probably in the mood for a break." She pointed at the wall of boxes. "You have my permission to take a year to unpack all those."

I laughed. "A year? Really?"

"Sure! A year sounds about right to me. Three kids, busy life, husband to keep happy, meals to cook. You can't do it all. Don't get sucked into thinking that you can."

I thought of Justine's talk the next day on organization. I did believe I could do it all with the right information. I nodded at Erica. "Yeah, I guess you're right."

She shook her head. "She got to you already, didn't she?" An amused smile played at the corners of her mouth.

"Got to me? Who?"

"The queen of Essex Falls herself. Justine Miller." She pointed at her house through my kitchen window. "I guess it couldn't be helped. I mean, she is literally in your backyard."

I shrugged and put down my cookie. I had already licked the filling out of the middle anyway, the sweetness still on my tongue. "She invited me to her mothers' group."

"I'm sure she did. Mothers' group is code for Justine Training Camp. Attend enough meetings and you'll be just like her!" I didn't miss the irony in her voice.

I couldn't figure out where Erica's animosity was coming from and I didn't feel comfortable asking. I remembered how she had slipped away when Justine showed up at the pool. "I figured the mothers' group would be a good way to meet people. Make some new friends here." I didn't know why I was defending my choice to Erica.

She nodded and smiled, the edge she had in her voice disappearing. "It is. You're right. Sorry if I came on too strong. I'm just not like those women so I tend to shy away from them." She tapped the Oreos. "Case in point."

I grinned at her and wondered idly if I had Oreos in my teeth. "There's nothing wrong with a bag of Oreos," I said.

She pulled another one from the bag. "Indeed." She chewed thoughtfully. "You be friends with whomever you want," she said.

"I just hope you'll include me on that list. You seem like a cool chick."

I nodded. "Thanks," I said. "You, too." Neither one of us looked in the direction of Justine's house, but I could feel it behind me, an uninvited guest at the table, frowning on eating store-bought cookies in the middle of the afternoon while unpacked boxes awaited my attention. I turned my body toward Erica and ignored Justine's house. I took the top off another Oreo and scraped the white filling with my teeth, the sweetness filling my mouth again.

CHAPTER 7

—

Ariel

Who was I kidding? It was 8:30 a.m., and the boys were still running around in various stages of undress, no one had eaten breakfast yet, and I hadn't put any makeup on my face. If I could even find my makeup, that is. "Boys! We need to leave in five minutes if we're going to make it on time!" I yelled up the stairs.

No answer.

"Boys? Do you hear me?"

A muffled "Yes, ma'am" came from one boy.

I let out an exasperated sigh as I marched up the steps to my room. We were going to be late and there was nothing I could do to stop it. Maybe I'd be better off to just announce, as Erica had, that I would never be any better. That this was as good as it gets. But I wasn't ready to give up on my promise to myself to get my life under control, and so far, this mothers' group was the closest thing I'd found to a guarantee of that coming true.

I stood in front of my bathroom mirror and took a few deep breaths, ignoring the clock's reflection from my bedside, its backward red numbers tolling the minutes that were slipping away. I rummaged in my drawer and hit the jackpot: my makeup bag. Justine had seen me only without my makeup, but I intended to show her another side of me. Never mind that it was going to make us later. I paused long enough to holler at the boys, "You have cereal on the table. Go eat as soon as you are dressed."

Returning to my room, I began applying base, eyeliner, mascara, blush. Normally in the summers I went without base or blush, but that was assuming I had spent some time in the sun. Our day at the pool party had been a nice start, but nowhere near enough. I heard a crash downstairs, and my heart began to race. I waited a moment for someone to call out or start crying.

"Mo-om," Donovan called out. "Duncan dropped his cereal bowl and it broke and there's milk everywhere."

I looked back at the mirror and tried deep breathing again. Who said Lamaze was just for childbirth? "Don't freak out," I warned the woman in the mirror. "Just go clean it up. Pretend you're not a raving lunatic." When I entered the kitchen, I found all three boys clustered over the mess. Donovan was trying to pick up the broken pieces of bowl. Dylan had a broom and was trying to sweep up the wet cereal, and Duncan had a washcloth and was smearing the liquid into an ever-widening circle. Their sweet attempt to clean up would have melted my heart if it wasn't making an even bigger mess and making us even later to the event.

"Boys, thank you. I'll take it from here," I said after taking a deep breath. I felt like crying. The microwave clock said 8:51. We should've already been in the car if we were going to make it even close to on time. I sighed. The boys stood rooted to their spots, Donovan holding pieces of broken bowl that thankfully hadn't cut his hands, Dylan with the broom in his hand, Duncan holding the dripping cloth. "It was an accident," I said to Duncan, who looked like he wanted to cry as badly as I did. They all exhaled in relief. "Go get your shoes on and then get in the van and wait quietly for me," I said. Thankfully, for once, they did exactly as they were told.

The church parking lot was quite full, the turnout surprising to me for a summer morning. My guess was that other moms needed the break that Justine described as badly as I did and would take any excuse they could get.

After dropping off the boys in the babysitting room, where I was surprised to see Erica's daughter, Heather, serving as one of the sitters, I headed toward the sanctuary. I heard Justine's voice before I entered the sanctuary. She was onstage welcoming everyone, her Southern drawl already familiar to me. I felt proud that she was my neighbor, especially as I stepped inside and saw the crowd of women hanging on her every word. That is, until the door's overloud click caused everyone to turn their attention to me. It felt like high school all over again.

With an exaggerated tiptoe, I made my way to a seat in the back beside a woman nursing a newborn. Justine found me, and our eyes met. She smiled warmly, the same bright smile I had admired that first day at her house. The exchange took less than a moment, but I felt welcomed by her. I ducked my head and was thankful that, with the lights low, she couldn't see me blush.

As Justine launched into her lecture on organization, I noticed the other women whipping out pens and notebooks. I sat there looking helpless as another woman passed me a sheet of notebook paper and a stubby pencil from the back of the pew. There was barely a point on the pencil, but I whispered a thank-you and obediently took notes. Apparently, it was expected to write down every word Justine said.

As I listened to Justine extol the benefits of planning out your menus for the week, I absentmindedly scribbled, "She makes it look easy." But as I continued to listen to her, I felt hope that I could be just like her. That with the right amount of planning and effort, I, too, could have a life like Justine's. When I looked around the sanctuary, I realized that every woman in the room had the same idea. We wanted to be just like her, and she was giving us the keys to make that happen.

One of the keys she held up was her "life-management notebook." The women ooohhed and ahhhed and murmured to each other as she went over the different divisions of the book: a section for each aspect of the busy homemaker's life, she said. I dutifully wrote down the sections: calendar, health, menus, goals, projects, prayer journal, notes, and a section for each child, all while trying to rectify the person wiggling to the music in the pool chair the other day with the poised, prim woman in front of us.

After the meeting, I milled around with the other women, smiling politely and repeating my name over and over as we sipped watered-down punch and ate cookies. I wondered if they would log the calories in the health section of their notebooks like Justine had suggested. I grinned at my own private joke as I noticed the line of women waiting in line to talk to Justine. She caught my eye and waved me over. As I approached her, I noticed the pairs of eyes staring at us. Was it envy in their eyes as Justine put her arm around my shoulders and said loudly, "Ariel, I am so glad you came"? Awkwardly, I put my free arm around her shoulders and squeezed back briefly.

"Y'all," she announced to the women around us, "this is Ariel Baxter, my new neighbor." They all nodded, and I cast my eyes downward. "She lives right behind me and has the most adorable little boys. And she's a fantastic photographer. You all know that portrait I have in my house of the girls in those white dresses?"

They all nodded in unison. I heard Erica's voice in my head: *"Stepford Wives."*

"Well, Ariel took that picture! Isn't it a small world?" The women nodded as they backed away, checking their watches and murmuring they'd be sure to call me.

Justine turned to me. "They have to get their kids or I'd introduce you to everyone. Those sitters are militant about picking up the kids on time," she said and giggled. "So, did you enjoy it?" She looked at me as if it really mattered what I thought.

"Yes, I did. Thank you so much for inviting me," I said.

"Oh good. I just knew you would. Listen, I want to help you make a life-management notebook. I even have some extra dividers at my house that I made that I'll bring over. I decorated them so cute! You will just love them." She lowered her voice again so that I had to lean closer to hear her. "That notebook is my lifeline. It's my Bible. I couldn't live without it."

Something in my heart hurt a little as she said it. Her Bible? I wondered what she thought about the actual Bible. I wanted to say something to that effect but at that moment, Justine narrowed her eyes as she stared at my shirt. "Oh dear," she said. "You've got something on your shirt." She leaned forward and plucked whatever it was off, then made a disgusted face. "It's mushy," she said, grabbing a napkin from the snack table. She held up what she had found on me: a piece of wet, mushy Lucky Charms cereal. A blue diamond, as a matter of fact. She wiped her hand on a napkin and looked back at me, pasting on her brilliant smile once again. "Better," she said.

I felt the red blush of embarrassment climb up my neck. "Well, you better go get your boys while I tidy up here," she said, turning to gather up the detritus of the snack table. I looked around to discover I was the only one left.

I found the boys with Heather. "Sorry, I got caught up in conversation," I offered meekly.

"No problem," she said and smiled, revealing her mouthful of metal. "I don't have anything else to do." She paused and toyed with a rubber band in her braces. "And I love kids. Your boys are cute." She smiled at the boys, then, shyly, at me.

An idea came to me. "Say, would you like to babysit sometime?" I asked her. I pictured sitting across from David at a grown-up dinner, smiling over our menus as we discussed the grown-up food we were going to order. It had been a long time.

"Sure," she said, brightening. "I love to babysit." She pulled a card from her back pocket and offered it to me. "Heather Davidson: Babysitter, Mother's Helper, Nanny" it read.

I smiled and pushed the card into my own back pocket. "Good to see you again, Heather. And please tell your mom I said hello." I wondered why Heather was babysitting at the very mothers' group Erica had such disdain for. Strange.

"Boys, can you say good-bye to Heather?" They waved good-bye as they followed me to the van, my little ducklings all in a row. I patted the card in my back pocket as we walked, a promise of romance to come.

That afternoon I took the boys out to jump on the trampoline. They smiled broadly as I suggested it, nodding their heads with the enthusiasm of the young. Seeing their faces, I remembered why I loved taking them out to jump. Although Justine's reproach about the trampoline was fresh on my mind, I concluded that I didn't share her concern. Yet her disapproval nagged at me for reasons I couldn't put into words.

The boys and I giggled and teased as we took turns jumping and being bounced by the other jumpers. I had to admit I loved the feeling of flying through the air. I also loved it when the boys and I lay down on the trampoline and watched the clouds, calling out the shapes we saw.

"Look, Mom," Dylan said, "it's a heart." I followed his finger to find a perfect shape of a heart in the sky. Dylan looked over at me. "God's saying He loves us," he said. My own heart clenched in my chest, and I wished for my camera. There were some moments in life I just couldn't preserve. If I were to take a photo of that moment, I would've somehow filled the frame with Dylan's profile, his cheeks ruddy from jumping, and his line of sight to include the heart-shaped cloud.

The loud crank of a lawn mower interrupted our afternoon reverie. We all sat up to see where the noise was coming from. A man was in Justine's yard. I assumed it was her husband and watched him, sizing him up. Did he look like he went with her? This was something my sister and I used to always decide about couples. To go the distance, we decided long ago, the couple needed to look like they went together. When I brought David home for the first time, I cornered her. "Be honest," I asked with my arms folded across my chest. "Do we?"

Knowing exactly what I meant, she beamed and nodded, hugging me. "I'm so happy for you," she whispered. Some women know they are going to marry their husbands when he says the right words, looks at them a certain way, makes some sort of gesture. But I knew I was going to marry David the moment my sister's arms slipped around me. He and I went together. Even my sister thought so.

Justine's husband went with her, too. He was as nice looking as she was beautiful. Tall with strong, handsome features. He had the evidence of a paunch under the T-shirt he wore but nothing some sit-ups wouldn't take care of. He kept his nose in the air and jutted out his chest like a man who was used to being in charge of things. He seemed like the kind of man who was more comfortable in a suit than the worn khaki shorts and Nike T-shirt he was wearing to mow the grass. Such menial tasks seemed beneath him. He looked out of place in his own backyard.

He turned around, caught us watching, and waved. The boys waved back, and after a moment, he stopped the lawn mower and left it sitting in the middle of the yard as he ambled over to the gate between our two yards. I hopped down from the trampoline and crossed over to say hello to my new neighbor, the boys hot on my heels. I felt shy and self-conscious as I extended my hand to shake his sweaty one. He smelled like cut grass and sweat as he flashed a smile that did not match Justine's brilliant one. He must not have visited her dentist.

"I'm Mark Miller. You must be Ariel?"

I nodded, pleased Justine had mentioned me. "Sorry we haven't met before now. I was sorry you had to miss the pool party," I said.

He smiled with one side of his mouth. "Yeah, business stuff. I don't have to travel much with my job, but when I do …" He looked toward his house and then back at me, shrugging. "Anyway, I'm sorry I missed it."

"These are my boys," I said as the boys all jostled to get as close to me as possible.

"Fine-looking young men," he said. "I've got girls, myself." He hitched his thumb in the direction of his house. He turned to the boys. "You boys like girls?"

They balked, shaking their heads vigorously. "Girls are icky," Dylan said.

He grinned. "Yeah, I remember I used to feel that way a long time ago. But my girls aren't icky. You should play with them sometime. They're always playing inside." He rolled his eyes at the boys, like the girls were missing out. "Think you'd like to play with them out here sometime?" He pointed to the coveted playset.

The boys nodded. If the playset was involved, they would endure the girls who came with it. I placed my hand on Donovan's shoulders. "They would love that, I'm sure. I think the boys may have played with your girls some at the pool the other day," I said, making conversation. "And of course we met Justine when she returned our dog to us."

He chuckled. "Yeah, I heard about that. Ended up in our garage somehow?"

Reflexively, I scanned the yard for Lucky's sleeping form. He had not moved from his position under the trampoline. Sensing my gaze, he lifted his big head and thumped his tail a few times before flopping back down. "Lucky's a bit of an escape artist if we don't keep this gate closed." I looked at the boys. "But we're learning about keeping it closed, right, boys?" Donovan ducked his head sheepishly. Dylan rolled his eyes like a miniature teenager. "I was glad he ended up with Justine," I added.

He shook his head. "Yeah, well, I guess dogs are attracted to her just like people are. She's pretty amazing."

I didn't know where to put his declaration about his wife. It was so unabashed, I almost felt embarrassed. "I got to hear her speak at church. She was inspiring."

He chuckled again. "She's got talent. That's for sure. I've been with her for ten years and even I haven't uncovered all her talents yet."

I tried to imagine David saying the same about me. I couldn't. "Ten years, huh?" I asked. "So that means you met her in college?" I was totally guessing.

"Right after. We both got our first jobs with this huge corporation but were on different floors. My boss asked me to take a package down to her department, and I got lost. Couldn't find the office of the man I was supposed to deliver it to. I asked her for help, and she made sure I found where I was going. After I handed off the package, I went back and found her. Ostensibly to say thank you but it was really just to see her again." He squinted into the afternoon sun and chuckled. "The truth is, I was actually engaged to another girl at the time. I tell her she saved me from a lifetime of being with the wrong person. But she came along in the nick of time and worked her way into my heart. I'm grateful every day that she did."

"That's a very sweet story," I said, taken aback by how open he was with me. I couldn't imagine David ever telling a complete stranger the story of how we met.

"Where did you meet your husband?" he asked, reading my thoughts.

"College," I said. "Fraternity party." I smiled at my confession. "It was another life."

He gave a knowing laugh. "Sounds like it."

I heard the door to their house shut and looked past his shoulder to see Justine crossing the yard toward us. Two little girls trailed behind, wearing the kind of sundresses I would dress a little girl in if I had one. They looked like Justine's clones with longer hair. Justine wore a concerned expression on her face. I waved at her, the look on her face making me feel as if I had done something wrong. She waved back and the look went away, her brilliant smile replacing it.

"Just who I wanted to see," she said as she reached us.

"Who, me?" Mark said, teasing her.

She smiled and looped her arm through his. "Of course," she said. She planted a kiss on his cheek and winked at me. They were cute together. My sister would approve.

"Mark was just telling me about how you two met."

"Oh yes, he loves to tell that story." She let go of him and pulled on my arm. "Well, let's go get to work."

"Work?" I asked.

"The notebook? Remember?" Her tone had a "duh" in it.

Mark dropped his hands to his sides. "Guess I'll go finish with the grass," he said. "Nice meeting you, Ariel."

I wanted to tell him how sweet I thought he was, how romantic it was for a man to still love his wife, to believe they had a love story worth telling. His shoulders were stooped as he walked away, and he seemed to push the lawn mower with less enthusiasm.

She held up a bag from an office-supply store and pointed to my house. "Oh," she added, gesturing to the two girls flanking her on either

side. "This is Cameron and this is Caroline." I smiled at the girls. I had
seen them from a distance at the pool but hadn't met them yet. They had
blonde pigtails that made my heart hurt just a bit. My one regret in life
was that I hadn't had a girl. God and I had had many discussions about
it, in which I made clear to Him that I really wanted to try a fourth time.
Of course David told me I was crazy.

True to form, my boys had drifted back to the trampoline and were
trying to eject one another from it. Justine's eyes flitted over to them
briefly. "Girls, how about you play on the playset and Ariel's boys can
join you?" She looked at me. "Is that okay?"

"Sure." I shrugged. She waved my boys over, who whooped and
hollered. Justine turned and headed toward my house, swinging her bag
of goodies as she did. I glanced back at my boys one more time before
following her inside. They were shoving each other as they clambered up
the stairs while the two timid girls stood at the base. I still hadn't heard
either girl say a word.

"How old are your girls?" I asked her as we entered the cool kitchen.
I walked straight to the refrigerator to retrieve a drink. I held a bottle of
water up for her, but she shook her head.

"Eight and five," she said. "Caroline starts school this year, praise
the Lord."

"Yeah, Duncan has another year." I paused. "I'm glad. I'm not ready
to have them all gone yet."

"Well, I for one cannot wait for August to come along," she said,
slapping the granite countertop. "I've got my life all planned out." She
giggled. "I started planning the moment she steps on that bus when she
was about two weeks old. I'm going to claim something for myself now
that I finally can. Maybe a business like yours."

"I guess you'll have time to go to lunch with Mark and stuff during the day," I said. "He seems so nice."

She turned her back to me, checking on the children from out my kitchen window. "Yeah, he is. He's a good guy. The best."

"Does he always get home from work this early?" I asked, pressing her.

"No," she said. "Mark's having ... issues at work."

"I'm sorry to hear that," I said, then became quiet to leave space for her to elaborate. She didn't take the opportunity, so I continued in an attempt to encourage her. "I wish David was home more often. It must be nice having his help around the house." I feared David wouldn't get to our grass until the weekend and I would end up taking the boys to the pool alone while he did. I was weary of doing things with the boys alone.

She turned away from the window. "Mark's job's just real up in the air right now. It's been kind of hard, especially for him," she said. She rubbed her hands together with anticipation, blinking her eyes rapidly as if blinking away the problems like a genie. "Now, let's make this notebook."

I tried to act interested in the contents of her bag, but my mind drifted back to the look on Mark's face as he talked about her. I glanced at the yard and saw him pushing the lawn mower, this time noticing the weight of the world on his shoulders.

CHAPTER 8

Justine

Sometimes when Mark asks me what I am thinking, I want to tell him. Like tonight in bed, in the dark, when we were lying together just before falling asleep and honesty seemed possible, even good. I wonder what being honest would do for us, if it would change things.

I want to tell him that I am thinking about the couple in that movie we saw when we went on one of our silent dates: Get in the car, ride silently to the restaurant, sit silently through the meal making the smallest of talk, then gratefully head to the movie theater where silence is accepted, expected. I want to tell him that, if you were going to pair up a couple for a movie, you would put us together every time. We look like we go together, just like that couple in the movie. He is handsome to my beautiful, reserved to my outgoing, sweet to my sassy. You could put us on top of a wedding cake. But looking like we go together, I discovered too late, isn't everything. There has to be chemistry. And that's something we lack. Mark is nice. He is courteous. He is safe. But none of those things curl my toes.

When I met Mark, we were working at the same place. And he took a liking to me instantly, finding silly excuses to come by my desk, bringing me little gifts, teasing me like a grade school boy with a crush. I was a year out from a terrible heartbreak. I got rejected. I got dumped. I got one of those phone calls that no one ever wants to get. The gist of it was "There's someone else." So when good-looking Mark Miller started pursuing me, I wanted it to work out. I wanted to be loved again. It didn't matter that he was engaged to someone else. She was easy enough to remove from the picture.

Mostly I just wanted to prove from afar to the one who hurt me that I was desirable. Mark held promise. And he had a good job. So when he held my hand the first time he took me out, I thought, well, that's it. He's the one. My parents loved him, which cemented the deal, my mother raving over how good we'd have it. "With that boy you'll never have to worry. Never," my mother said. That sounded good to me, the never having to worry part. The trouble was, my mother was wrong. Worry had curled up in bed with us at night, sleeping between us like a fitful child, poking us in the back and stealing the covers.

We were already engaged by the time I realized he wasn't the one. The wedding was planned. My mother had invited everyone in town. She had paid deposits. So I closed the door to my bedroom and cried bitter tears.

Then I dried them and walked down the aisle.

Don't get me wrong, it hasn't all been bad. Mark mostly loves me enough for both of us. Until recently he's been a good provider. He's a sweet man, a gentle man. He mows the grass and fixes things that break, and he loves our girls even though I know deep down he wanted a boy. I see him watching the little boys who moved in behind us when he thinks I am not looking. I remember how he shyly asked me when Caroline was only a few months old if we could try again for a boy.

"Lots of people have three children," he said.

"Not me," I said, not looking at him. I stared down at her instead, nursing away. She was a beautiful baby. Everyone said so. I had done my part. I had subjected myself to pregnancy and weight gain and varicose veins and sleepless nights as much as I was going to.

He rolled over in our big king-size bed and faced the wall. "Well, then, maybe we can adopt," he said to the wall. I didn't respond, but I knew that wasn't going to happen either. That night as I held my sleeping baby and listened to my husband's soft snuffly breathing that meant he was deeply asleep, I admitted something to myself. I didn't want any more children because I didn't want any more ties to Mark. Just admitting it was equally thrilling and frightening. To say it meant that I was thinking of a life after Mark, a life beyond Mark. Yet to say it was like crossing out the life I had spent ten years building, the position in our community I held, the home I had created. I had invested years into building this life, no matter how much of it was built on lies.

Did I even want to cross that out? What if something better didn't wait around the corner? What if I discovered that this really is as good as it gets? What if I messed up my own life because I was too selfish, too bold, too ungrateful?

I thought back to when the man who broke my heart said all the things I had longed to hear as we sat by a lake and dreamed about a future that never happened. His words still haunted me, coming back uninvited at inopportune times.

I told him about my parents and how their marriage had broken up. I confessed that I still held on to the hope that real love could exist. I told him that one time when I was about five years old I woke up and tiptoed down the hall because I heard music playing. Things with my parents hadn't gone horribly wrong yet. I stood outside the doorway and watched as my real father danced with my mother. She thinks I have no memories of him, but she's wrong. My father looked into my mother's eyes and sang the lines to a Barry Manilow song that was on the radio. "I could love you, build my world around you, never leave you till my life is done." I blushed as I told him this secret moment I'd been carrying all my life.

The truth is, I told him, my father had lied. He was gone less than a year later.

My long lost love pulled me to my feet and held me there by the lakeside, rocking slowly back and forth as he sang, "Baby, I love you. Come, come, come into my arms. Let me know the wonder of all of you." When we finished dancing, he cupped my face in his hands and smiled down at me. "I won't leave," he lied. "I promise."

Then he grinned and said, "And if you tell anyone that I know the words to a Barry Manilow song, I'll find you and torture you."

I could close my eyes and remember every moment of that evening—the crispness of the air as night settled into the mountains of North Carolina, the sense that summer was ending and so was our time together as counselors at the camp, the sound of birds singing in the trees and the water lapping at the shore. I couldn't remember how we came to be there together or why we were away from our duties, but I could remember the way he looked at me, picture his eyes as he looked into mine. If I closed my eyes and tried really hard, I could almost remember the sound of his voice.

Of course that night in my bedroom I knew the end of the story, saw the complete picture. But for just a moment I pretended that I didn't. I pretended that the man sleeping next to me was the one I really wanted, the one who made promises to me that night long ago. It was a dangerous moment, one I didn't let myself have very often. A moment when he felt so close I could reach out and touch him, never knowing that just a few weeks later he would show up at my pool with his wife, Betsy, and two children. Betsy, who took my part. Betsy, who took him.

The memories I let play out that night led to a thought that had been rolling around in my head ever since: How long should I be held to a mistake I made when I was too young to know how long "till death do us part" really was? More often I pushed the thought from my brain. Such thinking was not allowed, just like thoughts of driving down the highway as far as I could get until my car ran out of gas weren't allowed. Like thoughts of indulging in fattening foods weren't allowed. Like thoughts of skipping church weren't allowed. I told myself that it was just one of those things all women think about but never admit. I was no different than anyone else.

CHAPTER 9

⌒

Ariel

David's flight got in after I had fallen asleep, and he was gone to the office by the time the boys and I woke up the next morning. "Some homecoming," I said to myself as I woke up to find his side of the bed empty, his car gone from the garage. I wondered if I had dreamed him coming to bed in the dark, feeling his arms slip around me and his face press into my neck. I resolved to call him later as I set about smearing peanut butter on overly dark toast thickly enough that the boys wouldn't see the offensive burned parts and refuse to eat them. We were low on bread and milk and lots of other essentials. A trip to the store loomed in my future, and I dreaded it the way others dread a colonoscopy.

When the doorbell rang, I assumed it was Justine coming to see if I had made my list of acceptable breakfast choices in the menus section of my notebook, her first assignment for me. I wondered if cold cereal was an acceptable entry for all seven days.

Instead I found Kristy standing on my doorstep, her six-month-old daughter, Kailey, in her arms. "Do you think you'll need the car seat?" she asked.

I looked at her in utter confusion.

"Are you going anywhere?" she repeated, as if rephrasing it would make a difference. My mouth opened and closed but no sound came out. "While I'm gone to my appointment?" I could see the panic filling Kristy's eyes as she realized I had forgotten. I wondered if she could see the panic filling mine as I remembered, the details coming back to me in a rush.

Kristy had missed her period. She had called to tell me shortly after we had moved in.

I had assured her it was nothing. Women who have been nursing have erratic periods. It's normal. She couldn't be pregnant. I said all the things she wanted me to say, even though I didn't believe them and she didn't either.

"Will you keep Kailey while I go to the doctor?" she had asked that day, her words coming out in a rush.

"Yes, of course I can keep her. You just call me and tell me when they can see you," I had said. David had rolled his eyes and walked out of the room. I had hung up the phone and promptly forgotten all about my promise. When Kristy had called back, we were at the pool party. I never returned her call or listened to her message, which apparently was letting me know she was bringing Kailey by today, to leave her with me while she went to the doctor. I spotted the notebook sitting on the kitchen table where I had left it the night before. It mocked me: If you had used your life-management notebook, you would have these things written down.

Kristy shifted the baby onto her hip and bounced her a bit. I reached out to take Kailey from her. "You go. Kailey will be fine here," I said. "This is my fault. I am so disorganized. I've got to get things under control. This is just case in point."

Kristy patted me, looking relieved to be escaping the din of my house and the weight of her daughter. "Remember what I said to you when we talked on the phone? Don't look at what you do wrong. Look at all the things you do right."

I remembered now. My eyes scanned the room. The boys were still in their pajamas. The remaining moving boxes towered over me like prison guards reminding me of the hard labor I was sentenced to do. "I'll keep looking while you're gone," I quipped.

She shook her head. "You're going to get your life back on an even keel. You'll see. You're going to get on top of things and take this neighborhood by storm."

"Huh. That'll never happen," I retorted, although vaguely thankful for Kristy's blind belief in me. I thought of Justine, who was the reigning "queen of Essex Falls." Kristy ignored my negative remark and exited out the door she came in. I watched her walk quickly to her car and slide inside with the ease of the childless, if only for a moment. Her baby felt soft and warm in my arms. I inhaled her powdery scent and kissed her fuzzy head. I had watched her grow from squalling newborn to chunky baby when we lived across the street.

I turned back to face the boys, whose faces were covered in peanut butter. "We have a guest, boys," I said. Kailey started to fuss, and I bounced her a bit as Kristy had done. I watched Kristy back her car out of the driveway while Kailey stared at me like I looked familiar but she couldn't quite place me. "Have you forgotten me already, Miss Kailey?" I cooed to her. She broke into a toothless grin as if to say, "Ohhh, that's who you are." I lined up the boys and wiped off their faces one-handed as I balanced Kailey in my other arm. This is what it would be like, I thought.

Since Kailey appeared to be happy enough, I put her in her car seat and let the boys sit in front of her and make funny faces while I tried to unpack a box. I hoped that when David was home this weekend, we could finish the unpacking entirely.

Surprisingly, Kailey was mesmerized by the boys, and they were fascinated by her too. Just who was babysitting whom? I wondered if Kristy would start dropping Kailey off once a week so I could get some things done.

Soon enough, the fun was over. Donovan held his nose and tapped me on the arm with his free hand. "Kailey stinks," he said. "You better change her."

I sighed as I laid Kailey on the floor. Rummaging through her diaper bag, I found one diaper and a dried-up wipe left in the bottom of the wipe container. Kristy must have been upset. She was usually overprepared, a nervous Nellie about anything to do with her baby. "Hope this is all you need today," I told the wiggling baby. I peeled her diaper back and set to work cleaning the unfamiliar anatomy. I had changed only boys' diapers and was out of my element. I could change a boy lightning fast, but this took some concentration. I was just about to put her diaper back on when Duncan yelled, "Mom, wait!"

"What?" I asked.

"Somebody cut Kailey's wiener off."

I stifled a laugh as I finished diapering the baby and held her close, planting a kiss on her sweet-smelling head, inhaling her baby scent deeply, memorizing it. I used to have this every day, I thought. Now my children smelled like sweaty boys, not fresh-from-God infants. "Girls don't have wieners," I told Duncan.

Duncan furrowed his brow and stared at me. He wasn't buying it. Donovan and Dylan giggled and looked from Duncan to me and back again. "Look, guys," I said. "Why don't you ask Daddy about that when he gets home from work tonight?" It was low of me to push the questions off on David, but I wasn't prepared to give my eight-, six-, and four-year-olds a lesson on male and female anatomy.

"Daddy's going to be home tonight?" Donovan piped up. He was David's shadow, his biggest fan.

"Yes," I said. "And we need to get to the store today and get some food to cook a nice meal for him tonight." I said this even though I had no idea what I would cook.

"Mommy?" Duncan asked.

"Yeah, Dunc?"

"I still think you should tell Kailey's mommy about … you know …"

I smoothed a blonde lock back from his forehead and bent over to kiss him. "I'll be sure to tell her," I assured him. I would tell her, just not in the way he meant. I knew Kristy would get a good laugh over his concern.

I put Kailey back into her car seat, bagged the offensive diaper in two grocery bags and tied it, then chucked it into the trash can before returning to the boxes. The next box was full of books and weighed about two tons. I pulled one of my favorite childhood books out of

the box and rubbed my fingers across the cover lovingly. I had kept
it in pristine condition, even though it had been read hundreds of
times. I hugged it to myself before I opened the cover, remembering
my sister and me, dressed for bed, listening to my father's words
spilling over us as he read the story aloud. The memory was linked
to a happier time in my life, when my dad still lived with us and my
life was—in memory at least—perfect.

"Boys," I said. "How about I read you a story?" They nodded
eagerly. I took a seat on the couch, and they pressed in close.

I read about a little fawn that celebrates a birthday and the animals
that bring her presents, savoring the end when they present her with a
cake lit entirely by fireflies. When I was little, I had wanted a birthday
cake lit by fireflies, wanted to believe such things were possible, that
somewhere out of sight—deep in the woods—forest animals gave
each other such things. The boys relaxed into me, letting the peaceful
cadence of the story take us all to a more settled place.

"That was a nice story, Mom," Dylan said when I closed the
book. Duncan nodded with his finger in his mouth.

For a moment I just sat, not moving, not speaking, the five of us
savoring the quiet and each other's nearness. Then the phone rang,
breaking the moment. I rose slowly from the couch to answer it,
catching it before it rolled over to voice mail. "Hello?" I said. At
first I thought there was no one there. Then I realized that someone
was crying on the other end, making gulping noises as she tried to
compose herself to speak. "Hello?" I said again.

"Ariel?" came the weak reply, her voice thick with tears.

"Kristy?"

"They did a test."

"And it was positive?" I asked, already knowing the answer.

"Uh-huh," she said, sniffing loudly. "I can't stop crying. Is that terrible?"

"No, you're in shock. You need time to adjust to the news," I said.

"But I don't have time," she wailed. "I'm already three months pregnant. They're only going to be a year apart." She sniffed again. "I'm a wreck."

I felt her pain. Duncan was conceived when Dylan was still little, and I remember feeling confused and overwhelmed. "Listen," I said, glancing at cherubic Kailey in her car seat and thinking how ironic it was that now I would love to get accidentally pregnant so David wouldn't have anything to say about it. "You don't have to come get Kailey right now. Why don't you take some time, collect yourself?"

"Okay … I think I'm going to go to Josh's office," she said in a small voice.

"That's a good idea. You go see Josh. Talk to him. Kailey's fine here as long as you need. I think the boys would keep her if they could."

"Well, seeing as how I'm going to have my hands full now, that might not be a bad idea." She laughed in spite of her tears. "I'm really wishing you hadn't moved away," she said, and then said good-bye, still sniffling.

I hung up and looked around at the clutter of my new home. I noticed that the boys had disappeared, then saw a flash of movement outside and spotted them on the trampoline. Just before I could walk outside and warn them about trampoline safety as I always did, I noticed Lucky chewing on something on the ground. As my eyes focused on what it was, I blinked in horror. The dog was chewing on the book we had just read—my treasured childhood book. I ran outside like a maniac, screaming about the book, gesturing at the dog to my oblivious boys. They looked at me and stopped jumping.

"Who took this book outside?" I questioned them, reaching for Lucky's collar.

Donovan shrugged. Dylan looked away. Duncan popped his finger in his mouth.

"Who?" I asked again, as if I thought they just didn't hear me. I struggled to snatch the shredded book from the dog's mouth.

"Nobody," Duncan said, his words garbled.

"Well, somebody did and look what happened. You boys don't care about anything. You don't keep anything nice!" I held the ruined book close to my chest as tears of frustration leaked from my eyes, dog saliva sliming the front of my shirt. Through the open door of the house, I could hear Kailey crying. I turned and stalked into the house, angrily wiping at my tears and leaving my stunned children standing on the trampoline, mouths agape, eyes wide.

I picked up the screaming baby and went to the phone. I needed to tell someone what had happened. I dialed David's cell-phone number, choking back sobs. Unceremoniously, I dropped the book into the trash can. There was no hope of salvaging it.

As soon as I heard David's voice, I started crying in earnest. "Ariel?" he asked. "What happened?"

"It's nothing," I said. "I just miss you. You weren't here when I woke up and you got home after I fell asleep and I am just so tired of doing this by myself."

"Ari." His voice was a mix of understanding and exasperation. "We've been over this. I have to work. That was the deal. This job requires a lot more of me." His tone reminded me of when he lectured the boys. Is that what he thought of me? That I was just one more of his charges, his responsibilities, something to be endured?

"I know," I said, doing a terrible job of masking my whiny temperament. "It's just that things have been so hard with you gone and me trying to get used to everything and the boxes are never going to get unpacked and now I have Kailey ..."

"Kailey?" he asked. He exhaled loudly. "Why would you volunteer to keep an extra kid when you have so much on you already? You need to learn to say no."

"Well, in all the craziness I sort of forgot I offered, and Kristy just showed up here on our doorstep this morning and ... what choice did I have?" I shifted Kailey onto my other hip and looked out the window at the boys. They were happily jumping again, my problems forgotten. "Anyway, Kristy's pregnant. She's devastated."

"What?" David laughed.

"It's not funny," I said.

"Well, better them than us," he said.

My heart clenched as he said it. I forced myself not to say anything in return. "So that's why I've got Kailey. And then the boys took my favorite book from when I was little. Remember that book about the fawn?"

"I guess," he said. I heard a voice in the background and his muffled reply. "Listen, I do need to go," he said.

I sighed. "Well then, I guess I'll let you go." I seemed to be doing a lot of letting David go lately.

"What happened to the book?" he asked.

For some reason, just his asking made my heart leap. "The boys took it outside, and Lucky chewed it up and dragged it through the mud. It's ruined." Tears filled my eyes again. It was just a book, but at that moment it signified everything wrong in my life.

"I'm really sorry about your book. Maybe we can get you another one?" he asked.

"I doubt it. I mean it's an old book. I doubt that it's even in print anymore."

"Look, we can talk about this when I get home. Okay? I am really sorry you're having a bad day," he said.

"Yeah, me too," I said. "Will you be home for dinner?" I asked.

"Yes, I might be a bit late, but I will be home for dinner. We can all eat together." He said good-bye, and I hung up the phone. Though I felt a bit better after talking to David, my book was still ruined, and there was still no food in the house to make the dinner I had just promised David we would eat together. I had a busy afternoon ahead of me.

After an hour at the grocery store, with a full cart that had doubled as a jungle gym, the boys and I finished our shopping and made our way to the checkout registers. I was nearly exhausted from the effort. The only consolation I could muster was that at least Kailey wasn't with me too. While we shopped, the boys had invented a game of jumping between the cracks in the floor, paying no mind to other shoppers. Half the fun had apparently become how many times they had to say "Excuse me" after bumping into people. And at one point, we passed an old lady at the end of the aisle whom Duncan informed, "Girls don't have wieners," bringing up a subject I hoped he had forgotten all about. Checking out couldn't have come soon enough.

The cashier had the kind of disk earrings that enlarged the earlobes, a trend I just did not understand. What about after they took them out? Did they want extra-large earlobes for life? He looked at the boys. His name tag, I noticed, read "Chief."

"What's up?" he said to them. Duncan hid behind me, but Donovan and Dylan openly stared. I nudged them when the guy looked down to scan my items, but they wouldn't stop staring.

"What are those things in his ears, Mommy?" Duncan asked from behind me. Loudly.

"Earrings, honey," I said back and gave the cashier an apologetic smile.

"Boys don't wear earrings," he said. "And those kinds are weird." He pointed at the cashier just as he looked up. I moved to stand completely in front of Duncan. He popped his head out from behind me, looking at the cashier like one might look at a rare specimen in a museum: *Teenagerus Rebellious*. As I was swiping my debit card, Duncan looked at Chief. "Girls don't have wieners," he said.

"Duncan, shush," I pleaded.

"Nah, it's cool," he said, waving it off while I turned five shades of red. I certainly didn't want to discuss male and female anatomy with this person. "What's your name, little dude?" he asked Duncan.

Duncan was suddenly shy. Of course, now.

Donovan stepped in. "His name's Duncan. I'm Donovan. And this is Dylan." He pointed where Dylan stood quietly. "What's yours?"

"My name's Keith." He slapped Donovan five, then Dylan. Duncan hid his hand behind his back and refused to play along.

"But your name tag says 'Chief,'" Donovan countered, pointing at the evidence clipped to his polo shirt.

"That's a joke," he said, laughing. He turned to look at me. "And your name?" he asked.

"Ariel," I said.

"Ariel," he repeated. "That's a pretty name." He raised his eyebrows in a way that I could only describe as flirtatious. If memory served, that is.

I felt warmth crawl up my neck. This was new. No one really noticed me these days—at least not in *that* way. Even though the noticer was a would-be hoodlum with funky earlobes, it felt good to be noticed, gazed at appreciatively, singled out. I shuttled the boys quickly out of the store while Keith waved at us before turning to the next customer in line. I couldn't wait to tell David a teenager had flirted with me. It was the highlight of my day.

On Saturday morning, I woke to David standing over me, holding the phone out like an insect he found in his cereal bowl. "Phone's for you," he said.

I sat up in bed, blinking. "What time is it?" I asked.

"Seven. The boys are downstairs, and the neighbor—the pretty one from behind us?—is asking for you." He handed me the phone and walked away.

"Hello?" I said, not bothering to mask the sleep in my voice, feeling a bit unnerved by David calling Justine pretty and remembering how he wouldn't look directly at her at the pool.

"Ariel? Is that you? Are you asleep?"

"Not anymore." I groaned and flopped back down. I would have to find a polite way to ask Justine not to call so early.

"Let's go for a walk. It's time we get in shape for summer."

"I'm not a big fitness person," I said.

"Well, it's time you start," she responded. "We are going to start walking every morning early, before the kids get up and the husbands leave for work." I didn't remind her that David was out of town much of the time. "So, I am going to swing by there and get you. Can you be ready in five minutes? We need to beat the heat."

I mumbled in agreement and hung up the phone. Groaning loudly, I slid out of bed and went over to the box of my clothes I had been living out of. I was bent over digging through it when I heard David laugh behind me. I turned to face him. "Nice butt," he said, and smiled at me in a way I recognized vaguely.

I rolled my eyes and turned back to the box. "Apparently Justine thinks it could be much nicer and wants me to go walking with her every morning."

He leaned up against the wall. "You going to do it?"

"What choice do I have? She's trying to be my friend, and if this is what it takes to be her friend, then this is what it takes."

"I'm sure there are plenty of people you could be friends with in this neighborhood," he responded. "Give it time."

"Why do I need to find other friends? She's, like, in charge of the whole neighborhood, so pretty much if I'm friends with her everything will follow and—" He shook his head. "What?" I asked.

"You just seem a bit overly interested in this woman, is all. You mention her a lot."

I brushed aside his inference. "I'm fine. I'm not overly interested in her. I'm inspired by her. There's a difference."

"Just be careful, okay? I know she's this neighborhood bigwig and she's a nice person, but you're putting her on some kind of pedestal. And you know the danger in pedestals."

"That I'll never reach the same level?" I quipped.

He gave me a mock-reproachful look. "The higher the pedestal, the longer the fall."

———

"We should go at six tomorrow," Justine said as soon as I stepped out the door. She did some stretching exercises on my sidewalk while I looked up and down the street, vaguely wondering which of the neighbors had seen the tampon incident.

"I am not sure I can go tomorrow," I said, remembering David's words of warning. I gave a rueful smile. "And I know I can't go at six." This was as much as I could stand up to her. My heart raced as I said it.

She shot me a sideways glance. "Party pooper," she accused. "Don't you want to get in shape?"

We set off, her keeping a pace I would qualify as running but one that she called power walking. I had not had my running shoes on in years, except to wear with my jeans in the winter.

"So did you walk like this with Laura?" I ventured.

She shook her head, her blonde stubby ponytail bobbing from side to side. "No," she said, her breath coming out in huffs. "Laura and I went to the gym a lot."

We continued walking in silence. "I'm sorry that she's gone," I said, hoping to get her talking. Justine wasn't one for baring her soul, I was learning.

She waved her hand, dismissing my statement. "It's okay."

As we got closer to my street, I felt a burst of energy. The faster I walked, the sooner I would get into the air-conditioning. I was hardly listening when she began talking again.

"When Laura moved, it was one of the hardest times of my life."

I became focused on her once again, realizing that she was giving me a rare glimpse into her private thoughts.

"It shook my confidence in what I can count on. I mean, we'd planned this perfect future with our two families being together. And then one day all of that future was just gone. And then I lost this part in this church thing I usually sing in, and well, lately, it just seems like things have been going wrong. I know it might sound petty."

We had stopped in my driveway. "It doesn't sound petty," I said. "It sounds like you're having a hard time. Thanks for letting me know."

"So, I guess I just wanted to say to you that I'm glad that a nice family bought Laura's house. It's good to see life there again, happiness. It's helped me feel more … hopeful than I've felt in a long time. And it's been fun hanging out with you. You make me laugh. Mark said it's good to see me laugh again," she said, cocking her head and looking at me as if she'd never seen me before. "I'm glad you moved in."

I smiled back at her. "Me, too." I waited for half a second before I said more. "Maybe whoever lives in Laura's house is just destined to be your friend." I was careful not to say "best friend." That would have been too much.

CHAPTER 10

Justine

When I left Ariel at her house, I kept walking, thinking about how much I had grown to like my new neighbor. I liked how she didn't put on pretenses, how she let her faults show. I liked how she didn't seem caught up in the neighborhood politics, didn't jockey for position like I'd seen other neighbors do. Her house was messy and sometimes she was messy and her boys were definitely messy. I rarely allowed mess in my life. It felt too out of control. Lately I'd been wanting to be out of control though, straining to break free from the confines of my own ordered life. I had a feeling that Ariel could help me do that.

My feet took me to a destination that my brain seemed unaware of until I turned down the street. I don't know what I expected to happen. To see his house? To see his kids playing in the yard? To see him? I felt like a silly girl. The closer I got to his house the more my heart raced.

I replayed the moment that I saw him at the pool. I had been introducing Liza to Ariel, thinking how Ariel was my new project. I could tell Ariel was so taken with the whole scene at the pool and with being a part of Essex Falls. I enjoyed seeing the neighborhood through her eyes. The way she asked me questions like I knew everything, the way she held on to my every word and looked at me like I would lead her to the Promised Land or something. About all I could lead her to was uncluttered counters and the best playdates for her kids, but if that was enough for her, I was glad to do it. I remember Liza said that I needed to meet the new neighbors, and all I could think was *I don't need any more new neighbors to keep track of.*

And then she called them over, Tom and Betsy. He shook my hand. When our hands touched, I felt like someone opened a trapdoor in my life and I fell through. The only thing that was keeping me from hitting bottom was his hand, holding on. Our eyes connected for a fraction of a second—nothing that would give us away to Liza and Ariel and Betsy and the others standing around us, but enough for a flash of recognition, and revelation, to pass between us. His eyes said, "There you are."

And mine said, "Finally."

Walking toward his house, I wondered if I was being stupid. Mark always said I read too much into things, that I wanted things to be what they weren't. It was possible that was true with Tom. Maybe his eyes were just saying, "Nice to see you again." Maybe I just needed to let this go, turn around, and go home. Or maybe I just needed to look into his eyes again.

His house was "the one with the terrible backyard," a house everyone knew about in the neighborhood, mostly because it wouldn't sell. I came to a stop in front of the house, debating what my next move should be and what would possess someone to buy a house that no one else wanted.

"It was a steal of a deal," he said, coming up behind me. "I like people who get desperate. They make foolish decisions."

I looked around me as if he'd materialized out of thin air, willing my heart to stop pounding from the scare he gave me. "Where'd you come from?" I asked.

He smiled and held up an extension cord he'd wrapped around his arm. I turned my eyes from his strong hands as he gripped the cord. I couldn't start thinking about how those hands had once touched me or I'd be useless. He pointed at the house across the street. "Was at the neighbors' borrowing this. How about you?"

"Me?"

"Yeah, where'd you come from? I mean, you don't live on this street, right?" He smiled at me, and I knew he was teasing.

"I was on a walk. Was just wondering who bought this house after all this time and it turns out it was you. And here you are." We both knew my vagueness was a cover.

He shifted his weight and adjusted the extension cord, the orange coil looking like a snake he had tamed. "Here I am," he said and smiled. He held out his hand to shake mine, and I took it, happy for the excuse to touch him somehow. "Name's Tom Dean," he said. "Nice to meet you."

"Dean?" I asked just like I had all those years before, just like I had at the pool in front of everyone, a message to him that no one but us would know. "Like James? I just love James Dean. He's so ..."

"Sexy?" He was grinning too, both of us repeating lines from a moment that seemed inconsequential at the time.

"Cool," I corrected.

"Stick around," he said. "James Dean's got nothing on me."

We both laughed as a look passed between us, saying things neither of us would ever say out loud, so much history called up in just the acknowledgment of that one long-ago exchange. I changed the subject. "I thought I might invite you and your ..."

"Wife?" he asked, still smiling.

"I was trying to remember her name," I said.

He looked down at the ground, kicked at a stray pebble, and then looked at his house. "Her name's Betsy," he said softly, the smile gone.

Of course I remembered it, I just didn't want to say it out loud. "Yes, I'd like to invite you and Betsy to dinner," I said. "I try to invite all the new neighbors to dinner. My husband and I like to get to know them."

This was not true. Ariel and her husband had lived behind us for weeks and I had never even thought of inviting them to dinner. The truth was I would use any excuse to get to know him, even if I had to include his wife and kids.

"I'm sure we could work that out. We're new in town, so I know Betsy would love to get to know some of the other moms."

"Well, it sounded to me like she's getting involved quite well," I couldn't help but say. "And who would you like to get to know?" I added, unsure where my bravado was coming from except it's not every day that the one who got away is standing in front of you with an orange extension cord.

A look of shock passed across his face, as brief and fleeting as the flicker of a firefly. "Me?" he sputtered.

I nodded, pulling myself up into a proud stance and making myself look him in the eye.

"Well, let's just say I'd like to get to know *one* of the moms," he said. He looked away again, then back at me. "Can we meet to talk about … this?"

"What about this?" I countered, being purposely coy.

"About us being thrown back together. Here. Now. I'd like to talk about how we should handle this. I mean, do we tell people, or do we try to keep it quiet? There's just questions we should … go over."

"Sure. We can meet privately. But I'm still going to ask you all over. For dinner."

He shrugged. "You do what you need to do. If it eases your conscience." He gave me that teasing smile. "But in the meantime let's figure out how we could meet. Alone."

I thought suddenly about a coffee shop across town where I had met a woman a long time ago to pick up items for an auction at school. It was as if my brain had cataloged it for a time like this. The depths of my own depravity shocked me but didn't keep me from blurting out, "There's a place. Give me your number and I'll text you the address. We can figure out a time."

"Do you have something to write with?" he asked.

"Just tell me," I said. "I'll remember." And then, for the same reason that had made me walk by, made me say the things I'd said already, I added, "I remember lots of things."

Sitting in the coffee shop across town with sunglasses and a ball cap on, I felt a little silly and a little excited. I couldn't deny that this sneaking around added an element to my life I'd been missing before Tom showed up at the pool that day. I couldn't believe I'd agreed to meet him like this, away from people we knew, people I knew. And I couldn't overlook the fact that the same person I'd once fantasized about seeing again was about to walk through the door, that I was about to sit alone with him and get to ask all the questions I'd waited to ask.

The bell over the coffee-shop door jingled and I looked up, but it wasn't him. A frazzled mother carried a flailing toddler. The child kept screaming, "I want juice!" I scanned the room to make sure I didn't see anyone I knew, my heart racing. I wondered how people carried on affairs for years on end. Was that what I was doing? Carrying on an affair? I took a deep breath. No. I was seeing an old friend. That was all. I smiled at the man next to me and tried to look like I met men who weren't my husband in coffee shops every day.

The third time the bell jingled, it was him filling the doorway, smiling at me like we'd just seen each other, like I was as familiar as his own reflection, like we did this every day. What can I say? My heart soared. It literally soared, its wings beating on the inside of my chest. I stood up and let him hug me, let his strange familiarity engulf me. By the time I took my seat across from him, I knew I was in trouble and foolish to keep telling myself I wasn't, an addict in denial.

He ordered coffee for me, and a few minutes later the waitress placed it on the table, the steam rising and heating my face. I wrapped my fingers around the mug but didn't bring it to my lips. "So," he said. "Tell me everything. Everything I missed about you."

"Why don't you tell me everything you missed about me?" I teased him. I was pretending to be confident when I was anything but. Fake it till you make it: That had been my motto for as long as I could remember. It had served me well.

He smiled and cocked his head as if he couldn't figure out whether I meant it or not. There were little laugh lines around his eyes, and his hairline had moved slightly farther back, but other than that, I couldn't find a single thing that had changed about him. I wondered if he saw the changes in me—the pooch of my belly where I'd had the girls, the angry 11s between my eyebrows that had come from too much worrying, the fact that my eyes weren't the same vibrant blue they once were—more a washed-out denim color now.

"When we saw each other at the pool, I wondered if you'd remember me," he said. "I mean, I thought you would, but there was this part of me that was afraid you'd moved on so completely that you didn't." He looked at me. "That I didn't rank high enough to be worth remembering. A girl like you, I figured, has a lifetime of memorable loves. Who was I to think I'd be anything special?" He scratched at a mark on the table but gave up when he realized it was a stain. "So that's what I remember about you. I remember how truly remarkable you were." He looked up. "And how stupid I was to let you go."

I looked back at him, unblinking. His words pinged around my body, finally settling in my heart, expanding there, filling me up with something that had been missing for a very long time. "You sure know how to say the right things," I said. "You always did."

"It's not just words," he argued.

"It's all just words," I countered.

He reached out and peeled my fingers from the mug I was cling-ing to, lacing them in his own. "When I lost you—" he began.

"You didn't lose me. You let me go," I said.

He looked down. "I know. I did. And I've regretted that decision for a long time." He laughed. "I can't believe I'm getting a chance to tell you that after all these years. It's like I'm dreaming. The best dream ever."

"Whenever we'd go to a restaurant or a place like this," I said, gesturing to the shop, "I'd always have to sit facing the door, so I could see who was coming in. Mark teased me, said I was afraid of terrorists and stuff. And to be honest I never knew why I did it. But sitting here with you, I know that I was always watching the door, waiting for you to walk through. I guess somewhere deep inside I always hoped that we'd get to this moment. That one day the door would jingle and I'd look up and there you'd be, walking in with that smile on your face. And then my life could start again."

He squeezed my hand. "And now it has."

I nodded. "Now it has." The door jingled, but I didn't look up. I just kept staring into his eyes.

⌣

Days later, when I went to get the mail, I found a CD with my name on it waiting for me. My heart pounded as I opened the envelope and slid the shiny silver disk into my hand, a rainbow arc playing on the surface as I took in the handwriting I recognized from letters traded years ago. "Because I See You" it read. I held it for a moment, scanning the street to see if anyone was watching. And yet, as I walked inside, I was already wondering where I'd hide the CD. If Mark ever saw it, he'd know something was up.

I had to listen to it. The girls were outside playing with Ariel's boys and—later—I had promised to go over and teach Ariel how to bake her own bread. But first, I would listen to what he had made for me. I imagined him downloading songs late at night, burning them onto the CD, his wife upstairs asleep in her bed unaware. He was thinking of me, searching for songs that reminded him of me.

The music filled the den as I sat down on the couch, Barry Manilow's voice singing what to many would just be another cheesy love song. No one but him knew what that song meant. I marveled that he had remembered all these years later, that the memory hadn't been punched through with the holes of time. I thought back to that morning when we had spoken on the phone, how our conversations were growing longer, more frequent. How lately when something happened instead of thinking, *I can't wait to tell Mark* or *I can't wait to tell Laura,* it was his face that flashed across my mind, his number I automatically dialed.

"I want to see you," he'd said that morning. "How can we see each other for, like, more than an hour?"

"We could meet somewhere tomorrow night. I'll tell Mark I'm having a girls' night out with Ariel. He'll believe that."

"What about Ariel?" he'd asked. "How can you be sure she won't drop by your house or he won't see her in her backyard?"

"I'll make sure she's occupied. Don't worry. I'll figure something out."

He exhaled loudly.

"What?" I asked. "Are you worried?"

"No, just impatient. I don't want to wait. I think about you all the time. I can't believe I got through all these years without you. Now that you're in my life, I—"

There was silence on the phone as I waited for him to finish the sentence. I could hear both of us breathing. "You what?" I prompted.

"I don't think I can ever go back to the way things were."

"I know." Upstairs the girls were jumping up and down, singing and giggling. It sounded like they were coming through the floor. "I know."

"I keep thinking," he went on, "that this was supposed to happen. I mean, out of all the neighborhoods in all the cities we could've ended up, we ended up being neighbors. What are the odds for something like that? It's got to be a sign, right?"

"A sign of what?" I asked. I needed to hear his answer.

"That we're supposed to be together," he said. There was silence as we both processed what he'd just said. I didn't know what to say in response. That I thought the same but that it scared me to death? That the one thing I'd always fantasized about happening was happening to me? That I had never stopped loving him, only pushed the pause button?

"Are you there?" he asked.

"Yes, I'm here. I'm just ... confused. There's so much that would have to happen. You have Betsy and the kids, I have Mark and my kids. We have homes and bills and legal obligations. Not to mention morals."

"And yet here we are getting this amazing second chance. Do you see that we also have an obligation to us?"

"I see that. I do." I thought of the verses in the Bible that talk about divorce and adultery. I thought about Erica and how the women in the neighborhood talked about her, how they shunned her. I had even encouraged them to shun her for reasons I didn't want to think about. Did I want to be an Erica? Was I willing to sacrifice my position—my reputation—for another chance with Tom? My heart sang back its answer: *Yes, yes, yes.*

CHAPTER 11

Ariel

Justine and I sat down and had a cup of tea while the bread rose, and I couldn't help but wonder what Erica would've said if she'd happened upon our cozy little scene. And yet, I was having a lovely time. We had mixed up the dough together with a lot of little helpers. The girls' camp was over, so Justine brought them over for her lesson in bread making, just another of her many talents. Cameron insisted on doing everything we did, so we ended up with two large bowls of bread rising on the counter. The kids sat clustered around my island, staring at the dishcloth-covered bowls. "Dylan," I said, scolding him with a grin on my face, "don't take the cover off. Why don't you go outside and play and then we'll have lunch?"

"It's too hot," the kids all whined in unison. The five of them were fast becoming friends. The gate between our houses was hardly ever shut anymore, but Justine had learned to keep her fence bolted so Lucky was at least contained in our yards. I ushered the kids outside, promising them it was only for a few minutes.

Justine walked over to the bread and pulled back the dishcloth. "I think it's ready," she said, heaving the mass out of the bowl and onto the floured countertop. I watched her arm muscles ripple as she kneaded determinedly. "You know," she said as she worked and I watched, "you should come out with us for a girls' night out sometime soon."

A girls' night out sounded like just what I needed. "Sure," I responded, not even bothering to mask my eagerness.

"I think we're going out tomorrow night," she said, staring down at the bread dough.

"Okay," I said. A reminder of David earlier this morning standing beside the bed in the first light of morning, leaning over to kiss me good-bye, suitcase in hand, flashed through my mind. "Oh. Never mind. I can't."

She looked up at me. "Why not?"

"David's out of town," I said.

"Oh, too bad," she said. She looked genuinely disappointed. I couldn't imagine she was more than I was.

Donovan walked in from the deck. "Hey, Mom, where do we keep the umbrellas?"

"Umbrellas do not make good parachutes, Donovan. If I've told you once I've told you a million times, you are not to jump off the roof." He sighed deeply and returned to the deck to report that he had been unsuccessful in his mission.

I caught the look on Justine's face. It was a look that said she had never experienced such a request from Cameron or Caroline. I smiled at her. "See why I need a girls' night out?" I quipped.

"I guess you could never describe your life as dull," she said, studying the boys from the window like a scientist might study a rare breed of animal.

"When Donovan was about a year old, I took him to the park one beautiful day. I was pushing him in the swing when a little boy who was probably about four got on the swing next to us. His mom was pushing him, and with every truck that drove by, he would ask her what kind of truck it was. 'That's an earthmover,' she would say. Or, 'That's a cherry picker.' All these pieces of machinery I had never heard of or cared about. I stood there and pushed Donovan as long as he could stand it, just listening to this woman talk to her son in what was, to me, a foreign language."

I paused and smiled at Justine. "I went home that night and cried to David that God had made a mistake, that I couldn't be the mother of a boy because I didn't know any of the names of big rigs. The next day David brought home a book for Donovan with all these pictures of heavy equipment with the names under them. He handed it to me and said, 'You'll figure it out. God didn't make a mistake.' And I did figure it out." I looked out at my boys. "Now I could give that mom a run for her money. Show me any piece of construction equipment, and I can tell you the name and what it does." I giggled. "But I couldn't tell you where that book is anymore. We wore it out."

"David sounds like a great guy," she said. "A great dad."

"He is," I said. "I miss him being around more. It's hard."

Justine shaped the bread into loaves and placed them in the greased baking pans. I watched with the same form of respect I once held for that mother in the park. Could it be that easy?

Could I learn how to be her the same way I had learned to be that mom?

⌒

After Justine and the girls left to go home and whip up what was sure to be a gourmet three-course dinner for Mark, I decided to tackle the laundry while the boys vegged in front of a movie. I was untangling balled-up socks and separating whites and colors when my hand fell on the capris I had worn to the mothers' group meeting. I felt the crinkly feel of paper under my fingertips as my hand grazed the back pocket. Suddenly I remembered Heather, the babysitter. I pulled the card from the pants, thankful I hadn't washed it. Score one for not being on top of the laundry. Grabbing the phone in the kitchen, I hastily dialed the number.

"Hello?" a female voice said.

"Hi? May I speak to Heather?" I said.

"This is Heather." She giggled. "This is my cell phone so I am pretty much the only person who answers."

"Oh," I said. I wasn't ready for a child of mine to be armed with a cell phone. "This is Ariel Baxter, the one with the three boys? And, well, I was wondering if you could sit tomorrow night? My husband's out of town and a friend of mine—well, actually she's my neighbor. I mean, I haven't known her long enough to call her a friend yet. I mean, *friend* is a strong word. Oh. You might know her. Justine Miller? She led the mothers' group? Where I met you?" I sounded like a raving lunatic.

"Yes, ma'am," she replied. She sounded more adult than I did.

"Oh, great. Well, we live behind her. You know the house with the gate that connects to their yard?"

"Yes, ma'am," she replied. "I can walk to your house, actually."

This just kept getting better. "So you can do it? I mean, tomorrow night? You can sit?"

I heard her flipping through pages, checking her calendar. "Umm. Sure. What time?"

Justine hadn't told me a time because I had told her no so fast. "Let's say six?"

"Yeah, I can do it then for sure."

"Great! Thanks, Heather. You're a lifesaver. My husband travels a lot and it gets lonely here with just the boys for company. I could really use a girls' night out."

"Sure, no problem," Heather said, humoring me.

"Okay, well, I will see you tomorrow night." I made myself stop babbling to a teenager who neither knew nor cared about my need for adult interaction and hung up the phone, victorious. I kissed the business card and held it aloft. It was the golden ticket to a night of freedom.

———

I dialed Justine's number first thing the next morning, bursting with the news that I would be joining her and the girls from the neighborhood. "I got a sitter!" I said as soon as she said hello.

"Ariel?" she asked.

"Yes. I got a sitter," I repeated, a little embarrassed that I assumed she'd know who I was. "Heather Davidson? The sitter from mothers' group? I met her last week and forgot all about it, but after you left yesterday, I remembered. So I called her and she could do it. Isn't that great?"

"Oh," was all she said.

"Is something wrong?" I asked, willing there not to be anything wrong and the sensation I felt crawling up the back of my neck to be nothing more than prickly heat.

"Well, I hate to say this but we … well … we had a change of plans so we're not going."

I felt the air leave my lungs and sat down with a heavy thud at the kitchen table. Pressing the heel of my hand to my forehead I chastised myself for getting so worked up over a stupid girls' night out with women I barely knew. And yet, isn't this what I imagined when I dreamed of moving to this neighborhood? Togetherness? Friendships? Community? I was this close. "Oh," was all I could say.

"Hey, we'll do it again, though," she said. "And I will give you plenty of notice when we do so you can get Heather if David's out of town. How does that sound?" She sounded as though she was talking to a child. A silly, petulant child.

"Okay. Yeah, sure. That sounds great." I willed myself to sound perky, like her.

Donovan came in the kitchen and opened the refrigerator. "I'm hungry," he whined, his voice nails on a chalkboard, the soundtrack to a long day stretching in front of me.

I waved my arm at him to close the refrigerator door and pointed toward the den where he came from. "Go," I mouthed. He rolled his eyes and left with a deep sigh.

"Well … maybe you should keep Heather?" she said. "Nothing says you have to have a reason to leave. I am sure David wouldn't care if you hired a sitter for a break when you needed one."

"I couldn't justify that," I argued.

She laughed as though I had much to learn. "Has he had to justify leaving you for days on end with those boys, trapped in the house with no outlets?"

"Umm. No," I said, suddenly feeling angry with David. Why did I need to justify spending some money for a break I deserved? Justine was right. "I guess I could just go to a bookstore," I offered, halfway hoping she would say she wanted to go with me.

"Exactly," she said. "Invest some time in yourself. Get a pedicure. Eat a salad. Go for a walk. See a movie. You don't need me or any girls' night to do that."

I pictured myself all alone in a movie theater, something I had never done. I wanted to tell her that I did actually need her to do that. "Oh, of course," I said, trying to sound more positive about her suggestion than I felt. "That's a great idea. I'll do it." I did not think that I would, but I wanted her to believe I was the kind of confident woman who could do such things.

"Good for you," she said in a singsong voice. I heard one of her girls' crying go from faint to loud. "Listen, Cameron cut herself with scissors so I better go tend to her. You have fun tonight." The line went dead before I could say good-bye.

I set the phone down in the base and stood still, staring over at Justine's house through the kitchen window. I looked back down at the phone and willed it to ring, to be her saying she had worked it out after all. I didn't want to go out by myself. I didn't want to be the loser having dinner alone with just a book for company. But apparently, that's what I was.

———

I sat in the car and collected myself before I backed out of the driveway. Duncan was crying, Dylan was sullen, and Donovan was avoiding looking me in the eye when I left them with Heather, who tried hard to look like she wasn't bothered that the boys seemed to despise her. Just before Heather got there, Donovan said he hated me. He had never said that before, and I wasn't ready for it. I had heard it would happen, but that didn't make it any easier to hear. Was it wrong to leave them? I thought about Justine's admonishment to me earlier that day: that David didn't have to justify his frequent disappearing acts, so why should I? I put the van in reverse and pressed on the gas.

I eased out of the neighborhood, and when I slowed down as I passed Justine's house, I noticed her getting into her car. A thought nagged at me: What if they went out without me? What if she just didn't want me there? I feared that she didn't really like me and her invitation to me had only been out of pity. She recognized how much I wanted to be her friend; she felt sorry for me. I scolded myself for being insecure, for letting my emotions get the best of me. It seemed to be happening more and more.

Leaving the neighborhood, I swung out between the large brick pillars with the imposing-looking lions keeping sentry, the waterfalls continually spouting water into the air. The entrance to the neigh-borhood used to inspire a kind of reverence within me; already I barely noticed it as I sped past to somewhere else. I had planned to take walks with the boys to see the lions and sit by the waterfalls. But we hadn't done it once.

I turned into the parking lot of a little restaurant just past our neighborhood entrance. For all my running away, I hadn't gone far. I grabbed my notebook and Bible to take into the restaurant with me, a bastion against looking lonely and desperate. I ordered my food and found a table for one.

The restaurant was crowded with diners, and I ended up sitting close to an attractive man about my age. When he looked up and smiled at me, I smiled quickly and looked away. He fiddled with his cell phone while I made a production of turning to the prayer-journal section of my notebook and beginning to write. I opened to a psalm and read while I waited for the servers to call my number saying my turkey sandwich with sprouts and hummus was ready. Justine had said to have a salad, but I refused. I contemplated ordering a pastry just to make my rebellion complete.

The man's phone rang, startling me. I looked up in response to the ringtone it played. "I'm all out of love, I'm so lost without you." Air Supply. He smiled at me for the second time before answering. "Hey, you," he said in a voice that was so obviously happy to hear from the woman on the other end that tears came to my eyes. He laughed the laugh of a lover, a laugh charged with secret jokes and familiarity. "Yeah, me, too. Yeah, I'll be there. Of course. I'm glad you had a good day. That's all I want for you, you know. Your happiness. I was happy to do it for you. I love you too. Okay, see you then. Yes, I promise. Yes." He hung up still smiling, and I tried not to make it obvious that I could hear every word he had said. I noticed the ring on his left hand. How fortunate his wife was to have a husband who still talked to her like that. I looked down at my cell phone. David had not replied to my text.

Twice I looked up and caught the man looking at me, but I looked away before he could say anything. I didn't want to hear about his happy life with his happy wife. When Heather called, I grabbed the phone without checking the caller ID, hoping it was David since I hadn't talked to him all day. Heather just wanted to know if the boys were allowed to jump on the trampoline. I told her I would tip her if they were in bed asleep by the time I got home.

The man pulled a second cell phone from his pocket and dialed a number. "Hey," he said when the person answered, this time sounding totally different. "Listen, I am about to go into a meeting," he said. I looked around at the faces of the other patrons to see if they noticed what I was witnessing, wondered if the person on the other end could tell he was lying. "No, I told you I wouldn't be home for dinner. Yes, I said I would. Didn't I? Look, don't start in on me. I told you I didn't have time to talk." He didn't sound like the kind, gentle lover this time. He sounded like an angry, bitter man. "Yep," he finished. "Me, too."

He snapped the second cell phone shut and threw it into a brief-case on the floor, kicking the briefcase with his foot. I refused to lift my eyes and look at him. I didn't want him to see the betrayal I felt. He was not my husband. This was not my problem. Yet every bone in my body wanted to speak on behalf of his wife, to tell him what a putz he was, to tell him that his wife deserved love and understand-ing. His wife deserved the same tone that other woman got. She deserved happiness too. I looked back down at my cell phone, but there was no text. I finished my sandwich and got out of there as fast as I could. My big night alone had left me feeling worse than staying home with the boys would have. I wondered why I had listened to Justine.

I drove around aimlessly, past the library and the outdoor mall. I thought about going to see a movie, but there was nothing I wanted to see. I wandered around the bookstore and found nothing worth reading. I ambled up and down the aisles of a container store Justine recommended in an attempt to get our house organized but didn't have the energy or passion needed to buy containers for all our junk. It would have to stay unorganized at least for a while longer. I thought of how I would explain my lack of enthusiasm to Justine, who was always perky about organization. Finally, having exhausted all my efforts to fill my time, I aimed my car in the direction of the neighborhood.

As I pulled past the lions and waterfalls, I pressed the brake enough to slow the van down to a crawl. Hadn't I promised myself to stop there often? I pulled to the side and parked on the curb, out of the way of other cars. Grabbing my Bible and notebook, I walked toward the benches that the developer had added in hopes that the residents would enjoy the parklike entrance, I supposed. I had never seen anyone sitting there, however. Everyone was so busy working to afford their houses they didn't have time to enjoy the accoutrements of living there.

I sat down and closed my eyes before I began to write. I opened my Bible to the psalm I had read before, letting God's Word wash over my sorrows and renew my spirit. I wondered why Justine hadn't suggested this as an activity. Reading the Bible while I listened to the rush of water, the call of birds, felt the fading sun warm my shoulders. It was just what I needed.

I heard my name being called and looked up. Erica waved happily at me. "I thought you were out with Justine," she said as she got closer.

"She couldn't go. So I kept my sitter"—I smiled in reference to her daughter—"and went out anyway."

She gestured at my Bible. "Having fun?"

I looked around at the setting. "Yeah, actually I am. It's really pretty here."

She nodded. "I try to come here as much as I can. Since Heather was busy tonight, I decided to go for a walk, enjoy the evening." She looked at me pointedly. "Loneliness has its benefits, you know."

She had zeroed in on the theme of my night. I smiled. "I guess I'm still learning."

"Time, young grasshopper," she said in a deep voice. "In time you will learn much."

"Have a seat." I gestured at the space on the bench beside me.

"Don't mind if I do," she said. We sat and watched the waterfalls for a moment, the silence between us growing more awkward the longer it stretched. I barely knew this woman, but I wanted to know her better. I wondered what to say first, but she beat me to it.

"I've heard you are a good photographer," she said. "Justine is talking you up; word's spreading. Everyone's saying they're going to get pictures from you as soon as this heat dies down."

I couldn't hold my smile back. I would have to thank Justine the next time I saw her. "I love to take pictures," I said.

"Do you think you could take some for me?" she asked, her voice quiet, shy even.

"Sure. I'd love to. What's the occasion?"

She looked at the waterfalls as she spoke. "Heather and her friends. They're growing up, going to high school this fall. I just want to capture this time before it slips away—heat or not. I feel like this is the last summer she'll have any trace of that little girl I remember. By next summer she'll morph into a young woman. At least then I'll have the pictures." She turned to me. "I'll feel like I captured it somehow. You know?"

I nodded. "Yeah. That's one of the reasons I take pictures. It's my way of freezing time, of capturing what's precious before it can slip away."

"Can we do it soon? Do you have time this week?"

I grinned broadly. "For you? I've got all the time in the world."

She nudged me playfully and I nudged her back, falling into an easy conversation as we watched the sun set on Essex Falls.

CHAPTER 12

Justine

I watched Ariel drive past my house as I was getting into my car, part of me wishing I was going with her for a girls' night out. I hadn't had one of those since Laura and I went out the night before she moved. That hadn't been a happy occasion, though we'd faked our way through it, going to our favorite restaurant and even ordering dessert, a treat we rarely afforded ourselves. That night when I hugged Laura good-bye, I didn't let her see me cry, and now, as I drove toward Tom, I wondered why I hadn't.

The good news was, I was forgiving Ariel for being the one who moved into Laura's house. She was becoming a good friend.

I felt bad for deceiving her so I could be with Tom. I thought about the hurt in her voice when she called to say she could go out. Her finding a sitter was not something I had planned for. I was glad she'd gone out anyway like I'd suggested. It would be good for her, I told myself. And she wouldn't be around where Mark could possibly spot her.

I turned down the empty street and parked in front of a skeleton of a house abandoned to the economic downturn. Some builder had begun this neighborhood near Essex Falls, then bailed, leaving the street developed but not settled. Tom's car was parked exactly where I'd told him to meet me. I got out of the car and slid into the front seat beside Tom like I'd done it a million times. I wondered how many other illicit meetings had taken place in this exact spot.

The heat of the night settled on our skin and in our throats as we sat in silence, enjoying just being together. He took my hand, and I knew he could feel the sweat on my palms. His palms were dry. Every so often a faint breeze would float through, teasing us with its fickleness. Tom almost turned the engine on so we could run the air-conditioning, but I stopped him. "I like the heat," I said. "It reminds me of those summers in the mountains."

He laughed, an exhalation of breath that came out like a sputter. "Who said the mountains are cooler in the summer? I remember it being sweltering."

I smiled, thinking of a photo of him from one of our summers that I had tacked up on the bulletin board in my dorm. He was shirtless, tan, and the expression he wore on his face was nothing short of alluring. I could still see that picture when I closed my eyes. Truth was, I had it tucked away in easy reach even now.

"I remember you being sweltering." He turned to face me. The air in the car suddenly felt closer.

I leaned my head against the window, away from him. The glass felt cool against my cheek, like a caress. "Have you ever done this before?" I asked. Why it mattered, I couldn't say.

"Done what?" He looked out the windshield as though he needed to see the road. But all that lay ahead of us was woods. Along with obscure coffee shops, it seemed my brain had also cataloged out-of-the-way parking spots where people could hide. Our two cars sat parked together in the dead end conspicuously. Before I had gotten in his car and closed the door, I had told myself that I was only there to catch up with an old friend. Lying to myself, it turned out, was just as easy as lying to Ariel, to Mark, to Betsy, to my girls.

"Lied to your wife. Snuck around with someone else." I wanted to be the only one.

"I've never done this before," he said. "I need you to believe that." He turned toward me.

"So, why are we here?" I asked. I wasn't going to go easily.

He reached across the space between us to run the tip of his finger along the line of my jaw. A shiver traveled the length of my spine as he did. I turned to look at him. By now I knew the look he was giving me. After more than ten years of silence he was becoming familiar again. "I needed to see you, to be near you."

"You left me," I said, even though we had already been over this. "You chose her."

"I was a scared kid," he answered me. "I did what was expected of me because it was what I had done all my life. I married Betsy. I made a lot of people happy." He paused, sighed. "And I made myself miserable." We both sat in silence for a few minutes. I could hear the sound of his breathing, smell the cologne he wore. Something I didn't recognize, but liked. "You were the only one who touched my soul."

Dusk had collected in pockets in the edges of the cul-de-sac. I was surprised by how easily the lies had rolled off my tongue about where I was going and who I was with, how much I was willing to forfeit if it meant seeing—or talking to—Tom. All my little deceits were starting to collect, a compost pile of discarded truths, fertilizing the tender growth of our relationship.

There was no clock around, but I could tell it was time to go. Mark would be expecting me, the girls would most likely be waiting up even though he'd told them to go to bed. I wondered how I would explain all this to them someday. Would they applaud my courage to go after what I wanted or condemn my selfishness? Would they want to be like me or anything but? I nodded my head, and the girls disappeared.

When we both agreed it was time to go, Tom leaned over, kissed me, and repeated the promise he'd made all those years ago. This time I didn't intend to let him break it. If someone was going to get hurt this time around, it wasn't going to be me.

CHAPTER 13

‿

Ariel

We shot Heather's pictures at the neighborhood park. I bailed on Justine and my morning walk so I could get to the park before the sun climbed too high in the sky and baked us all. The teens groaned good-naturedly about being up so early but got into the spirit of the shoot pretty easily with a few sips of the sodas Erica brought for us all. I brought the boys, and they played on the fringes of the action. Occasionally I had to get a shot of them, too. I couldn't resist.

Through my lens I watched the dynamic of friendship play out among Heather and her friends: the familiarity laced with timidity, the chance to open up paired with the fear of being exposed, the awkward dance of really knowing another person. Heather and her friends, Sophie, Grace, and Nicole, had been close since elementary school, Erica told me. They had weathered two parents' divorces, the critical illness of one mom, and numerous squabbles and friendship breakups. But somehow the girls always found a way to come back together, to find what made them stick and hold on to that. I envied their natural rapport, the ease that can only come with time together. How ironic, I thought as I focused and clicked, that these girls already had what I couldn't seem to find. I couldn't record the whispers and giggles and "had to be there" references with my camera, but I could catch the smiles, the wide eyes, the dimples, the comfort. I could, as Erica requested, capture what was there.

"I think I'll have these for you this afternoon," I told Erica as I wrapped up the shoot. "I'm anxious to get home and edit them." I was always this way with new shots—couldn't wait to get home and see how I could make the shots better with a little editing. If only life came with editing software, I often thought. Take out the ugly parts with a click of a button.

"Wow! This afternoon? That's amazing."

"Yeah, I'll just give you a disk with the pictures on it. Then you can make prints of the ones you like."

"I'm sure I'll like them all!" She put her arm around Heather's neck and yanked playfully. "I'm a sucker for pictures."

Heather rolled her eyes and nodded. "You should see my baby books!"

"Well, just let me know if you need good references for places that can enlarge them. I'm happy to help," I said.

"Okay, well, I'll stop by for the disk later this afternoon then?"

"Sounds good!" I said. I could tell I'd made her day, and that felt even better than I'd expected.

"Thanks, Miss Ariel," Heather said shyly after I saw Erica whisper in her ear to do so.

I packed my camera into my case. It had been my first splurge when I started making real money from photography. Every art form has its tool: a musician has an instrument, a painter has paints, a writer has a pen. I had my Nikon D3S. I shut the case and looked up at Heather, into the sun. It surrounded her head like a halo. "No problem," I said to her. "I was glad to do it."

"Well, it was very nice of you. It meant a lot to my mom. Not many people go out of their way to be nice to her. So, thanks for that."

I did my best to not let my smile falter at her brave admission. "Good friends are hard to find. You're a lucky girl. I think your mom knows that." I did not add that I envied her.

She turned to look at Sophie and Grace on the swings, being pushed simultaneously by Nicole. They were all laughing at Nicole running back and forth from swing to swing. "My mom's always telling me I'm lucky to have them in my life. I'm starting to believe her."

"You're a smart girl," I said to her, and winked. "And your mom's a smart lady." I hoisted the camera bag on my shoulder and motioned for the boys to follow me as I headed to the parking lot. I waved at Erica as I loaded our things in the minivan and drove away, finding myself excited that I would see her later.

The next morning Justine was at my door bright and early. We made a slow progression walking with the kids in tow, but we were sticking with our exercise plan. I noticed how easily I had allowed her exercise plan to become my own. Oh well, I rationalized, exercise was good for me, no matter how I came into the idea. I trudged on with determination, ignoring the boys' requests to turn around and the girls' complaints that it was too hot. We were a motley crew.

"You know who I shot pictures for yesterday?" I asked Justine, trying to swing my arms to get my heart rate up like Justine had instructed me. Walking and swinging my arms was, it turned out, like rubbing my head and patting my stomach. I could do it, but I really had to focus. If I started talking, I would forget all about it and my arms would fall to my sides, useless.

"Who?" she asked. Justine had no trouble keeping her arms moving, and she always outpaced me.

"Erica Davidson," I said.

"Yes, I know Erica." Justine's tone changed from upbeat to strained.

"She's very pretty. Exotic." I had taken photos of her and Heather together, their hair the same inky black, their eyes the same unique shape, same gray color. Heather would one day be a beautiful girl when her braces came off and her acne cleared up. I wondered if her friends would still like her as much then.

Justine stifled a laugh. "*Exotic* is a good word for Erica," she said, her fingers over her mouth as though she was holding in more words she wanted to say.

"What do you mean?" I asked. My heart began to pound as if in danger.

"Just keep her away from David," she said.

"Why?" I asked.

"Because she has a reputation. She can't be trusted. I wouldn't get too friendly with her if I were you." She tugged the brim of her visor farther down on her head. "You're not doing your arms," she reminded me.

I thought of how Erica made me laugh, how she seemed to get the way things were around here. After yesterday and our night by the entrance, I had hoped we would be friends. And yet, the one friend I had made was telling me not to get close to her. I looked over at Justine's determined face, the set of her jaw, the intensity of her eyes. She was not kidding.

"So you think she's dangerous?" I pressed.

"I think Erica was married to a very sweet man who loved her very much. She wanted the divorce, and he did not. He even gave her the house out of the goodness of his heart. And now she flaunts her single-ness and flirts with married men and drinks entirely too much. I am fine with a glass of wine now and then, but she drinks like a fish and acts like a college girl. It's just not good. She's not a good influence." Justine put her hand on my arm, slowing me down. "I'm just trying to warn you, as your friend. It's what I would want if the tables were turned. I would hate for you to ask me later why I didn't warn you." She smiled and began walking again. Her short ponytail bobbed in time with her steps.

"Of course," I said. "I'm glad you told me the truth."

"She was probably trying to buddy up to you before you found out the truth about her. She doesn't have too many friends in this neighborhood, as you can imagine." I thought about Heather's words, how not many people were nice to her mom. It made more sense now.

I thought about the cracks Erica had made about the neighborhood, how she put down the people who lived here, but her reason for doing so became more suspect in light of what Justine was saying. Erica was not someone I should be talking to. I would be more careful in the future. I wouldn't want my reputation around the neighborhood to be sullied by being linked to her. And I certainly didn't want my husband exposed to more temptations that I had imagined he was already exposed to, thinking of the situation with the man in the restaurant. "Thank you," I said to Justine. I was so glad I had her.

"No problem whatsoever," she said. "What are friends for? Now let's get that heart rate up. Move those arms."

One afternoon I watched the boys jumping on the trampoline, their bodies lifting and falling like popcorn. They were getting tan from our afternoons by the pool, their olive complexions darkening a bit more each day. They looked healthy and handsome. I watched them as a stranger might. Lulled by their acrobatic dance, I found

Our summer days fell into an agreeable rhythm. Mornings were spent walking and cleaning house. Lunch was packed and eaten at the pool, then home in the afternoons to play outside or watch a movie while I made dinner. It was Justine's schedule, and I marveled at how easily I fell into it. Usually Cameron and Caroline were at my house or my boys were at Justine's. It felt … comfortable, perfect, just what I dreamed of, except for the fact that my husband and I were barely speaking.

myself swaying by the window just like I used to when I held them as babies, the mother's dance.

When I saw Cameron and Caroline begin to climb on the trampoline, the spell was broken and I flew outside, arms flapping like a fierce mother bird. "No, girls. You are not allowed to be on there," I said.

Caroline pointed back toward her house. "Daddy said we could," she said.

I followed the direction of her finger to find Mark standing on the deck with his hands on his hips. He waved. I relaxed and gave him the thumbs-up sign, guessing that he and Justine had decided trampolines weren't so bad after all. A smile crept onto my face as I realized the boys and I were rubbing off on them, too. I helped both girls get on the trampoline and reviewed the safety precautions with them. They all stared up at the clouds overhead while I talked. Moms were boring, always fussing over safety. I gave up and went in the house where it was cooler. I could keep an eye on them from there.

The phone was ringing when I walked in, and I grabbed for it, hoping it was David calling. Instead I heard Kristy's voice, just calling for our occasional chat. I looked out the window at the kids. They were trying to coax Lucky to jump up onto the trampoline, as if the poor dog could hope to jump that high.

After awhile I moved into the laundry room and was simultaneously chatting on the phone while throwing clothes into the basket to be folded, when I heard the screaming. "I have to go," I said briskly and hung up. I ran out to the yard. Mark was running from his. I looked at the trampoline. Cameron was holding her mouth, from which blood streamed between her fingers. The boys and Caroline clustered around her with worried looks on their faces, the air around them charged with danger and fear.

"Mom," Donovan said as I got to the trampoline, his hand on Cameron's shoulder, "she's hurt!" *Thank you, Captain Obvious.* Dylan was holding his knee, which was also bleeding slightly. He rocked back and forth and wouldn't look me in the eye when I asked what had happened. "Dylan's knee hit her mouth when they were jumping," Donovan said. "Now she's bleeding."

I nodded and reached for Cameron, pulling her from the trampoline and cradling her as she cried. Mark joined us, panting. He smiled at me. "I need to exercise more," he quipped as he reached for his daughter. "Shhh," he told her, palming her face with his mitt of a hand, a gentle giant. "Let me see your mouth."

Instead she opened her fist and presented him with her front tooth. "It's gone," she wailed.

"Hey, hey, it's okay. You're supposed to lose baby teeth," he told her, ruffling her hair and holding her closer. "That just means the tooth fairy's going to come tonight."

I felt myself relax because he was relaxed. I had a feeling his calming presence was working on Cameron as well. She giggled as she tried to guess how much money the tooth fairy would leave her. I went in the house for some wet paper towels to mop up the blood, smiling to myself that the crisis hadn't been worse, that Mark had handled everything so well.

By the time I got back with the paper towels, Mark was holding her, and Justine was bent over the two of them. She looked at me, and a flash of anger flickered across her face before she could compose herself. I walked up to them, holding the wet towels out like an offering. "I'm so sorry," I said.

"It's fine," she said stiffly. I could tell she wanted to say more but was restraining herself.

"I'd be angry at me if I were you. I let them do something you asked me not to," I said. "Maybe we should just get rid of the trampoline."

"Mom, no!" Donovan said. I narrowed my eyes at him, and he bent his head down. I noticed Dylan's shoulders heaving, his head tucked between his knees.

"Dyl?" I went over to him and held out my arms as he crawled into them. From the corner of my eye, I saw Justine lead the still sniffling Cameron toward their house. Mark looked nervously between the two of them and us.

"It's all my fault," Dylan said. "I knocked out Cameron's tooth." I looked down at his knee. Blood dripped down his leg in a fine trickle. He would have a large bruise. I could see the mark the tooth had left, the beginnings of purple radiating out.

I laid the cool, wet paper towels on his knee. "There, there," I said, just like I imagined a good mother would. "It's okay. Cameron's going to be fine," I assured him. I smiled over his head at Mark. "She is," I said to him.

He nodded. "Sure she will," he said. "But Justine might be another story." He ruffled Dylan's hair and walked slowly across our yard and then his own, climbing his deck stairs with legs made of clay.

CHAPTER 14

~

Justine

As soon as I could, I was going to call Tom and tell him what had happened. Lately he was the only one I could be honest with. He would listen to how angry I was with Ariel for letting my girls on that trampoline, with Mark for standing by while they disobeyed the one thing I'd asked. And now my little girl was maimed. Okay, maybe not for life. But it could've been worse. And then what? What would Ariel's apology do for her then? I paced around the kitchen, stewing. Cameron was settled in front of the television, her tongue continually feeling the space where her tooth used to be. I wanted to run from the house, jump in my car, and drive straight to him. I wanted to stop playing pretend in front of all the people who were standing in the way of us.

"I can see the steam coming out of your ears," Mark said from behind me. He stood in the doorway that led to the deck. Caroline hovered behind him, looking scared. I pasted on a smile and pretended everything was fine.

"It's fine," I said to Mark. "It was an accident."

He crossed the room and took me in his arms. "I'm proud of you," he said, squeezing the breath from me in his strong embrace. His hugs always felt like he was choking me. Tears filled my eyes as I nodded and smiled.

"You're changing," he said. "You seem happier." He pulled away from me, turned my chin to look in his eyes. His eyes were brown. Tom's eyes were blue. "That makes me feel really good, to know you're happy in spite of all that's going on. You know that's all I ever wanted for you, right?"

I nodded again, doing my best to meet his eyes. I wondered if he could see the pity in mine. If he only knew the real reason I was more at peace, happier. He pressed his lips to my forehead. "Thanks for not being angry. About any of this," he added. "I promise I'm going to fix things for us."

I pressed my lips into a smile. "No problem," I managed. I had gotten so good at saying no problem. No problem that I feel nothing for you. No problem that our money never seems to last long enough. No problem that my entire life is an act and you don't even notice. Later I would find an excuse to go to the store and call Tom as I drove, my new MO. I would cry to him, vent to him, give it all to him. Mark would never know what he was missing. I just wondered how long this strange limbo we were living in would be enough. Mark looked at me and smiled in that warm, genuine way that would charm any woman but me. "You're so pretty," he said, as if he hadn't seen me in a long time. The truth was, he never had.

Tom was outside talking, "away from big ears in his office," he had said. Whenever I called, he would stop what he was doing and find a quiet place for us to talk.

"Sorry to bother you in the middle of the day," I said.

"You could never bother me," he replied quickly. Birds were singing wherever he was. I wanted to be where he was, hear the birds' songs together, lie back on a blanket, and feel the warmth of the hot sun on our bare skin. Desire rose up in me as it always did whenever we spoke, the sound of his voice an aphrodisiac.

"Is everything okay?" he asked, reminding me of why I'd called. "Where are you?"

"In my car," I said. I was parked outside the grocery store. I had lied to Mark that we needed some obscure ingredients for a dish I was making. All I had to do was spout off some names of herbs and Mark would wave me out the door.

I sighed and told Tom about the trampoline accident, how it was something so simple but it felt like something more significant. How I had pretended not to be angry so as not to raise suspicion but what I really wanted was to cry and scream at all of them.

"I hold so much in so that I can hold on to you," I said.

"What does that mean?"

"I can't let on how unhappy I am. Mark thinks I'm so happy. He thinks we're so happy. He doesn't see and I can't let him see. The fact that he's not looking leaves an open door for … this. And Ariel, well, she's my cover with him. He thinks I'm with her when I'm with you. He thinks I confide in her when I confide in you. She can't know how unhappy I am either. I just have to keep up this facade so I can keep talking to you, keep seeing you." I paused, exhaled into the phone. "But I don't know how long I can keep lying."

"You're not really lying," he said. "You're just not telling everything. Does anyone ever really tell the people in their lives everything?"

"I tell you everything," I said quickly.

"I'm sure you don't. There are things you can't say to me, things you don't want to admit, things you've withheld because you're unsure or you just don't want me to know. It's the nature of a new relationship, to keep things to yourself. I'll bet you're already thinking of something you haven't told me."

I thought of his wife taking my part, how mortified I'd be if he knew. I never intended to tell him, and I never wanted him to find out from anyone else either. "No," I said. "There's nothing I can think of."

He chuckled. "You might think you're a good liar," he said, "but you're not. That's okay. You'll tell me when you're ready. Hey, I gotta go. You sure you're good?"

"Yeah," I said as I watched Erica and her daughter cross the parking lot into the store, which meant I wouldn't be able to go in there. I laid my head on the steering wheel. "I'm good." I was a better liar than he knew.

CHAPTER 15

Ariel

After mothers' group the next day, I nibbled on fancy crackers and eyed Justine. She wouldn't look at me, and I feared our friendship was over as soon as it had begun. I was about to give up on her when she showed up at my elbow, her smile as in place as her outfit. She was as good at being perfect as I was at being a wreck. I made myself smile back at her.

"I'm sorry," I said after I swallowed my mouthful of cracker. "I should have told the girls they couldn't be on the trampoline. I should have respected your wishes."

She waved my words away like stinky cigar smoke. "Bygones," she said. "I've already forgotten about it."

"But—"

She patted my shoulder and pointed toward the emptying room. "Better go get your boys," she said and whisked away. I slunk out of the room feeling chastised by Justine's dismissal and unconvinced of her profession of forgiveness. She didn't seem like one who moved forward quite so easily.

— ⁓ —

Later that afternoon I was calling the boys down to lunch only to be completely ignored except by Lucky, who always showed up when food was being offered. I headed in the direction of their playroom, grumbling and snatching up stray toys and discarded items as I walked. "Always look for things you can tidy up while you're on your way somewhere else," Justine had instructed me. I carried the items up the stairs and moved to the doorway of the playroom to find Donovan with a flashlight looking up Dylan's nose while Duncan sat beside them on his haunches, a worried look on his face. He glanced sideways just in time to spot me.

"Uh-oh, guys," he said and pointed. Donovan dropped the flashlight and looked at his brother as if to say, *I tried, but you're on your own.*

"Dylan, what's going on?" I asked, not wanting to know the answer yet compelled to ask.

I looked down to see Dylan pointing to a Star Wars action-figure gun jammed halfway up his nose. "It's way up there, Mom," he said, sounding like he was afraid to breathe. He moaned. "Is it going to be stuck there forever?"

I resisted the urge to scare him by saying yes and instead walked to the phone to dial the number for the pediatrician. After I had made an appointment, I directed the boys into the minivan. I only *thought* I was going to have the afternoon at home. Not wanting to sit for an undetermined amount of time with three wild boys in a small waiting room, I impulsively dialed another number. Justine answered right away, as if she was waiting by the phone. I explained what had happened and asked if she would watch Donovan and Duncan while I took Dylan to the doctor's office to retrieve the offending weaponry. Justine was only too happy to come to my rescue.

As I drove away from her house, I thanked God for good neighbors and hoped that, if nothing else, we could at least be that to each other.

I smiled at the receptionist as we walked in, and she waved us to the waiting-room seats. Dylan ran off to play with the trains in the kids' area, and I tried not to think of what kinds of germs could be lurking on those surfaces. I hadn't thought to bring anything to read, and the doctor's office typically had only medical magazines. There was only so much information on treating chicken pox and head lice that I could enjoy. I sighed and leaned my head against the wall, closing my eyes. The low noises of the office lulled me into a twilight sleep—aware of my surroundings but resting at the same time. It was as close as I came to a nap, and I welcomed the chance to sit quietly and think of nothing at all.

When I opened my eyes, Erica and her daughter were sitting right across from me. She smiled, and I smiled back without showing any teeth, then busied myself with the magazines that I hadn't been interested in earlier. Heather snuggled against Erica, and while I wanted to ask why they were there, how long they had been coming to that doctor, and other things, I kept my head down and didn't say a word to her.

When they called my name and I looked up, our eyes met again and something like recognition flashed in her eyes. Recognition and hurt. I collected Dylan from the train table and followed the nurse to the exam room, not looking back at Erica so I didn't have to see the look on her face again. Part of me wanted to run back and apologize to her, but another part of me remembered Justine's words of warning. I hardly knew her, after all. I owed her nothing. The doctor retrieved the toy without much fanfare. Thankfully, Erica wasn't in the waiting room when we left.

I swung by Justine's house to get the boys, and she invited me in as though the trampoline fiasco had never happened. We talked about the mural she wanted to help me paint on the large blank wall in my bathroom, and she showed me pictures of some of her other work. When I congratulated her on her talent, she shrugged, spots of color blooming in her cheeks. She looked away, showing the boys a space mural she had painted for a friend, which of course prompted them to beg her to do the same for them. I told them I needed a bathroom mural first. She leaned in, smiling. "I used to beg Laura to let me paint that wall. I know just what we can do. It'll look perfect."

Just before we left, I told her about seeing Erica. "I didn't talk to her," I said. I hoped she would tell me not to be ridiculous, that we should treat people with basic kindness and that I had taken it too far. I waited for her to say something like that, something the leader of a large Christian mothers' group would say.

Instead she patted me on the shoulder. "That was probably a good thing," she said. "No use in encouraging her. You are smart to protect yourself and your family. Your *marriage,*" she added, raising her eyebrows.

I nodded soberly and ushered the boys out the door. As I drove toward home, I ignored the gnawing feeling in my stomach, writing it off to hunger because I still hadn't eaten lunch.

CHAPTER 16

Justine

For once Mark didn't drop his briefcase by the door. He walked right past me in the kitchen and went to sit on the couch we were still paying for. The decorator I hired said I had to have it as the focal point of the den. At the time I agreed with her. But as I watched my unemployed husband sit uncomfortably on the edge of a couch we still owed money on, it suddenly didn't feel so urgent for us to have a focal point in our den.

I sat across from him on the coffee table. We still owed on that, too. "What are we going to do?" I asked. He stared ahead, not speaking. He wore a jacket even though it was 100 degrees outside. He held on to his briefcase like it was a security blanket. He'd called four hours earlier to say he'd been fired, and I couldn't help but wonder where he'd been since then. I didn't dare ask. It wasn't really my business. What right did I have when I'd spent the last hour on the phone with Tom telling him that Mark had been fired, only hanging up when I heard his car pulling into the garage?

I watched Mark, trying to determine what I felt for him. It wasn't love. It wasn't affection. It wasn't really even like or respect. What I felt for him, I decided in that moment, was family. He had become my family in the years we'd been married. He was family like my mother was family, my sister, my stepfather. How could I hurt someone who was my family?

I reached out to him, patting his hand. "We can do this," I said. I tried to use my most encouraging tone, willed my eyes to look sincere. Because the truth was, we couldn't do this. He had been given very little severance. We had no savings. Our credit cards were maxed out. We had lived a life built on his paychecks showing up regularly. We weren't prepared for this hurricane that had come blowing into our house, pulling the roof off so the rain could pour in. Mark had to believe he could do this so he could go find a job. Even a few weeks of no paycheck could bring the house down.

He looked at me as though he'd never seen me before, as though he was trying to place me. "I can't do this," he said.

I patted his hand again, noting the scar he'd gotten when he fell off the ladder while cleaning the gutters. Hadn't I taken him to the hospital and sat by his side while the doctor stitched him up? Hadn't I been there for him? I wasn't a terrible person. "Of course you can," I said.

"No," he said. "I've been driving around thinking about this. I'm not going to be able to find another job. The economy's too bad and what I do is so specialized there's not going to be another job just around the corner, Justine. It's going to take too long." He looked directly at me for the first time. "And we can't afford to wait." He broke my gaze and looked at his lap. "So I think it needs to be you. You are the talented one, the one who can hold our family up. I'm just a loser."

"Me? Mark, what do you mean?"

"You need to find a job."

I laughed, my commitment to being supportive evaporating with his ridiculous suggestion. "That's crazy talk, Mark. You're not making any sense."

He looked at me. "I'm totally serious," he said. "You're this capable, smart, beautiful woman. You've got what companies look for." He sighed. "I don't. It's going to be up to you to keep our family from going under. I can't."

Anger flickered, then burned inside me as I looked at him. "You can't ask this of me," I said.

"I can. And I am. All I hear is how together you are, what an amazing person you are. Everywhere I go in this town, people stop me and talk about you. No one talks about me that way. No one. If one of us has to find a job in a hurry, it's got to be you. It just makes the most sense."

"No." I shook my head, and though I tried to stop it, the thought entered my mind too quickly: Tom would never ask this of me. I stood up and walked into the kitchen. I couldn't start comparing the two of them; holding Mark up to Tom wasn't fair. We hadn't spent enough time together for me to truly know what Tom would do. And then another thought torpedoed through my brain that was even more dangerous than the first ... one simple word: *yet.*

I shivered a little in the air-conditioning as I came to a stop at my
kitchen sink. From there I could see the cul-de-sac of my street. If I
strained, I could make out the roof of Tom's house.

I felt Mark's arms go around me from behind. He pushed his
head into my neck, burying his face in my hair. He had held me like
this that one time I tried to break up with him, when I first knew that
marrying him was a mistake, before things had gone too far. I had
given him his ring back, saying I needed time, that we had rushed
into things. We'd only been dating less than a year, I told him. Didn't
couples need more time to know if marriage was the right thing to
do? I'd been at his kitchen sink in his apartment, washing dishes.
He'd come up from behind me and held on to me, his tears wetting
my hair. "I love you," he'd said. "I don't need more time." And I'd
turned into his embrace, into his chest, and cried too. Because he
really was sweet, a dream come true for any other girl but me.

Now his body shuddered, and I stiffened, but he seemed not to
notice. "I'm sorry I let you down," he said.

I knew what I was supposed to say. I was supposed to say that
he hadn't let me down, that we were going to be okay, that together
we could get through this. But I said none of those things. Instead
I said quietly, "Me, too." After he left the room, I went to hide on
the screened-in porch so I could text Tom to tell him what had happened. "That didn't go well," I wrote. As I put the phone in my
pocket and waited for him to respond, I couldn't escape the feeling
that this had happened to punish me for what I was doing. But now
more than ever, I couldn't stop.

In spite of Mark losing his job, we had no choice but to go ahead with the plans to have Tom's family over for dinner. It was too late to cancel, and besides, I looked forward to seeing Tom any way I could. I stood in front of my bathroom mirror, applying lip gloss and practicing my "everything's going to be fine" smile. I couldn't fool Tom, but it was imperative that I fool Betsy. I needed her to believe that all was well with me, with my marriage. That I didn't despise her for taking my part, even though she had no clue that she had. If she believed that, she wouldn't look too closely. She'd believe exactly what Tom had told her when she figured out who I was: that it was just a crush from when we were young, no lasting effects, no harm done. I believed in keeping my friends close and my enemies closer. Besides, I could learn a lot about Tom by befriending Betsy. I finished with the lip gloss and practiced another look entirely—the look I would give Tom if we got a moment alone.

"They're here!" I heard Cameron announce. "Mom, Dad."

"Coming," I called out, listening for the sounds of unfamiliar voices coming from downstairs. Above all the others, I heard the one I was listening for and smiled. This smile wasn't practiced.

Dinner was grilled hamburgers and hot dogs. I had made baked beans, and Betsy brought coleslaw and potato salad. Tom hung out with Mark on the deck while I made small talk with Betsy. We talked about the schools the kids would be attending, the best sports and activities to sign up for, where to find the best bargains on groceries. Mom stuff. Betsy was cute and easy to talk to, and for just a moment, I felt bad for talking to her husband behind her back. Then I thought of her standing in front of my church in a few weeks on the Fourth of July, singing my solo. And I didn't feel bad anymore.

Tom walked in from the deck, and our eyes met just long enough for me to know that I was kidding myself if I thought talking to him would be that easy to stop. I stifled a smile and turned to the sink, where I was slicing a tomato for the hamburgers.

"Where should I put this?" Betsy asked, holding up the large platter I had out for the hamburgers. I had painted the platter myself with the verse "Trust in the Lord with all your heart." Did I ever really believe that? Was I really the woman who had painted those words on that platter? I focused elsewhere and asked her to carry it out to Mark, who was presiding over the grill.

When she was gone, Tom came over to me. "I've missed you. It's weird seeing you, with her here too." He pulled me to him with a devilish-looking smile on his face. "But kind of exciting."

I pushed away from him and slapped at his hand, trying to see where Betsy was. I spotted her talking to Mark over the grill. Wouldn't it be nice if we could all switch places? Trade spouses like the reality TV show?

"Stop it," I said to Tom, like a mother speaking to a child. But I bit back a smile as I turned back to the sink. Sneaking around did feel … dangerous. To someone whose idea of pushing the limits was being overdue on a library book, dangerous felt good.

Tom came up behind me, leaning his weight against me. I could feel his breath on my ear. "I listened to our song today. Thought about you."

I shuddered, wanting so badly to turn around and kiss him that I had to grip the counter ledge. He moved away and turned to pretend he was getting buns out of the bags just as Betsy came back in the house. His timing, I noticed, was uncanny. I exhaled, unaware that I'd been holding my breath. Betsy laid her hand on my arm. "You okay?" she asked me, concern etching her face. I was a horrible person.

"Yes," I said. "I was just telling Tom about the news we got today." She didn't know I had already told Tom hours before. I started to peel off lettuce from its core, saving the best pieces to put out for the burgers. "Mark lost his job today," I said, fumbling for an excuse for my clear exasperation.

Betsy's hand flew to her mouth. "I'm so sorry." She put her arm around me and squeezed. "Well, of course you're not okay." She looked over at Tom. "This is terrible," she said to him.

"I know," he responded, not meeting her eyes. He looked over at me. "It is terrible." I knew he wasn't talking about Mark's job.

"Well, what can we do? Tell me what we can do," Betsy said. She stood between Tom and me, which was, I thought, appropriate.

I shook my head. "There's nothing really. Mark's going to start looking, of course." That was not true. He'd said nothing about looking, only that I should. "And I'm going to try to find something too. We need all hands on deck." I gave her my practiced smile, and she fell for it, smiling right back.

"You're a hero," she said, her eyes kind and warm as they looked into mine. I looked away.

In a bold move, Tom walked over to me, put his hand on my shoulder. "She is a hero," he said, looking at Betsy. "And we should help however we can. Why don't I give you my cell-phone number and that way I can offer you counseling? I'm in HR at a huge company, and I can help you with your search, your résumé … whatever you need."

Betsy's face lit up. "That's perfect, Tom. You could totally help her."

He smiled at me. "I hope you don't mind me offering. To help you," he said, every bit the concerned old friend/neighbor he was pretending to be just then.

"Not at all," I answered him. "That would be nice, actually." I looked over at Betsy, shaking my head. "I've been a stay-at-home mom for eight years. I am totally out of my element in the corporate world." Betsy clapped her hands together as she looked from me to Tom and back again. I went to call Mark and the kids in for dinner. I had to hand it to Tom, he was one smart cookie. He had just cleared the way for us to have sanctioned contact. I couldn't help but wonder if he'd planned that or if it had just come to him suddenly. Oh well, what did it matter?

CHAPTER 17

Ariel

On Monday before I slipped out the back door, I told the boys, who were watching a movie, that I was just walking across the yard to Justine's and to come and get me if they needed me. Lucky wagged his tail from under the coffee table as if to say, "Don't worry, Mom. I'll watch out for them!"

I tapped on the glass door of the Millers' deck and saw Cameron and Caroline sprawled out, still in their pajamas, watching TV. I hadn't seen any of them for several days and Justine hadn't responded to my phone calls. I worried that she was angry about the trampoline incident and was avoiding me, but David said I made too many things about me and to just go find out. From what I could see as I peered through the window, there was definitely something wrong. Justine had a strict rule about TV watching and an even stricter rule about remaining in one's pajamas after eight. Cameron came to the door and opened it, blinking at me like one of those children who can't be exposed to sunlight.

"Hi, sweetie," I said. "Is your mommy here?"

She opened the door wider so I could walk in. "She's upstairs," she said. "In her room." She pointed toward the staircase. I stood there awkwardly as Cameron turned back to the TV.

"So I guess I'll just go up and see her then?" I asked.

Cameron said nothing in response. I walked to the stairs, expecting her to stop me, but no one said a word. The only noise in the house was from the cartoon the girls were watching and the mechanical hum of the Sub-Zero refrigerator in the kitchen. At the top of the stairs I looked around, trying to determine which room was Justine's. I got it right on the first try, the door revealing a large master bedroom, the bed unmade, its floral comforter slipping onto the floor like discarded clothing.

I had never been beyond their family living area—the acceptable place for an acquaintance to go. But a true friend? A true friend waltzed into your bedroom and jumped in bed with you, saw you in your pajamas with no makeup, talked to you while you tried on clothes. It felt monumental to be stepping past the threshold, beyond the acceptable limits we had in place before that morning. I eased into her bedroom, expecting her to call out for me not to come any closer. Instead I heard no sound, not even breathing. I was alone in the room. "Justine?" I whispered, sounding more like a hiss. "It's Ariel."

I was about to leave the room and search for her somewhere else when I heard a noise. "In here," came a muffled reply from behind the closed door of her closet. I stood for a moment and pondered what she was doing in the closet. Hiding out like that would be bizarre behavior for me, unfathomable for her. Something was really wrong.

I walked slowly toward the door and turned the handle, opening the door to a large, dark walk-in closet. I flipped on the light to see her better, and she shielded her eyes. "Turn it off," she whispered at me.

I switched the light off quickly, got down on all fours, and crawled toward her, forgetting all about my dignity. As my eyes adjusted to the dark, I could make out her form. The light from the open door lit her face softly. I could see a ring of black mascara around her eyes. "What are you doing in here?" I asked her softly.

She shrugged. "Hiding," she said in a very small voice. It was not Justine's confident, assertive voice. It was Cameron's or Caroline's.

My mind raced as I struggled for something to say. I was used to Justine providing the answers, not me. "Hiding from what?"

"Life," she said, drawing a crumpled-up piece of toilet tissue to her nose and daintily dabbing at it. She sniffed and looked at me. "Reality."

"What reality?" I pressed.

She sighed, a long inhale and exhale. "Mark lost his job. They gave him hardly any severance. They took his company car, his company phone, his company computer." She looked at me for a beat. "Our company life, I guess you could say."

"Where is he?" I asked. Mark had been nowhere in sight when I walked through the house.

She shrugged. "How would I know? I can't call him. He doesn't have a phone." She fiddled with the shredded piece of toilet tissue. She laid the tissue in her lap, picked it back up again.

I sat silently, running through options of what I could say next, but nothing sounded right. "I'm sorry," I offered. It was nothing, two words as flimsy as that piece of tissue she was holding.

*

She nodded. "I know. I know you are. I guess I just need Mark to come home and tell me this is going to be okay. That nothing has to change. That he'll take care of it." She smiled grimly. "I want him to come home and lie."

"So, what—what are you going to do?" My mind raced with possibilities of what I could do. Call David? Help organize a job search? Make a meal?

"There's nothing I can do. Get a job myself like Mark wants? Be his cheerleader while he looks for another job? Because he has to find another job." She waved her hand at her closet, the line of clothes hanging up, the rows of shoes and purses and accessories all around us. "All of this came with a price. We can't go without a job." The tears began to roll down her face again. "We won't make it. We weren't prepared for this. We didn't save for a rainy day or whatever it is you're supposed to do."

I thought of the many arguments David and I had had over his propensity to save instead of spend. How angry I got over his frugality. And yet, if something like this happened to us, I reasoned as I knelt in Justine's closet, we would be okay because of the very thing I railed against. Shame colored my face, and I was grateful for the darkness.

I thought of the time I found my mom hiding out in a darkened room. I crawled into bed with her and asked her if she was sick. She pulled the covers back, and I snuggled underneath them, curling up beside her in the shape of a comma. Our faces were so close I could feel her breath every time she exhaled. I remembered it was raining, and for a while the only sound in the room was the rain hitting the roof and the window. Finally she spoke. "I'm not sick," she said. "I'm sad."

"Why are you sad, Mommy?" I asked. I was eight years old.

"Because Daddy went away," she said.

The night before, my daddy had read me a story and tucked me into bed. He hadn't mentioned going away. He hadn't packed a suitcase or promised to bring me back a surprise like he usually did. I remember rubbing her shoulder. "Don't worry, Mommy," I said. "He'll be back soon."

"No, Ariel, honey, you don't understand," she said. "He's not coming back. He's left us." She corrected herself. "Left me."

I remembered trying to absorb the meaning of her words. My daddy had just read a chapter of *The Boxcar Children* to me. Who would read the rest? How would I find out what happened? Did the children's adventures sound so good he'd wanted to go on one of his own? And if that was what had happened, did that mean his leaving was my fault?

Years later in a class on child development I learned that children nearly always try to take responsibility for a divorce. That it's up to the parents to communicate to the children that they did nothing wrong. My mom said nothing more that day in her dark room, as though the mere effort of telling me my dad was gone took the breath right out of her. When I got up from the bed and went to find my sister, she reached out and stopped me. I looked back at her in hopes that she would offer some words of comfort or perspective. My eyes had adjusted to the dark and I could just make out her face. "Yes, Mommy?" I asked.

"You have to work hard to keep a man, Ariel," she said. "You better take care of him, or be prepared to take care of yourself." I nodded as though I understood, but the truth was—all these years later—I was still trying to understand her words to me.

I noticed Justine staring at me and laughed. "Sorry," I said. "My mind wandered." I hurried to add something. "I'd like to pray for you before I go." I felt lame as I said it. The emptiness of my words echoed around us. Why did I always feel like I was offering a consolation when I suggested prayer? It wasn't that I didn't believe in it—I absolutely did. It just felt so … passive in the face of such a huge issue.

Justine stared back at me blankly. "You can pray if you want," she said, sniffling. "God and I aren't really on speaking terms right now."

I put my hand on her shoulder, the lightest touch, ready for her to brush it aside. But she didn't. I wanted to pull her into a hug, but I feared her stiffening against me. Justine was not the hugging type. So I sat motionless, silent, my hand resting awkwardly on her shoulder as I prayed quietly for her. She dabbed at her eyes, and we sat that way, saying nothing. But inside I was saying a lot.

That night David arrived home after dinner was cooked and cleaned up, after the boys had surrendered to sleep, after I had given up on flipping through reality television and courtroom dramas and headed to bed alone. He slunk into the room, his head ducked as if he was already prepared to be assaulted. "Sorry I wasn't here for dinner. My flight was canceled. I had to take a later one," he said, not looking me directly in the eyes, a disobedient child waiting for his reprimand.

I put down the book I had been pretending to read. "It's okay," I said and smiled.

He set down his suitcase on the floor. "What?" he asked. "No lecture about why I didn't call or wasn't more considerate?"

I shook my head, my smile widening. "I'm just glad you're here."

He crawled onto the bed, smiling back at me. I didn't even tell him to take his shoes off lest he mess up the bedspread. He nuzzled his face in my neck. I felt his warm breath as he kissed me. He was looking me in the eyes now. "Why are you glad I'm here?" he asked, his eyes saying much more.

"I missed you," I said. I gave him a look that was meant to be coy. I wanted to be a mystery to him again, a conquest. I would not tell him until later that I was just relieved that he had a job, that he took care of us financially, that we weren't in Justine and Mark's boat. Just for tonight I would let him believe it was nothing more than him and me and passion resurfacing, like a glimpse in a magic mirror of the person you once were. I helped him remove his shirt and counted my blessings, still smiling as his mouth covered mine.

CHAPTER 18

⌒

Justine

I didn't know how to get a job, but I knew how to throw a party. Mark didn't say anything as I busied myself with throwing a party for Ariel's birthday. He didn't mention that we didn't have money to host a party or that he wasn't really in the mood to have a houseful of people. Instead he slipped away at odd times, really only smiling if I smiled at him first. I saw the light go out in him, watched it flicker and die. I offered nothing in response, no oxygen for his dying flame. We barely spoke that week, giving each other a wide berth as we passed each other in the hall. Sometimes I made myself reach out and pat his shoulder. He always stopped and closed his eyes when I did.

Here is what I know about throwing a party: I know that lighting matters. Overhead lighting is a no-no. Lamps and candles make everything glow, including faces. Music is a must. I try to pick good background music: piano, acoustic guitar, something like that. Hors d'oeuvres should be easy to eat standing up, preferably in a bite or two. The less formal and stuffy the party feels, the better. A relaxed, informal atmosphere will get guests talking and socializing. Get a good cake, and grown-ups will gather around it and ooohh and ahhh like kids. And finally, don't let couples hover together. Find a way to split them up.

David had grudgingly gone along with my idea when I caught him in the yard and proposed the party. He always looked at me funny, as though I had said something about him behind his back or kicked his dog when he wasn't looking. He was a handsome man, and handsome men didn't usually look at me that way. There was usually more appreciation there. His lack made me work harder, want it more.

That day in the yard I leaned over the fence, knowing that the V-neck of my shirt slipped down as I did. I saw his eyes flicker there and away. But instead of the look of appreciation I was used to seeing from a man, the look in his eyes was different. Not discomfort. Not anger. Not revulsion. It took me a few days to name it, but when I did finally determine what it was, I felt ashamed. David had looked at me with pity. As I told him about the party I wanted to throw, I looked instead at the fence, picking at the peeling white paint with my red nails. Our exchange lasted mere minutes but stayed with me for days.

I worked hard to make the party all it could be, even inviting some friend of hers I didn't know like David had suggested. I also invited new people from the neighborhood I thought she would like to meet. It was part "welcome to the neighborhood" and part "happy birthday, new friend." That's what I told myself. But the truth was, it was a nice diversion from what was happening with Mark and a guaranteed way to be in the same room with Tom again. I wanted to breathe the same air, eat the same food, talk to the same people. Most of all I wanted to feel the way my heart raced whenever he was nearby. It made me feel alive, and alive was good after years of feeling dead. There had been another brief time when I'd felt that way, but that was a long time ago and best forgotten. This was entirely different.

What I had with Tom was real, and it was going somewhere. I thought of each time he had kissed me since that first kiss in the car. Three stolen moments, relived in my mind again and again, savoring the smell of his skin, the intimacy of his mouth on mine, our mingled breath, the softness of his lips. Sometimes when I was sleeping, the memory would wake me. In my dreams I struggled to get to him. Sometimes I sat bolt upright in bed, the longing seizing me like a lightning rod shooting straight through me. I would catch my breath and look beside me at Mark, sleeping away, entirely unaware of the secret thoughts I carried. I would relish standing beside Tom at the party, knowing the scent of his skin from memory, the same scent I had inhaled as I kissed him. More and more I wanted to possess him. More and more stolen moments were not enough, and we both knew it. This ... affair ... was moving faster than both of us were prepared for.

On the day of the party I went over to Ariel's with a recipe for play dough for the kids to make. She had no idea about the party, and I relished the thought of seeing the surprise on her face. Whatever David saw, his wife did not. When I knocked on the door, she always looked grateful to see me standing on her doorstep. She welcomed whatever I had to offer in the way of instruction—bread baking, organization tips, a new recipe. When I left her house, I wished just that was enough: that her approval, her friendship, would distract me from wanting Tom. That somehow I would be cured of the disease of adultery just by basking in her unabashed admiration. As much as I wanted to see Tom, I also found I wanted to spend time with her. She made me feel good about myself. When I was around her, I believed I could actually be what she saw in me. I just had to keep her from knowing the truth about what I was doing, or her friendship would be gone. Ariel was a good person. And good people, I had learned, did not tolerate following your heart.

Before I left that day, I offhandedly said something about her birthday, as though I had given it little thought. I saw a flash of disappointment in her face and had to stifle a smile. Later she would understand why I hadn't come over and made a fuss. Later she and I would giggle about how I had kept her party a secret. Later I would pretend that the party was all about her. And she would believe me. That's what I loved about her.

CHAPTER 19

⌒

Ariel

For my birthday, David took me out for a nice long dinner that didn't involve cutting anyone's meat or scolding anyone for burping at the table. Okay, well, one time I did have to scold David for shaking his knee up and down so hard the table was wiggling. "What are you nervous about?" I asked as I gently laid my hand on his knee. We were sitting side by side.

He shrugged, looking sheepish. "I just want tonight to be special for you. Are you having fun? I mean, it's your birthday after all."

I took a bite of my steak and chewed for a moment with a rapturous look on my face, then smiled at him. "Yes. It's perfect," I said.

"Wow. I hardly ever hear you say something's perfect."

"I admit I want a lot," I said, laying my fork down.

He gripped my hand and leaned his forehead against mine. "It's sometimes hard to keep up with."

"I'm sorry," I whispered. "For the pressure I put on you. For the way things have been between us. I just get so … worried."

"About what, though? What are you so worried about?"

"That if things aren't perfect it'll … fall apart."

He ran his hand through my hair and looked at me. The noise of the restaurant dimmed, and the surroundings faded away as I willed myself to really hear what he would say next. "We have everything I ever wanted. The boys, the house, you." He laughed. "Even Lucky. When I pictured my life, I couldn't even imagine this life—it was too good. It seemed impossible. That's not going to fall apart." He lowered his voice. "This is not your past, Ariel, this is your present. And it will be your future."

"But how do you know?" I asked.

He looked at me intently, a smile playing at the corners of his lips. "I don't know what will happen. But I know that every day I get up and do my job and look forward to coming home to you. And to our boys, our life. A life I chose. A life I would choose over and over again. Please don't think differently of me, always accuse me. I'm not going away. I'm not your dad."

I nodded, blinked away tears at the mention of the real reason I wanted an ironclad life. I had lived the reality of a life that was fragile, easily broken. I had grown up vowing that I would one day have a real family, not the fractured farce I had grown up with.

David excused himself from the table and returned a minute later clutching a square, flat, wrapped package. He placed it on the table in front of me. "I got you this. I hope you like it," he said shyly. I tore into the paper, smiling at him with a question in my eyes as I did. The paper revealed a copy of the book I had lost weeks earlier when the boys took it outside and let the dog chew on it. My beloved childhood book, now out of print, yet restored to me. I held it to me and felt the comfort of being a little girl dressed for bed, dampness still clinging to my hair after my bath, the timbre of my father's voice rising and falling as he read to my sister and me. That was before he left and the stories stopped.

"How did you—"

"The miracle of the Internet. Turns out there's quite a network for out-of-print books. I found the ruined copy in the trash so I had the title and author." He smiled proudly. "Do you like it?"

Still holding it with one arm, I reached out with the other and hugged him. "It's the best gift you've ever given me." I pulled away, my eyes shining with tears. "Really."

"I love who you are." He covered my hands, holding the book with his own. "I love that you are passionate about kids' picture books. I love that you are most likely to be found running crazy, always scurrying around because you've lost your focus. I love that your biggest focus is on me, and the kids." He laughed. "I love that when you get distracted it's most likely because you've found one more thing you can't resist capturing on film. You intrigue me, still. Nothing's going to change that."

"But you said—" I stopped, realizing he never knew I heard him talking to the moving-van guy.

He pursed his lips. "What did I say?"

I shook my head and grinned. "I heard you, talking to the moving-van guy that day. You said you were frustrated with me. I thought—"

He smiled. "I'm going to get frustrated when you forget stuff. That doesn't mean I'm going to stop loving you, or that I'm going to leave. You've got to trust me more. Trust us more."

He was right. "I'm sorry. I kind of freaked out. And between you traveling and Justine's impossible standards and hearing the man cheating on his wife, I've been feeling just crazed lately."

"The man cheating on his wife?" he asked. "What are you talking about?"

I laughed. "We really need to talk more," I said.

"I'm all ears," he said.

As the server cleared our plates away and brought us after-dinner coffees, I told David the story of the man and my night out. It felt good to tell my husband everything, to lean on him and just be heard. It occurred to me that I wanted nothing more than just what I had at that moment.

CHAPTER 20

Ariel

When we pulled into Justine's driveway instead of our own after dinner, I looked at David, confused. He smiled. "She wanted to do something for you … for your birthday. It was her idea." He got out of the car and came around to open my door for me. "Act surprised," he said as we walked to the front door. He held my hand.

Justine opened the door, and I noticed many of the neighbors I had seen at the pool this summer behind her. "Surprise!" she said, her eyes wide and her smile as brilliant as I had ever seen it.

I hugged her, and she didn't shrink away. She looked pleased with herself as she led us into the house, where people I barely knew smiled and told me happy birthday. I tried to ignore the fact that I hardly knew anyone at my own birthday party. I would soon enough, I supposed. My eyes scanned the party for Erica, but she, of course, wasn't there. Down deep I still felt bad for blowing her off at the doctor's office that day. I accepted a glass of wine from Justine and watched as David drifted toward the deck, where many of the men stood. I smelled cigar smoke when the door opened and wrinkled my nose.

Justine grinned at me. "I know how you feel. It's a man thing. Anyway, how was dinner?"

"It was great. So nice to eat a grown-up meal."

She rolled her eyes. "Tell me about it. I'm glad you had a good time."

"Justine," I said. "I can't believe you're doing this with everything … else going on. You didn't have to."

Her eyes scanned the room. She looked back at me. "Oh, don't you go worrying about that." She appeared uncomfortable talking about Mark losing his job, and I understood that. Sometimes you just want to forget your problems. "So did David give you your gift?" she asked. "He said he had something really special planned." She scanned my neck, my wrist, my hand, my ears, then wrinkled her brow.

I tried to brush aside the thought of her and David having a private conversation of any sort. She looked especially beautiful that night. Even my eyes were drawn to her. I pushed aside my insecurities and instead remembered David's face as I opened his surprise gift. "It was a book from my childhood. The boys let the dog chew it up right after we moved in. I … was really upset about it, and he … found me another copy. Even though it's out of print."

Justine's brow stayed wrinkled. "Oh. Well, isn't that … sweet."

I didn't expect her to understand, though I had hoped somehow she would. "It's a sentimental thing for me," I said. Someone tapped me on the shoulder. I turned to find Kristy, wearing a maternity shirt and holding her arms out for a hug. "Kristy!" I squealed, equally as grateful to see a familiar face as I was for that face to be hers.

She folded me into her arms, and I felt the unmistakable bump of her stomach as I hugged her. "Look at you," I said, gesturing at her stomach. I looked around the room. "Is Josh here?"

She nodded and pointed toward the deck. "With the menfolk out there." She pinched her nose. "Gag."

"Yeah, now David's gonna come home smelling like those foul things." I rolled my eyes like it bothered me, though nothing could mess up this perfect night. Not even stinky cigars.

Justine leaned over and extended her hand to Kristy. "I don't believe we've met beyond my quick invitation to this little soiree. I'm Justine Miller."

Kristy shook her hand and smiled, her hand falling onto her belly out of habit. "Kristy Duffey."

"And how do you know Ariel?"

"We were neighbors before she moved here," Kristy said, a wistful expression crossing her face as she did.

"And you're pregnant?" Justine asked, even though it was obvious.

"Yes," Kristy answered, looking down at her stomach as though she was just noticing it. "About four months along."

"This your first?"

Kristy looked embarrassed. "No. Second."

"And your first is a girl? Boy?"

"A little girl. Kailey. She's eight months old." Kristy rolled her eyes, already used to the response of others.

Justine clapped her on the back. "Girl, don't you know what causes that? So they're going to be how many months apart?"

"Just over a year," Kristy said, taking a drink of her water and scanning the deck for a glimpse of Josh, I knew. She looked back at me and smiled.

"Well, better you than me," Justine said, giggling. Couldn't she tell that Kristy was self-conscious? I wanted to steer Kristy away from Justine—even if it meant going out to the deck around the cigar smoke. Instead we were interrupted by Tom Dean, who came up to us and leaned into our circle of three.

"Ladies," he said, smiling at us. He was handsome, and he knew it. I preferred men who were unaware of their looks. "Happy birthday," he said to me and smiled.

"Thank you," I said. I took a sip of the wine Justine had handed me.

"Having a good night?" he asked.

"Very good. Thanks," I said.

He sipped from his bottle of beer and surveyed the crowd. I noticed his wife, Betsy, in a group of women, talking away. I wanted to make my way over and talk to her, get to know her better. I leaned over to Kristy. "Tom and his wife, Betsy, moved in about the same time we did," I said.

"Yep," he said, nodding. "Sure did. Moving here was … quite the coincidence." He looked at Justine.

"Justine told me she knew you a long time ago," I said.

"Well now, it wasn't that long," he said with a laugh. He put his arm around Justine briefly, and I swore she moved in closer to him for a fraction of a second before they both pulled away like two magnets with the same pull. I think my eyebrows might have risen slightly. I took another sip of my wine. "Justine and I knew each other at summer camp when we were both counselors."

She jabbed him with her elbow. "But I was a junior counselor and you were a senior counselor."

"Are you trying to rub it in that I'm older?" he asked. I glanced around to see if Mark was anywhere nearby, if Betsy noticed who her husband was talking to.

"Well, if the shoe fits …," she said and grinned, showing him all her beautiful white teeth. They held each other's glance just a little too long, I thought. Kristy shot me a look. I would explain to her later that it was just harmless flirting, the result of Justine's efforts at being a good hostess and maybe a bit too much wine. Kristy didn't know Justine like I did. She hadn't seen her in front of the women at the mothers' group, didn't know that her house wasn't this clean just for the party. Later I would tell Kristy what a role model Justine was, that everyone needs to cut loose every so often, feel appreciated, admired.

"Has Justine told you that we dated back then?" Tom asked. My eyes widened, and I looked from him to Justine.

Shock crossed her face, but she quickly smiled to cover it and placed her hand on Tom's shoulder. "It's true," she said. I watched Kristy eye Justine's hand, resting there proprietarily.

"Oh, how cute!" I wanted to be agreeable amid my discomfort. Was anyone else weirded out? "For how long?" I asked.

Tom smiled at Justine and then looked at me. "Well, we had a few summers together when we were in college."

Justine nodded. "I was eighteen, and he was twenty."

Tom picked up the story again. "We would go our separate ways after each summer, but we stayed in touch. Back then it was through letters." He turned back to Justine. "I wonder whatever happened to all those letters?" he asked.

She shrugged. "Goodness, who knows?"

"Wouldn't they be fun to read now?" Tom asked her. They looked at each other for another fraction of a second too long.

Justine waved her hand, dismissing the idea. "Those old things are long gone by now," she said. She looked at me. "We were just a couple of crazy kids then." As if that explained everything.

I looked back at Justine, whose eyes were darting around the room. She spoke again. "Kristy, didn't you say you had a baby girl?"

Kristy blinked back at her, not able to make the awkward segue as fast as Justine had. "Umm, yes?"

"Well, I have a bunch of adorable little dresses my girls have outgrown that I've been meaning to give to someone. Would you like to come and look at them? I mean, while you're here?"

Kristy looked from Justine to me and back again. "Umm, sure?" she said.

"Now, Tom, stop boring poor Ariel with that old story," she said as she walked off with Kristy trailing behind her. Kristy looked back over her shoulder at me as she left. *Your new neighbors are kind of strange,* her look said.

Tom took a sip of his beer, and I watched as his eyes followed Justine up the stairs and then scanned the room, resting on his wife. He raised his beer to her, and she nodded, then looked back at the woman she was talking to.

"Your wife seems very nice," I said. I wanted to run outside on the deck with David and the stinky cigar smoke. "I'd like to get to know her."

"Betsy's a sweetheart. You won't meet anyone nicer," he said. He laughed. "She was the one who broke me and Justine up actually," he said.

"Really?" I asked. The admission shocked me. I couldn't imagine Tom passing up beautiful, confident, striking Justine for demure, sweet Betsy.

"Yeah, Betsy and I were together all through high school and college. We had planned to get married from the beginning. Our families were friends. You know how it goes. I still remember wondering if I was making the right call. It was so hard to know," he said. He looked again in the direction of where Justine had gone with Kristy. "It's just so hard to know."

I nodded, trying to discern if he meant then, or now.

CHAPTER 21

⌣

Justine

"You shouldn't have said so much to Ariel," I said when Tom and I were pretending to politely chat at the party. "She's going to suspect something. I haven't told her about our … past." To every oblivious person around us, we were just two neighbors making friendly conversation at a party. I wondered how they couldn't feel the electrical charge in the air. How could they not feel the heat coming off us in waves?

And yet, all around me, people were moving through life as if Tom and I didn't matter. It was amazing. Betsy was talking to Michelle, Susie, and Liza, charming them with her cuteness, no doubt. Mark was on the deck smoking cigars, most likely thinking that the worst thing that could happen to him was me insisting he shower before bed tonight. Ariel was talking to that annoying girl from her old neighborhood. When they glanced over at me, I smiled and waved. They waved back.

"You worry too much," Tom said.

Mark often told me the same thing. I thought of the lines between my eyes formed by worry, evidence of this bad habit. At church the pastor said not to worry, to let God take care of everything. Somehow I didn't think God wanted to take care of this for me. And yet, hadn't He brought us together? Didn't we deserve this chance?

"It's maddening to be this close to you and not be able to touch you," he said quietly.

I nodded, sipped my wine, and looked down into my glass, away from his probing eyes.

"Can I see you this week?" he asked. "Can you get away?"

I could always get away. That wasn't the problem. *Staying* away with him was becoming more and more what I thought about. "You look really nice tonight," I told him. He was wearing a golf shirt that brought out the blue in his eyes.

He smiled with half of his mouth. "You're not answering my question."

"I will meet you somewhere this week. Yes. The usual spot?" We had met in that dark, empty street a few times since our first rendezvous. I remembered the feeling of that first kiss we shared in his car and the many since then. As the memory settled, I looked up and saw Betsy glance over at us. I waved at her, but she turned her attention back to the women she was talking to.

"Sure. I'll meet you anywhere, anytime," he said slyly.

"Fine. But we can't keep doing this."

"You mean you want to break things off?" he asked. Concern crossed his face.

"I didn't say that," I said. Around me the party was in full swing. I could see the periphery of movement as people talked and gestured, hear the clinks of glasses, the buzz of conversations taking place all around me, the sound of laughter erupting every few minutes. And yet it all receded as I looked directly at him, allowing myself to dive fully into his presence for the first time that evening. I couldn't afford but a few seconds or I would give myself away. "I mean we've got to figure out a way to move … forward."

He took a sip of his drink, swallowed, glanced around as if someone might be eavesdropping. "I've been having the same thoughts," he said. "I'd like it if we could be together for an entire night. Do you think that might ever be possible?" He smiled at me and dropped his glance just as quickly. Neither of us said anything.

He looked up at me as though he was about to say more, but just then Betsy came up and put her arm around me, telling me what a great party it was. I found myself inviting her to do something together the next day. Whether I was trying to deflect any suspicion or make myself feel less guilty, I didn't know. Tom and I didn't get a chance to be alone again for the rest of the night. It was probably for the best. The conversation had headed into a dangerous direction I didn't know if I was ready for. And yet, it seemed headed there no matter what kind of detours we attempted.

CHAPTER 22

———

Ariel

That morning I sent David off to work with a smile, not minding the suitcase that was swinging from his hand as he walked away from us. He kissed me so long before he left that the boys made gagging noises and collapsed into a pile of giggles when David dipped me dramatically. "You boys be good for your mom," he said, rubbing his hand over their heads on his way out the door.

He paused at the door. "I'll hurry home," he said and raised his eyebrows at me.

"I hope you will," I said, and he was gone. My eyes filled with tears as he backed out of the garage. I realized this was the first time he had left that I had thought about missing him instead of just being angry that he was gone. Later I would send him a text telling him how much I appreciated him working hard for us.

I took out the ingredients to make chocolate-chip banana muffins—a recipe so basic a monkey could make it. The boys gathered around to watch, begging to lick the bowl and the beaters, fighting over whose turn it was to stir. I was making the muffins for Justine. I envisioned handing them to her, tucked into a basket with a decorative cloth covering them, giggling with her over the therapeutic benefits of chocolate as she took the first bite with a rapturous look on her face. I imagined her hand on my arm, the earnestness in her eyes as she thanked me for being there for her. She would tell me their plans for Mark to get another job; I would talk to her about how to be a support to him. We would strengthen each other, and in the end, our marriages—our lives—would be better. Someday we would talk about "that time" and we would say things like "We are all the better for it." I closed the door to the oven and called out to my sons, who had lost interest in the muffins.

"Boys, why don't you get dressed for the pool, and we'll go see if Cameron and Caroline would like to come with us. I think their mommy would like a break," I said. I was on my way to becoming friend of the year. The boys whooped with delight. They would've lived at the pool if I let them.

An hour later I had warm muffins and barely contained boys making a procession across our yards. They wore matching swim trunks and no shirts, looking the epitome of little boys on summer days. It occurred to me that I hadn't snapped a photo in weeks. I had phone messages to return from clients anxious to schedule their fall appointments, but I hadn't carved out a moment to call them back. Justine had been true to her word to send me more business than I could handle.

When I knocked, Mark came to the door, looking disheveled and confused. His eyes fell to the basket of muffins in my hand and traveled back up.

"Is Justine here?" I asked. I held up the basket. "I brought muf-fins," I said, master of the obvious. "They're still warm," I added hopefully, as though I must say the magic word to get him to open the door the rest of the way and let us in to find Justine.

"She's not here," he said. "She's meeting someone for lunch," he said. He shook his head. "Her parents came and got the girls yesterday so it's just me here. I have no idea when she'll be back." A cloud crossed his face, dark like a storm gathering.

"Oh," I managed. Like a jealous suitor, I wanted to ask him who she was with but refrained. Who else was she confiding in? I handed him the basket of muffins. "Well, then, you should enjoy these."

He looked at me. "I couldn't," he said, his hand frozen in midair. I knew he wanted to take them, so I forced them into his hand.

"It's the least I can do." A look passed between us. He understood that I wanted to say more but lacked the right words. The muffins would have to do. He nodded.

"I'm glad Justine has you," he said. "I was worried about her, after Laura moved away. Worried how she'd cope. You two seem to have become good friends. I like that you guys go out as much as you do and that she can talk to you as much as she does. It gets her mind off things."

Go out? Talk a lot? I stood blinking back at him. "Oh, well, okay. Yes. It's good," I stammered. "The party last night was really great, by the way."

"Yeah, sure. No problem. Thanks for these." He held up the muffins and scratched his stubbly cheek with his free hand. "I'll tell her you came by."

"That would be nice," I said, backing away from the door so he could shut it gently and go back to where he came from.

What did Mark mean "go out"? Justine and I never went out. And she rarely confided in me. Maybe he was confusing me with another of her many friends. Or maybe he just meant that we saw each other often thanks to proximity. Either way, I couldn't fault him for his confusion. He was under a lot of stress.

———

I was debating leaving the pool that afternoon when Justine arrived with Betsy, Tom's wife. They were laughing like old friends, and I hated the jealousy I felt as I watched from across the pool. I never imagined her being friends with Tom's—her former boyfriend's—wife. It struck me as odd, and I wondered why Betsy would go along with it. Probably for the same reason I wanted to be friends with her. She was pretty and poised and influential and smart. Who wouldn't want to be in her company? I watched Betsy look at her and knew she was as taken in by her as I was. Perhaps this is who Mark meant when he said he was glad we went out often. Maybe Justine and Betsy were chummier than I knew. How very *progressive* of them.

Eventually she separated from Betsy and plopped down beside me, smiling. "Did you have fun last night?" she asked. "I did."

"I came by your house earlier," I said. "I brought muffins." I sounded put out, even though I didn't mean to.

"Muffins?" she said. "What kind?"

"Chocolate-chip banana," I said. "Warm."

"Mmm," she said, her face dreamy as she closed her eyes and rocked back and forth. "Warm chocolate-chip banana are the best." She opened her eyes. "Wish I'd been there," she said.

"It was the least I could do. To thank you. And to come alongside you," I added hesitantly.

"Come alongside me?" she asked, her eyes wide. "About what?"

I narrowed my eyes at her. "About Mark's job ..."

She waved her hand in the air as though she were swatting a fly. "Oh, honey, that's no tragedy. We'll be just fine." She smiled at me pitifully, as though I were a dramatic child instead of the woman who found her sobbing in her closet. She pointed over at Betsy. "Tom's even going to help me find a job if Mark can't find one first. Isn't that great?"

"You—you're going to—work? But I thought you said he was going to find another job."

"Well, I mean, the market's tough out there. I think it would be foolish of me to not try to do my part, don't you?"

All I could think of was the hole that her working would cut into my life. What about our morning walks? Carpool plans? What about freezer cooking? What about our friendship? I felt panic rise up in my throat like bile. I didn't know if I was disgusted with her for thinking of working or with myself for being so selfish that I could even make her husband's job loss about me.

She waved her hand again. "Well, this is all getting ahead of ourselves, now isn't it? We have no idea what's going to happen, so let's just not worry about it before we have to." She smiled again, though something behind her eyes looked different, uncertain. "What I really need is to get away. What would you think about that? Do you think you could do a girls' getaway weekend?"

"Umm, sure. Yeah, that'd be great. But I mean, umm …when?" Like it mattered. Of course I would go. I would do whatever I could to go on a girls' weekend with just Justine and me.

"This weekend. Let's be spontaneous! Of course, if you can't go, I could ask someone else…."

"No, I can go. Let me work it out with David."

"Great. My parents have a place down at Myrtle Beach, and we could drive down there. What do you say?"

I nodded even as my brain was still scrolling through my to-do list, checking my mental calendar. Where was my life-management notebook when I needed it? "I'd love to go," I said, matching my smile with hers, tooth for tooth.

"Fabulous!" she said. She gave me a high five like we were kids. "This is going to be fabulous. All we'll need is our bathing suits and some clothes to wear out to dinner." She hopped up to go back to Betsy. I prayed she wouldn't invite her, too, hating my territorial side. "I think I want to go dancing," she said, doing a little dance move right there and smiling at me before she walked away, leaving me to try to picture our middle-aged selves dancing at some club in Myrtle Beach far away from our husbands, kids, and middle-aged lives. I was sure she was just kidding. I fished around in my beach bag for my cell phone. I had arrangements to make.

CHAPTER 23

⁓

Justine

What kind of person spends the day with a man's wife, all while planning to meet that woman's husband alone at the beach that same weekend? Tom had asked me to figure out a way we could spend the night alone, and I had, the idea popping into my brain even as Ariel and I were talking at the pool. My plan was brilliant, and no one would suspect a thing. I just tried not to think about Betsy as I stood in front of the display of bras at the lingerie store. There were pink and red and black and white and beige ones. There were leopard print and heart print and zebra print and stripes and polka dots. There were lacy ones and plain ones and racerback and strapless.

I fingered the silk, wondering whether buying sexy underwear would automatically make me guiltier. That just the act of picking out a lacy black bra with lacy black underwear to match (when all I currently owned were dingy white granny panties, most of them with holes) would make the next step irreversible. Plucking it from the rack and paying for it was adultery by proxy. As I strode toward the checkout registers, I thought of Tom's eyes on me in the set I had in my hand, the appreciative smile that would spread across his face.

Betsy's face kept playing in my mind as I waited for my turn to be rung up. She had been so kind, so complimentary. "I was a bit skeptical at first," she had confessed to me by the pool. "I was a bit worried there might still be something … between you and Tom." She had giggled. "I guess there's a bit of high school left in all of us."

I hadn't flinched. "Well, we all grow up, don't we?" And I had grown up enough to even forgive her for taking my part. Of course, I had taken her husband as the consolation prize. That made it easier.

I wanted to hold it against her that she was so trusting, blame her for not looking both ways before crossing the road. Because the car was coming that would knock her into the air, crush her in its treads. I could see it coming. Why couldn't she? A part of me wanted to tell her to be more careful, to fight harder, not to welcome me with such open arms. I waffled between pitying her and despising her for not being stronger. She trusted God, Tom told me. I told him I used to.

When Betsy mentioned Erica as we floated on our rafts, I said nothing derogatory. I listened as Betsy went on about how much she liked her, how nice she was. If things went the way they seemed to be heading, Betsy would need a friend who understood what it was like to lose a husband to another woman. Erica certainly understood that.

Walking to my car with my secret purchase swinging from my arm, I didn't think so much about what I was doing—or was about to do. I thought instead of Erica and how she had already run the gauntlet, already shaken herself free from the bonds of marriage. Oddly enough I longed to be in her shoes.

———

My parents were keeping the girls for a few hours so Ariel and I could get on the road and not wait for Mark to get home. He was "job hunting," which was code for sitting in a coffee shop and staring at his laptop mournfully. I knew he wasn't really doing anything, just waiting for me to announce I'd found the job that was going to save our family, even though we hadn't spoken of it again since the day he lost his job. My blood coursed through my veins, hot and pulsing, at the thought of it. I could feel it throbbing in my temples as I stowed my last items in the bag I was packing. Caroline draped herself across my bed, looking like her dog had died. "I wish you weren't going, Mommy," she said into her arm.

"Sometimes mommies need a break. You'll understand that someday when you're a mommy." She didn't look up. "I'll bring you a prize?" I tried.

She raised her eyebrows, and I could see the hint of a smile from where her mouth was hidden in her arm. "What will you bring me?" she asked.

"What would you like?" I asked, zipping up the bag and backing out of the room, like one would move away from a dangerous animal: slowly, with caution.

She slid off the bed and followed me. "Umm, I don't know."

"Tell you what, you think of it, and Daddy can tell me."

She hopped down the steps, already reeling off the things she thought I should bring her. I lugged the heavy duffel down behind her, not listening. "Caroline, honey, hop on down. Quit stopping," I said when I nearly ran into her.

I heard Cameron calling out, "G-ma's here. G-ma and G-per are here. And they brought the car." She and Caroline went scrambling for the driveway while I carried the duffel out to my car. I thought about the things I had put into the bag that I would never want Mark to see, the texts on my phone that I needed to erase. I loved organizing my home but was finding organizing an illicit relationship mentally exhausting. I opened the garage door and plastered a smile on my face so my mother wouldn't suspect anything.

The whole group was standing by the restored 1930 Model A Coupe that had become my stepdad's retirement project. The sun bounced off the hood, which he had lovingly painted a dark green color. My stepdad rocked back on his heels, his face radiating pride. My mother rode around with him as though she liked all the attention the car garnered, but I don't think she did. I think you just do things to keep your husband happy, things you'd never suspect were going to be part of the vows when you stood there in a white dress. I thought the two of them looked pretty silly puttering around town well below the speed limit, but I knew better than to say so.

The girls had climbed in, and Cameron was pretending to drive. Caroline was in the rumble seat waving at no one. My mother squeezed my shoulder. "All set?" she asked. She had a sad expression in her eyes, even as she smiled at me. She was worried about Mark losing his job. It took us both back to darker times in our family's history. Times we didn't mention once my stepdad came into our lives and rescued us.

"It's fine, Mom," I said to her. "Thanks for coming to get the girls. Again."

She squeezed my shoulder again. "You just need to get away, get your mind off things. Now, who is this person you're taking with you to the place?"

My parents always called their condo at the beach "the place." Not "the beach place," not "the condo," always "the place." They rarely went there, and my mom admitted to me she didn't really even care for the beach. "All that sand," she had said disdainfully, sticking her tongue out. "I wanted to get a place in the mountains, sit on a porch overlooking the mountain range, sipping coffee and going for walks." She had shrugged. "Oh well, this is nice. And the girls enjoy it."

"Ariel, the girl who moved in behind me, is going. The one who bought Laura's house?"

"Well, that's an interesting choice," my mother mused. "You hardly know her."

I didn't tell her that was precisely why I had asked her. "Well," I said, "it's a good chance for me to get to know her."

My mother shrugged her shoulders. "I guess." She paused. "I just hope you're not trying to replace Laura with her. You might be disappointed if you do."

I wanted to laugh. If my mom was trying to protect me from disappointment, we were long past that. "It's fine, Mom," I said again. I turned to my stepdad to change the subject. "The car's looking good," I said.

He chuckled. "These girls sure do love it," he said, pointing at Cameron and Caroline, who had switched places. "I said I'd take 'em on a ride. They're saying they want me to drive it in the neighborhood parade for the Fourth."

I ignored the pang that came with him mentioning the Fourth of July. Ordinarily I'd be in rehearsals by now, practices dominating our lives as the date moved closer. "They'd love that," I responded mechanically and put my arm around him. He'd been married once before my mother but lost his wife to cancer before they could have children. We became his family, and he never seemed to want more.

"You know I got that car from a guy who had it in his family for thirty-five years. It just sat in an old shed, all but forgotten. He couldn't believe I wanted it, wanted to pay him for it." He smiled at me. "And I couldn't believe he'd let me have it for such a steal."

I nodded. I'd heard this story at least three times. Then he went on to add something he'd never said before. "That's what any good collector does. He finds someone who doesn't know what they have and talks them out of it before they can realize it. If someone doesn't see the value in something, you can take it from them much easier." He looked at me meaningfully. The smile on my face didn't falter as I nodded and tried to keep his words from penetrating my heart.

"Well, I better get going, Dad," I said. "Ariel's waiting on me." I waved the girls over to hug them good-bye. They all stood in the grass as I got into my car and backed out of the driveway. My earlier purchases and my stepdad's words tangled together in my mind like clothes in the washing machine. I waved to the girls as I drove away, leaving them to watch my car disappear as I cranked up the radio and let the music drive my guilt far away.

CHAPTER 24

⌣

Ariel

"Okay, so I put chicken in the Crock-Pot and all you have to do is stick these baked potatoes in the oven for dinner about five," I proudly instructed Heather. I was successfully putting into practice several strategies I had learned from Justine. The girl nodded, an intense look on her face as though she was memorizing my every word.

"I left a list of instructions here for David so if you'd just make sure he sees it. He should be home about six. But that's if his flight is on time and if nothing comes up last minute." I looked around the house, suddenly convinced I had forgotten something despite my best efforts at organization. Guilt laced my thoughts as I wondered what kind of mother leaves three small children with a sitter so she can go have fun. Are mothers even allowed such luxuries?

"It's fine, Mrs. Baxter," Heather said, reading my mind. "Go have fun." She looked over at Justine, who stood in the doorway twirling her keys like an anxious teen ready to drive for the first time.

Justine smiled at her and then looked at me. "She's right," she said with a sympathetic smile. "They'll be just fine without you."

I thought about David's words to me that morning. "We won't even know you're gone," he had teased. When I was home, I wanted to be less needed, but as I stood readying myself to leave for two days, I wanted to be irreplaceable. Go figure.

"Wait!" I said, digging my camera out of my bag. "Let's get a picture together before we go!" I looked at Heather. "Will you take it?"

She nodded and followed us out to the car while we posed with our thumbs up, mugging for the camera. When we were done, I tucked the camera back into my bag and turned to the boys. "Okay, hugs good-bye!" I pressed each one of them to me, memorizing their dirty little boy smells. I looked into their eyes and said that I loved them, that I would be home soon. They nodded politely, looking bored and maybe a tiny bit sad. Really they just wanted me to go so that Heather would play games with them.

I sat down beside Justine in the car, and she rolled down the windows, letting the thick, humid Southern summer air wash over us as we backed out of the driveway and pointed the car toward the entrance to the neighborhood. It felt decadent to be using Mark's sporty sedan instead of our requisite minivans, and I rested my elbow on the windowsill and let the rush of air take my breath away. We passed by her house on the way out, and I noticed Mark and the girls in the front yard. I started to wave at them, but Justine didn't even look over. I quickly lowered my hand and kept my face forward as she did, focusing on the adventure ahead and not on what we were leaving behind. It seemed I needed to be taught how to leave.

Justine had our day all planned out from the moment we arrived until the moment darkness fell. As I slumped on the bed, pleasantly exhausted from a kid-free day of sunbathing and a visit to the spa on her parents' condo property, I smiled to myself. I scrolled back through the photos I'd taken during the day. Justine relaxing on a raft in the pool. Me getting my toes done at the spa. Both of us posing beside the sign that read "Massages Included!" I smiled and stretched luxuriously as I rolled over to watch Justine. She was out on the condo balcony, talking on her cell phone again. She had fielded phone calls all day from Mark and the girls. I tried not to rub it in, proud that Heather and the boys were apparently doing fine. I hadn't received a single call. As she slipped back into the room, tucking her phone into her beach cover-up pocket, I smiled at her. "Everything okay?" I asked.

She nodded, biting back the smile that played on her lips.

"Is Mark missing you already?" I teased.

"Are you having fun?" she asked.

I gave an exaggerated *ahhh*. "I could get used to this," I said.

"I'm glad to hear it." She looked around. "I could get used to this too. It's always nice to get away. I don't do it enough, ya know?"

"Yeah, if I had this place at my disposal, I'd be here every weekend," I said. I turned to watch the ocean waves crashing in on each other. A family on the beach was packing up to go in. The mom chased a little girl, picking her up and carrying her once she caught her, while the girl thrashed. She was a chubby toddler in a pink bathing suit with a spiky ponytail on top of her head. My heart lurched. Even when I wasn't on mom duty, I could muster up a serious case of ponytail envy.

Justine and I had spent the afternoon at the condo pool—a fancy affair with a long, lazy river. I had mentioned taking a walk later, before dinner, but she had never answered me. "Think you'd like to walk before dinner?" I repeated, hoping she would want to squeeze in a walk. I loved the beach in the evenings when it wasn't so hot, the sun wasn't so brutal, and the sand wasn't so crowded with people. I'd love to get some shots of us out on the beach in the soft evening light.

"Maybe after?" she said, slipping out of her cover-up and grabbing towels for the shower. "Let's get ready and go get an early dinner. I thought tonight we'd just watch movies here in the room? We can save our big going-out night for tomorrow."

That sounded lovely. Every minute of this weekend had already been exquisitely lazy. I sighed deeply and lay on my back, propping my head on my arms. "I could stay right here for the rest of the night," I said. "Just bring me some food and I don't need to move. If there's a good chick flick on, all the better."

She giggled. "That's why I brought you, Ariel," she said. "You're so easy to please." I heard the shower door shut and closed my eyes. I thought of her saying I was easy to please and knew David would beg to differ. Funny how I was different with different people, I mused as the noise of the water lulled me to sleep.

When I woke up, Justine was fully dressed and standing on the balcony again, the wind from the shore whipping her hair around as she spoke into the phone, an angry expression on her face. With the door closed, I couldn't hear what she was saying, but I knew it wasn't good. I wondered what had happened—and whether I should ask. I watched as she lowered the phone and stood for a few minutes, staring out at the ocean. Then she dialed a number and started talking again. Mark followed by her mother? I wasn't sure, but I wondered why she didn't just come and talk to me. I would've understood. Feeling like a voyeur, I turned away and slipped into the bathroom to shower before she caught me watching. She would tell me when she felt ready. This weekend was about growing closer and forging a new kind of friendship. And it was only just beginning.

⌒

Justine was gone when I woke the next morning. I looked around the room, remembering that I was there without the boys or David, far away from family responsibility. I grinned and kicked my feet like a little girl waking on Christmas morning. The hours ahead of us stretched out long and blissful. I sat up and decided to make coffee to get myself going, ready for whatever adventure the day would bring.

I was nearing the end of my second cup when Justine bounced into the room, glistening with sweat and smiling broadly. "This place has a great gym," she said as she reached into the refrigerator and grabbed a bottled water. She took a long pull from it. "I didn't dare wake you though. You looked like you were enjoying your sleep."

I smiled and drained the last of my coffee. "Yeah. Sleep is a precious commodity. I can exercise another time."

"Hmm. Not me." She bent at the waist and touched her toes as silence filled the kitchen. I looked out the window at the beach. I had never been to the beach before and not gone out on it.

"Think we can go to the beach today?" I asked, sounding like one of her children instead of an adult with an equal vote. Why, I wondered, was I letting her call all the shots?

She made a face. "I know this sounds weird, but I just don't care for the beach all that much. All that sand everywhere."

I suppressed the urge to say, "The sand's the point." I shrugged instead and pulled my knees up to my chin, wrapping my arms around my calves. "So then what would you like to do?"

"Shopping?" she asked. "Lunch somewhere we'd never take the kids?"

I thought about it for a moment. Unwilling to let her entirely plan our day, I countered, "How about we shop and have lunch, then come back here and lie by the pool for a bit, get some sun?"

"Sounds great. Then we'll get all prettied up for our big night out!"

"Do you have something planned?"

"We're going dancing!"

I rolled my eyes and looked out the window. I had thought she was kidding that day at the pool. "Eh, you might need to go without me. I am not into grinding with a bunch of young kids. We're sort of past that stage of life, aren't we?"

Her tone was cutting. "Speak for yourself." I looked over at her, shocked. She grinned like she was just joking around, but there was that—something—behind her eyes that made me think she was very serious. My friend wanted to go dancing for some reason, something apart from me and my mature outlook, apart from rationale. This weekend was about more than just a new friendship; it was about doing something different from the norm. Justine didn't want to be the queen of the neighborhood this weekend. She wanted to be anonymous, out of character. Some part of me understood that.

"Fine, you win," I said with a laugh that sounded more playful than I felt. I was irritated. "If you want to go dancing, then we'll go dancing."

"Salsa," she added.

Oh brother. "You want to eat Mexican?" I teased, masking my consternation. It wasn't that I was afraid of salsa dancing, it was just that it was the opposite of my idea of relaxation.

"No, silly. Salsa dancing. It'll be fun!" She did a little pivot right there, moving her arms back and forth. She looked over at me. "We'll need clothes for salsa dancing. Hence the shopping trip." She seemed to be suddenly catching my antisalsa vibes. "Come on, Ariel, live a little. Cut loose. You're far away from everything and everyone you know. You can be anyone you want just for tonight. Doesn't that excite you?" She smiled the most genuine smile I had ever seen on her face. For just a moment I saw the real Justine—not just the one she wanted me to know. This Justine was passionate and vivacious, uninhibited. This Justine was, frankly, a little scary.

"Sure," I lied, to be agreeable, to make her like me. "That sounds just perfect."

CHAPTER 25

Justine

Ariel picked pieces of lettuce out of her salad, making a little pile on the side of the bowl. I pointed. "Don't you like lettuce?"

She chewed, swallowed. "Not the stalks." Her eyes scanned the restaurant, and she leaned back against her chair. "This is so nice. I never get to have lunch with another grown-up." She pointed to her salad. "And this salad is delicious. Is something wrong with yours? You've barely touched it."

I thought ahead to what I had planned for that night, thought of the dress I'd just bought: short, black, sexy. Knowing Tom was probably arriving at Myrtle Beach at that very moment made my stomach lurch. I couldn't do much more than pick at my lunch. "No, it's fine. I'm just not very hungry," I said.

She pointed at my plate. "Then can I have your pita bread?" she asked, as if she was one of my daughters. The way she asked me for things, the way she hung on my words, the way I knew I was very important in her eyes. I liked it, but I also hated it. I wanted her to see the real me and still want to be with me. I doubted there was much chance of that happening. Like everyone, Ariel saw a product I had developed, packaged, and sold. Maybe Mark was right: I should go into sales.

I passed her the bread and glanced around the restaurant, thinking of how fortunate I was to be eating out, to be able to use such a beautiful condo whenever I wanted. If you didn't know me better, you'd think I was wealthy. I guess I was, but it hadn't always been that way, and sometimes the poor girl inside me woke up, looked around, and said, "How did we get here?"

"I was poor growing up," I said, surprising myself with my outburst. But for some reason I felt I owed her something in return for providing my alibi, for trying to be my friend. "I don't know why I said that!" I covered my mouth in embarrassment.

"That's what girlfriend getaways are all about," she said, a genuine smile crossing her face. "Getting to know each other better." But I wasn't into all this disclosure. "You can talk to me about anything, Justine."

Little did she know that I, in fact, could definitely *not* talk to her. Especially not about why we were really in Myrtle Beach. But there was no harm in telling her my background, to appease her. "My mom had no way of earning money," I found myself continuing. "We were so poor I went hungry a lot. I had three outfits to my name. We had to get government help, and even then it was hand to mouth. I remembered being scared all the time we were going to lose our house, which wasn't much to begin with. Eventually we did. I was pretty insecure and a fashion nightmare back then. We ended up moving in with my aunt, who hated us being there. She always put my mom down for marrying my dad, for his leaving, as if it was my mom's fault."

In my mind's eye I could see my aunt Susan, single and homely, yet prideful that she had the one thing we couldn't seem to ever get and keep: money. My mom was the pretty sister, but my aunt Susan was quick to point out that beauty didn't get you very far. She always looked at me when she said that, as if my mother's beauty was a curse I had inherited instead of a blessing. She had nothing to worry about. Boys didn't look at me with my thrift-store clothing, bad teeth, and acne.

"But now?" Ariel asked, her open expression making me want to tell her more. "I mean, your mom's married, and your dad—or the guy I thought was your dad—is a dentist, right?"

"Yeah. She married him when I was fourteen. I was in middle school." Before she could think I was some kind of pity case, I added, "I wasn't picked on because we were poor or anything like that. I was just … kind of invisible. Eventually, after my mom married my step-dad, who had money, I was able to focus more on my appearance." I gave her my most confident look even though thinking of this story was making me more uncomfortable than I expected. "Soon enough all the boys were asking me out. It was nice. I was visible." I looked down at the table, pushed my salad around with my fork. I couldn't meet her sympathetic gaze. "I pretty much vowed that I'd never be invisible again." I squared my shoulders, smiled, and took a bite of a tomato.

Ariel picked up her fork. Her warmth almost irritated me. "Well, it worked. You're the least invisible person I've ever met." I laughed along with her. A moment later she took a bite of salad and followed it with a bite of my pita.

I forced myself to eat another small bite and chewed methodically, thinking of the only person who had ever really seen me. My cell phone in my pocket vibrated as if on cue. It was a text. He had arrived.

CHAPTER 26

⁓

Ariel

I tugged at the hem of my dress, trying to get it to cover more of my thighs. "I'm not sure this dress was a good idea," I said to Justine, who had set up camp in our bathroom and was fussing over herself like a beauty-pageant contestant. I studied myself in the full-length mirror, arching my eyebrows with a surprised look, pouting, making kissing noises, faking laughing. Glancing over my shoulder to make sure Justine wasn't watching, I attempted a dance move. I wondered if I looked beautiful or … ridiculous, a middle-aged woman trying too hard. Justine had talked me into a red minidress I would never have bought without her salesman-ship. I justified the purchase because (a) it was on sale and (b) I planned to wear it out to dinner with David for our anniversary in another month. If I had the guts, that is. The more I wore the dress, the more I realized that it wouldn't exactly fit in a suburban scene.

Justine came out of the bathroom looking stunning in a black minidress that showed off her tan and her legs. "Ooh la la!" I said with a soft whistle. "The exercise is really paying off," I added, pointing at her legs. I aimed my camera in her direction and took a few shots of her before she could pose.

She grimaced at me and waved the camera away. "You really think so?"

"Yup. You look gorgeous."

She looked over at me and gave a nod of approval. "You look gorgeous too."

I groaned and pulled at the hem of my dress again. "I feel ridiculous." At least I was tanner than I had been at the summer-kickoff party. There was that.

She walked over and stood beside me in the mirror. We took in our reflections. "We are two hot chicks," she said and bumped me with her hip, grinning. I wondered what she was like as a teenager, if we would have been friends then. "You are beautiful, Ariel. Don't let anyone tell you any different. Just because you're a mom doesn't mean you can't be stunning."

"I know, but—"

She put her hand up. "No buts." She giggled. "Speaking of butts, does mine look big?" She turned around and craned her head to see her behind in the mirror.

"Trust me," I told her and patted her arm. "Your butt looks fantastic. Mark would be all over you."

She snickered. "I don't know about that. Now … let's go salsa!"

The noise of the club was vibrating in my head after two hours of exposure to bass so hammering I felt like my teeth were coming loose from their sockets. I watched as Justine danced with yet another man. She had moved from man to man all night, bumping and grinding like a seasoned salsa-dancing pro. The short lesson at the beginning of the night had been all she needed to get started—the rest she seemed to improvise in the heat of the moment. Of course, the lesson did nothing to make me any smoother than a robot, so after a short while of pretending to enjoy myself on the dance floor, I finally resigned myself to being lame and stepped off to the side. I wished I hadn't left my camera back at the condo. At least I would've been entertained by taking pictures. Somehow, though, I had the feeling that Justine didn't want this night recorded.

The longer the night went on, the more impatient I became. This was *not*, as I had suspected, my idea of a happy getaway. Once again, I found myself questioning my devotion to Justine. I cared for her, but the constant reminders of how different we were had started to wear. I pulled my cell phone from my purse and texted David. "Salsa dancing with Justine," I typed in. "Supposed to be fun. But I just want to go home."

I looked up to see Justine searching the perimeter. When she caught my eyes, a broad, happy smile crossed her face. In that moment I realized it: I was her home base. Her safety net. She needed me. With pride, I smiled back and gave a playful little hip shake. So what if she wanted to escape for an evening. It was only dancing. It was harmless.

My phone vibrated. David had written back. "Wish I was there to do a little dirty dancing with you."

My skin became prickly. "Me, too," I typed, smiling broadly. I tucked the phone back into my purse.

I returned my gaze to the dance floor when a man—handsome, young—approached me. "You have a beautiful smile," he said.

"Thank you," I replied, looking away. No sense in encouraging him.

"Wanna dance?" He pointed to the dance floor.

"No, thanks," I said. I didn't want to shoot him down. I pointed down at my feet, hoping he noticed the diamond on my left hand as I did. "My feet are killing me." It wasn't a lie. The strappy high-heeled sandals that Justine had talked me into that afternoon on our shopping spree looked much better than they felt. I looked at the door. I yawned and covered my mouth. I was every bit the middle-aged mom I was pretending not to be.

He smiled at me. "I'm with you. I'm not really into these places," he said, probably in response to my yawn. He gestured at the dance floor. "I was dragged here by some friends." I noticed he did not wear a ring. "Can I at least buy you a drink?" he asked.

I intended to turn him down, so I was surprised when the word "Sure" came out of my mouth. This was a night for doing things out of character, right? He walked me over to the bar, putting his hand on the small of my back as he did. I held my breath, partly mortified that another man's hand was on my back, partly relishing the attention, if only for a moment. I moved slightly out of his reach and waited as he ordered me a glass of wine. I had had one earlier in the evening but could justify one more.

I looked around for Justine but couldn't find her. I knew now that if she needed me, she'd find me. When my nameless acquaintance pointed to the patio door, I followed willingly, happy to get some relief from the noise and crowd.

He set the drinks down on a patio table and took a seat. He was very handsome, far from the cheesy sort I imagined would frequent a Myrtle Beach salsa club. He ran his hands through his hair, a shock of it falling into his eye. He looked at me shyly from behind it, like a little boy caught doing something he shouldn't. His eyes were blue. David's were green. His hair was a dirty blonde. David's was jet black. He voluntarily came to salsa-dancing clubs, even if he wouldn't willingly admit it. David would have to be tied and dragged.

He raised his glass to me. "Cheers," he said. I clinked it with him and sipped. "My name's Brian, by the way."

"Hi, Brian. I'm Ariel." He extended his hand, and I shook it from across the table. He held it for a bit too long.

He turned my hand over, stared at my wedding ring. "What's that?"

"What do you think it is?" I smiled.

He dropped my hand and held his own to his chest like he was appalled. "You're married?" he gasped, feigning shock.

I giggled. "Yes. I assumed you knew."

He held his hands up. "I had a feeling," he admitted. "Figured I'd get it out of the way before we went any further. Give you a chance to confess."

"Confess?" I asked.

"Yes. You've been dying to clear the air. I get that."

I bit my lip and looked away. I was more transparent than I thought. The red dress wasn't fooling anyone. You could take the wife out of the house but not the house out of the wife. I held up my hands. "You got me. I am not as mysterious as I thought."

He looked at me seriously across the table for a moment. "There's nothing wrong with being transparent. Or loyal." He took a sip of his drink. "I wish more women were." He smiled, shrugged. "I was supposed to be getting married next week. She called it off. Found someone else." He shrugged as though he wasn't hurt. "That's why my buddies dragged me here. They're all inside having a blast. Thought it would get my mind off my troubles."

"Instead you're out here talking to me, a married woman."

He held up his hands. "You seemed safe. Safe is good for me right now."

I tried not to feel hurt. What did I care if this guy chose me to hide out with? I was married, and in reality, I had no business being there at all. I wished for the ability to teleport myself back home to my bed with David snoring softly beside me and my three boys tucked into their beds down the hall.

"You just looked like a nice person," he added, not making it any better.

"The red dress didn't throw you off?" I teased.

"It was in your eyes," he said. "You're a nice person. You care about people. Sometimes too much?"

I thought of Justine dancing inside with total strangers, drinking and behaving in a way I was having a hard time justifying. "Yes, sometimes too much. I guess I just want to believe the best about people."

"Trust me," he said, "it can burn you sometimes." He raised his glass, and I raised my own. "To seeing people for who they are and not who we wish they were." As our glasses clinked, a cold shiver ran down my spine. Justine had emerged from the club, a fine coating of sweat making her skin glisten. She caught my eye and smiled, gave me an approving thumbs-up. I shook my head. She had it wrong.

"Will you wait here?" I asked. "I need to speak to my friend," I said, rising before he could answer. I walked quickly over to Justine, my bare feet on the warm patio bricks, the painful stilettos still under the table where I had kicked them off.

She pointed at my feet. "Aren't we cozy?"

"No. Not cozy. In pain," I said. "But definitely not cozy with that guy. He just broke up with his fiancée. Wanted to talk with someone 'safe.'" I gave her a mock-pathetic smile, but secretly I was hoping she'd follow my lead and keep her interactions with these men nice and safe.

But she just waved my explanation away. "I'm not here to judge," she said. "Listen, I am going to go on to another club with some people I met. Can you just take a taxi back to the condo?" She dropped a key into my hand and smiled. "Don't wait up," she said and giggled like a college girl who club-hopped every weekend instead of a mom of two who presided over our neighborhood back home.

Whoa. This was nowhere near safe. But before I could ask any questions, suggest coming along, or argue, she flitted back inside the club and was swallowed up by the crowd. Shocked and flustered, I couldn't seem to hatch any plan except to do as Justine had suggested. I turned back to the table to collect my shoes, say good-bye to Brian, and go hail a cab. As I reached the table, I realized that I didn't have enough cash to get home. I sat down and shook my head. So much for being Justine's safety net.

"What?" he asked, clearly sensing my anxiety.

"My friend, she … just left me here," I confessed. "And I'm not sure how I'm going to get back." I lifted my hands, unable to stop the whine that escaped. "I don't have enough cash to get a cab." I put my forehead on the table as if he wasn't there at all and wished again that I was home. What had possessed me to go on this stupid trip anyway?

Brian reached in his wallet and pulled out money. "Here," he said. "This should be enough."

I looked at him in shock. "No, no … I didn't mean … I can't—"

"You were nice to me. You helped me pass a few minutes of this ridiculous outing. So keep it. As a thank-you."

I took the money. "If I wasn't desperate at the moment I would argue with you."

"How many kids do you have?" he asked out of the blue.

"Kids? Is it that obvious?" Was it my childbearing hips? The permanent worry lines between my brows? The outdated haircut? I knew it wasn't the red dress or stiletto heels that gave me away.

"Moms just have a certain look to them. You can just tell. Motherhood seems to … change a woman."

I smiled. He was right. "Fair enough. I have three boys." I smiled, then rose from the table, bone tired. It was way past my bedtime.

He stood with me. "I'll walk with you." He fell into step beside me as we made our way out to the curb, where an assortment of cabs idled, waiting for those who had imbibed too much to drive. I stuck my head in the window of one of them and gave the driver the address of the condo, then looked back at Brian.

I extended my hand to him once more. "It was nice to meet you," I said.

He held my hand for a moment too long, and I knew that—if I wanted it—things could go a different direction. With one word he would be in the cab with me headed to the condo. With one word my entire life could change. Seeing the look on my face, he kissed my cheek, his lips as momentary as butterfly wings grazing my skin. "Go home," he said. "You're one of the good ones." He laughed. "Thank you."

"For what?" I asked. He was the one paying for my cab fare.

"For proving that good ones still exist." He waited for me to get into the cab and shut the door behind me. I watched him through the window until he faded from sight, then leaned my head back and closed my eyes until the cab pulled up to the condo. I opened my hand and looked down at the folded bills Brian had put in it. He had tucked his business card in with the money. I squinted at it under the dome light and smiled. I paid the driver with Brian's money and left his card on the seat of the taxi. When I got inside the house, I sat down and called Justine, wanting to tell her what had happened and find out when she'd be back. But she didn't answer. Then or the other times I tried before I finally fell asleep, the phone in my hand.

CHAPTER 27

~

Justine

It was dark when Tom and I headed to the beach. He held my hand, and I walked blindly toward the sound of the surf, my feet sinking in the powdery sand. The moon was hidden behind clouds, and the blackness was so complete I couldn't see my hand in front of my face. Slowly my eyes adjusted to the darkness and I could make out his form, like a ghost emerging from the shadows. He smiled over at me as he pulled me toward the edge of the surf. I slipped off my shoes and let the water cover my toes.

"Thanks for meeting me," he said. "I know it was a risk."

"For both of us," I said. "You have as much to lose as I do."

"And yet, tonight, we have so much to gain." He pulled me into an embrace, our bodies lining up as we stood there, shoulder touching shoulder, leg touching leg, stomach touching stomach. I could feel him breathe, smell the scent of his skin. I had never wanted anything more, not even when we were kids.

"I'm just sorry I couldn't get away sooner. I had to figure out a way to get away from Ariel. Luckily, she got distracted." I smiled to myself, thinking of Ariel slipping away with that good-looking guy. It alleviated my guilt and gave me ammunition in case she started asking too many questions. I guess nobody was immune to the temptations of life outside the bounds of marriage. Even Ariel with her continual broodings about how much she loved David.

"Where does she think you are?" he asked, pulling me onto a patch of dry sand so we could sit. I tried to sit down gracefully in my too-short dress but gave up and sort of fell onto the sand. I thought of what I was wearing underneath the dress and felt guilt surge, then die out. I could deal with guilt later. Tonight was for us.

"She thinks I went out dancing with people I met at the club."

"You party animal," he said, elbowing me in the side.

"Yeah, that's me. A party animal."

His voice changed, deepened with what I recognized as longing. "I'm glad you chose to come here with me." He reached over and pulled me to him. Kissing him already felt as natural as breathing. As though I had never stopped.

We kissed for a while, the heat between us deepening and intensifying. He broke away, and I felt my lips burn, my entire body crying out for … more. "My hotel's right there," he said.

He seemed hesitant, unsure, which I liked. I didn't want to be a foregone conclusion. Every part of my body was saying yes, even as my head fired off reasons I should say no. I knew that standing up, taking his hand, and following him up to that hotel was against everything I had said I believed up to that point. I had stood in front of the mothers' group and talked about honoring your husband, sang solos in church about allegiance. I knew that making this one choice would follow me for the rest of my life. I knew that the people who waited for me at home would be affected by me whispering the word *yes*.

I thought of Mark and his kindness, the look on his face when he came home after he'd been fired. I thought of my little girls—how they loved their daddy, how they trusted me to take care of them. I thought about taking the only home they'd ever known—their security—from them. I thought about my mom and dad standing in the driveway as I drove away, unknowingly enabling me to get to this place, this moment, the trusting looks on their faces. Tom kissed me again, ran his hand through my hair and sent shivers up my spine.

I pulled away.

"What? What is it?" His hand traveled up my arm to my face and caressed my cheek. "Are you scared?"

I nodded, swallowed, waited for my lips to stop tingling from his kiss. If I stopped now it would be hard, but I could still go forward. I could tell Mark. We could go to counseling. We could try to heal from the job loss and this … indiscretion of mine. We could sell the house, get away from Tom, and somehow make a new start. I could do the work it would take to save my family. I was good at fulfilling the expectations of others. I could do that.

"It's okay to be scared," he said, interrupting my thoughts, tracing his hand up and down my arm. "You don't ever let anyone see you scared, do you? You think you have to be so brave for everyone. To put on this face of perfection and never let anyone down."

He pulled back and studied me for a moment. His voice was hypnotic as he said things I had waited all my life to hear. "It's time for you to let someone—let me—take care of you for a change."

The moon came out from behind the clouds, and I could see his face as clearly as if it were daylight. I saw real love reflected in his eyes. I saw this face that I wanted to look at for the rest of my life. And in that moment I knew I had to have it.

"Will you let me take care of you?" he asked.

I thought of Mark telling me it was my turn to take care of the family, assuring me I had what it took to support us. I saw the way he sat on the couch, never reaching for me that day he lost his job. Mark never saw me clearly. Even on a dark night, Tom saw me. He saw through to my soul. How could I turn away from that?

"Yes," I whispered. "Yes. I will let you." I lifted my hand to him, and he took it, pulling me to stand and walk with him toward his hotel.

When dawn broke, I slipped from the bed as Tom slept. I pulled on my black dress and disappeared to avoid a morning encounter I wasn't ready for. I knew that everything had changed, that I could never go back. But during the cab ride back to the condo, I knew I wouldn't want to. Bad or good, I had a new future now.

CHAPTER 28

Ariel

I woke to the sound of Justine creeping into the room and slipping into the other bed. I looked out the window and saw light between the slats of the window blinds. In a few hours we would pack up and head home. As she settled into bed, I smelled a new wave of the cigarette smoke that had attached to us both over the course of the night. Where had she been? Who was she with? She had been gone all night. I lay there feeling like the snotty little sister who had the power to expose it all. But to whom? David? Mark? The neighborhood? The mothers' group? Obviously she was counting on my discretion. I wondered if that had been her plan all along. I was safe, but not in the way I had thought. I was malleable. She could shape our friendship into whatever she wanted.

I rolled over and willed myself to doze again. My body floated on the waves of consciousness, begging to be pulled under into the sweet abyss of sleep.

—⁓—

The next time I woke, the sun had climbed higher, and I could hear happy shouts of children by the pool. I looked over to see Justine's blonde hair on her pillow, the sheet pulled over her face. I stretched noisily and tossed back the covers, hoping the interrupted silence would wake her. We needed to get on the road. My longing for home was even more acute than it had been the night before at the salsa club. I crossed the room to the bathroom and turned on the shower. I would be ready to go before her, my things packed and waiting so she knew I just wanted the weekend to be over. So much for a time to get to know her better. She had only succeeded in alienating me further.

When I emerged from the bathroom, I found her sitting on the bed, her suitcase packed and her hair thrown into a sloppy, stubby ponytail. She had her keys in her hand. "If you're ready to go, I'm ready," she said.

She looked terrible. I wondered what excuse she'd offer to Mark when she got in. I could still see the effects of the evening on her skin—the dark circles under her eyes, a slightly green complexion from the alcohol. "A shower might make you feel better," I said.

"We need to get on the road. I know your family's expecting you," she said. She twirled the keys around on the ring.

"And your family's expecting you, too," I said pointedly.

She looked out the window at the view of the pool and the beach beyond. "We never got to the beach like you wanted," she said, changing the subject of her family.

"It's okay," I said. The beach was the furthest thing from my mind.

"Sorry about that. And sorry for leaving you last night."

"I was ... surprised. When you left."

"Well, you seemed to be having a good time with your new friend."

"What? Justine, I told you. I wasn't—"

"Hey, it's okay. This weekend was about getting away from your normal life, feeling like someone exciting, someone different. I get that." She stood up and smiled at me, as if I was her partner in crime. "It'll be our little secret."

"Justine, please understand me. I don't have any secrets. I can tell David honestly what happened every step of the way last night. And I will," I added. I had already thought about what I would tell David when I got home. He might get a little jealous, but I had to tell the truth. I had never withheld information from David before, and I didn't intend to start.

"Are you sure about that, Ariel? I mean, you wouldn't want David thinking that you aren't trustworthy. That you might do more next time. That's how it starts, you know. A little harmless flirting that leads down the wrong path." Justine plowed ahead, building her case. "Let's just keep this weekend between us. What happens at the beach stays at the beach kind of a thing. Okay? No sense in letting people get the wrong idea."

"I'm not worried about David. He trusts me."

"Don't be so sure," she said. "These things have a way of snow-balling." Suddenly tears filled her eyes, and she sat back down on her bed. She put her head in her hands, and I moved to put my arm around her. I could still smell the perfume she had worn last night underneath the smell of alcohol and cigarette smoke from the club.

"I just can't take any more drama. Laura moving. Mark losing his job," she said, her voice muffled by her hands. What if all of this weekend was just a delayed reaction for her, an act of rebellion against the hardship that had befallen her? What if she needed me to be a true friend to her and to see her through the drama? What if God put me in her life to love her no matter what? I wondered what God had to do with any of this and realized I had not given Him much thought throughout the weekend. It was as if I was dehydrated—I could feel a physical lack of God and a desperate thirst for Him. I silently prayed in that moment for wisdom and grace.

Justine looked up, her eyes red-rimmed. "So will you let this be just between us? For the sake of our friendship?"

"Sure," I said, though something inside me hated myself for saying it. "For the sake of our friendship, this'll stay between us." The only problem was that I didn't know what "this" was. All I knew was that she had flirted with men at the club and then disappeared until morning. I both wanted and didn't want to ask her for specifics. Aside from the fact that I could pretty much guess what had happened, I feared that asking her would only anger her and force her to push me further away. Her friendship had become too important to me. No matter how evasive she had been, she was the first woman to welcome me to the neighborhood. She was beautiful, smart, influential. She had a powerful magnetism that I simply couldn't resist. Not to mention that I now felt that God had given me a special role in this friendship.

She gave me a hug. "I knew I could count on you, Ariel." As I turned to make my bed and finish packing, I tried to decide if that was a good or a bad thing.

———

Neither of us said much for most of the ride home. Every so often I would catch Justine looking at me from the corner of her eye, as though she wanted to say something. But I pretended not to see. I didn't want to talk unless she had an apology for me instead of more justification. No matter what she said about my harmless exchange with Brian, it was not the same as her disappearing act. I tried to put my finger on what I felt—betrayal, rejection, shock, anger? No single word summed up the range of emotions I'd experienced in the three hours we'd been riding quietly.

As if reading my thoughts, Justine spoke up, clearing her throat first like a warning. "I have something to tell you."

Finally. She was going to come clean. Whatever it was, we could move forward from here, start fresh with the truth between us. I would listen and not judge. I would offer helpful advice. "Okay," I offered, willing my voice to sound kind and open.

"I'm getting a job."

I tried to make what she was saying fit with what I had been thinking. Where was the tearful confession, the rational explanation? Maybe this was it. This was the explanation for her odd behavior. "Oh?" was all I said.

"Remember I told you Tom was going to help me?" she asked.

"Yes," I said.

"There's a job at his company he's going to help me get. And with Mark out of work now, well … we just can't make it if he doesn't get a job. And with this job market we have no idea how long that will take." She looked over at me again briefly and returned her eyes to the road. "This opportunity just sort of came up, and we decided it would be best for me to pursue it."

"Oh," I said again. We were nearing home, and I couldn't get there fast enough. I wanted to escape from the thoughts that were circling in my head about what Justine was really up to the night before. It was impossible to take in that my perfect friend could step even one toe outside the line of decorum. Yet not only had she, but she'd done it right in front of me. And now she expected me to smile and go along with it like nothing had happened. I wanted to throw myself back into normal life, get far away from the realities that were pressing in on me in that enclosed car.

"So this was my last hurrah before I go back to work, so to speak. Thanks for letting me get a little crazy." She smiled at me as if that explained it all.

"I guess everyone's entitled to get a little crazy every now and then," I said, hoping I sounded earnest.

"Exactly. I knew you'd understand." She turned on a CD of old love songs, the car filling with some cheesy Barry Manilow song. I turned to look out the window at the scenery rushing by, faster than I could take it in.

Later that night, after I had successfully answered David's questions about how the weekend went without saying too much and hugged on the boys until they gave in to sleep, I lay beside David in bed. He was snoring softly beside me while all the things I hadn't said ate at me from the inside out.

I thought about breaking my promise to Justine and waking David up so I could spill it all: Brian's kind words to me, the way he looked at me just before the cab left, the way it felt good to have another man's eyes on me and how guilty I felt about it. I wondered if I could tell all that without breaking Justine's confidence. I knew his questions would follow. "Where was Justine? Why were you in a cab alone? When did she get home?" So instead of waking him up, I lay quietly beside him, my stomach churning. It felt like there was a poison within me, a poison I had to get rid of one way or another. I had never kept anything from David before, and I wondered what kind of friend would ask me to start now.

CHAPTER 29

⌒

Justine

The night we got home from the beach I made dinner—hoagies with all the fixings and a side order of guilt for my plate. After dinner, Mark watched TV, and the girls slept peacefully in their beds, content that I was home and all was well. I slipped out to the deck to look at the stars and wonder what I'd just done, wondering why my family couldn't see traces of him on me. Mark didn't look up from ESPN as I closed the door behind me.

The night was not quiet. Crickets, frogs, and cicadas blended together to perform their summer symphony. From across the yard I could hear Ariel's neighbor, a recluse I'd waved at but never met, playing music as he often did. Tonight was '80s music. Toto sang, "All I wanna do when I wake up in the morning is see your eyes." Even after dark the air was still hot, though not as humid. I wore a tank top and fantasized that I'd stayed long enough to wake up with Tom this morning, that the slight breeze I felt on my arm was his touch as we woke up tangled together in his hotel room. It was hard to imagine that just the night before we'd been on the beach together. I tilted my head back, breathed deeply, closed my eyes, and heard a noise—a movement in the yard.

I yanked my head back down, scanning the yard for the source of the noise. There was movement in the playset tower. I saw the faint outline of a profile, a white shirt. "Who's there?" I asked, foolishly heading toward the culprit instead of going inside like a smart woman would.

A girl stuck her head out from the cover of the tower. "Miss Justine, it's me, Heather."

I stopped in the yard and watched as she climbed down. "Heather?" I asked. "What in the world are you doing out here?"

She stopped at the bottom of the tower and leaned back against it. "I come here sometimes," she said. "To think. I'm sorry. I'll go." She started to walk away. I could see her clearly in the light coming from our house windows.

"No, Heather, you don't need to feel like you have to leave. I was just going inside," I lied.

She reached up and pulled on her ponytail, shifting her weight and looking around like she was trying to find the fastest escape route. I hadn't really looked at her in a long time, I realized. She'd grown up while I looked the other way.

"You've gotten so pretty," I blurted out.

She blanched and looked away. "Umm, thanks," she said. She wrapped the end of her ponytail around and around her index finger, then let it go.

"I mean, you're not a little girl anymore." I smiled. "I still think of you as a little girl."

"You and my dad," she said.

"How is your dad?" I asked. I could feel the blades of grass against my bare feet, sharp on my skin. I shouldn't have asked about him.

"He's good. Working a lot. He lives not far from here. I see him some." She looked at me with eyes that told me she knew more than she was supposed to. "I remember he built this playset with Mr. Mark."

"Yes, he did." I thought back to that day years ago. Caroline had been so little I was afraid for her to climb the stairs of the tower. The men had looked so handsome, so capable, climbing around hoisting lumber. Erica had come over, and we'd cooked dinner, laughing as we worked. Heather had helped watch out for the girls. "That was a good day," I added.

She smiled with one side of her mouth. "Sometimes I like to come here and remember when things were better with my parents. When we were all happier."

I wondered what to say in response to that. "That sounds like a good idea," I said. "It's good to remember the good times."

She paused and looked at the house. "I know," she said. "About what's going on with you and Mr. Dean."

My heart started pounding. "What?" I asked, laughing. "Nothing's going on with me and Mr. Dean."

"I saw the two of you together. You were in his car on that dead-end street where they stopped building houses. I saw your car and I saw his, so I went over to see what was going on. And I ... saw you. Together."

If she only knew that I was trying to figure out which time she saw us. We'd gotten pretty crafty at inventing excuses to meet there. It was "our place." "Listen, Heather, I don't know what you think you saw, but ... there's nothing going on with me and Mr. Dean."

She looked me in the eyes for the first time that night. "My dad denied it too, when my mom caught him."

I didn't try to argue further. We stood for a moment and looked at each other, neither of us saying a word. "I might be a kid," she continued, "but I'm not stupid. And the truth is, I came over here tonight to try to figure out what to do about it. The Deans live across the street from us. They're nice people. They love their kids. You and Mr. Mark are nice people. You love your kids." She sighed. "So I came here just to watch your house and try to remember what that felt like—to be like Cameron and Caroline. To still have a mom and a dad who loved each other." Her eyes flashed in the darkness. "Do you really want to take that away from them?"

I looked away, ashamed. "No," I said quietly, thinking of the guilt I'd been carrying since I slipped away in the first light of dawn. "I don't want to hurt anyone." I couldn't explain to Heather that Cameron and Caroline didn't have a mom and dad who still loved each other. That argument was pointless, and she was, after all, just a child. A wise child, but a child nonetheless.

"Then stop, Miss Justine. Just stop. It's not too late." She kicked at the grass with her flip-flop. "I won't tell anyone. It'll be just between us." I saw desperation in her eyes. The poor kid needed to believe that I could do what her parents could not. In that moment, I wanted to be the person she believed me to be.

"Okay," I said, because it was all I could think of to say, and because I just wanted this confrontation to be over. I raised my eyes to look into hers. "Thank you."

She left without another word, and I wondered if she thought I was thanking her for not telling or thanking her for helping me see that I had to do the right thing. She was right, and I knew it. I was a grown-up. I had to stop, for my girls if nothing else. I stood in the yard for a long time after she left, figuring out how to do just that, watching as the lights in the houses around me went out, one by one.

The next morning after Mark had gone to a coffee shop to hide behind his laptop screen and the girls were busy playing upstairs, I called Tom and was relieved when his voice mail picked up. Between Heather's visit and the overwhelming guilt I felt, I knew what I had to do even if my heart wasn't in it. I was worried that if I actually spoke to him, I wouldn't say what I had to say. His voice made me weak, drove me to promise things I had no business promising. This promise wasn't for me or for him. This promise was for my family.

"I think that we both know the other night was a mistake," I said, my voice barely more than a whisper. "I'm sorry, but this just isn't me. I'm not this person. And I know once there was something between us, but now … there just can't be now." I glanced around the kitchen and thought of him trying to pull me to him the night we had him and Betsy over, how happy I was just from his nearness. "I'm sorry," I said into the phone and ended the call.

Later I would tell Mark we needed to sell the house. He would agree because of our finances and his job loss. He would never suspect the real reason I wanted to get away. He might even congratulate me for being willing to sacrifice my house to save my family. He would never know what I was sacrificing. I wiped away tears and turned to face the rest of my life without Tom.

CHAPTER 30

Ariel

I was in the kitchen, mixing up a batch of Justine's play dough for the boys and trying to break my habit of watching Justine's house for movement, when I looked up to see her standing on my deck, about to knock on the door.

I let her in but did not look her in the eye. "Hey, Miss Justine," Duncan said. He threw his arms around her legs and squeezed, but she barely noticed, absentmindedly patting him on the head as she made her way to the kitchen. Undeterred, he pressed on. "Where's Cameron and Caroline? We want them to come over and do play dough with us." He jumped around, the energy in his body escaping in short, contained bursts.

"They're home with their daddy," Justine replied as she took a seat at our kitchen table. Her voice was flat, emotionless.

Duncan tried unsuccessfully to snap his fingers. "Rats," he said. "Will you tell them that we've got play dough here? 'Cept this time it's blue. Not pink. But they can still play with it."

She looked at me as she answered. "Sure." She sighed. "Hey, Duncan, can you let your mommy and me talk for a second?"

He continued jumping around, adding the flourish of waving a gun in the air like a choreographed routine. "Dunc," I said, my voice raising to be heard over the sound of his feet hitting the floor again and again.

"What?" he asked.

"Can you give Miss Justine and me a minute to talk? Go upstairs and see what your brothers are doing. Tell them play dough will be ready in a minute."

"Can we use your cookie cutters?" he countered before leaving. He needed something exciting to tell his brothers.

I knew when I was beat. "Sure," I said as he pumped his fist in the air and ran up the stairs, all thundering feet and movement, the Tasmanian Devil in motion, whirling up the stairs. I smiled at the sight of him.

As I turned to face Justine, my smile faded. "What did you need to talk to me about?" I asked, as if my mind wasn't on the same thing hers was.

"I barely slept last night," she said. "I needed to come over and clear the air between us."

Relief escaped from my lips in the form of a sigh. "I feel the same way."

"Listen. I should not have gone on to that other club. It was stupid. I put you at risk. I put myself at risk. I just got caught up in the moment. I felt young and daring and … not myself." She gave me a wry smile. "I guess I just didn't want to be myself, just for one night. Can you understand that?"

I nodded. I did understand. The need for escape was exactly why I had gone on the trip in the first place.

Justine continued, "The realities of the changes in my life caught up to me, and I dealt with it by acting crazy. I just hope you can forgive me. I'm not that woman you just spent the weekend with. I hope you know that." She had voiced my previous rationalizations. Yet I wasn't convinced.

"But are you the woman I've spent the last several months getting to know either?" I asked, pushing my fear of going too deep with her aside. I stared at the grain of my hardwood floors, thinking how just six months ago I had actually believed the right floor, the right granite, the right house would bring me the right life.

She shook her head. "I don't think so," was all she said. She rolled her eyes. "Suddenly I'm learning that I don't know who I am."

"Are you really going to get a job?"

She looked away, out the window at her house. I wondered what she thought when she saw it from this vantage point. Did she see it as beautiful, as perfect, as I did? "I don't know," she said without looking back at me. "Maybe. Probably. We'll probably sell the house."

"I'm sorry to hear it. I like being your neighbor."

Her shoulders slumped forward. "Mark told me I had to get a job. He said he's tired of doing all of this, that I am capable of helping. And we—" She pinched the bridge of her nose and closed her eyes. "We have too many bills to make it for very long." She looked around the room, and I wondered what she saw—my attempts at order and decorating, or the many ways I still fell short? "I don't expect you to understand. Things seem much ... simpler ... for you. You make it look easy."

"Me?" I gasped. "*I* make it look easy?"

"Of course. David just took a great job," she said. "You've been smart with your money. You told me that—how frugal David is, how he made you wait to buy this house till you could afford it, how you don't have credit cards."

"But I was complaining," I said, stunned at the turn of events.

She didn't miss a beat. "Maybe you shouldn't complain," she said.

Our eyes locked. She blinked slowly and turned to leave. "I came to say I was sorry."

"Okay," I said. Her hand was on the doorknob, her nails still polished a vixen red from the night at the beach, but the red nails no longer seemed to suit her. "I appreciate you coming by."

She shrugged. "You're welcome," she said. "Thanks for hearing me out."

I smiled. "That's what friends do." She tried to smile back, but her smile lacked its usual fervor. I watched her walk back to her house slowly and wondered what could've made her look so sad.

CHAPTER 31

⌣

Ariel

When the phone rang, I was in the midst of making table center-pieces for the neighborhood Fourth of July party out of red, white, and blue colored sand. There were granules all over my counters and floors, and so far the centerpieces didn't look a thing like the pictures. "Why did I say I could do this?" I wondered aloud to no one.

I reached for the phone, expecting it to be Kristy. We had been playing phone tag the last three days. The voice on the other end was female, but it wasn't Kristy. "Is this Ariel Baxter?"

"Yes, it is," I said, walking over to clean up the sand from the counters and find a safe place to store the glass centerpieces.

"Hi, Ariel, this is Betsy Dean. Tom's wife?" She sounded as if she'd been crying. "I met you briefly at the pool, and I was …" She paused. "I was—well, it sounds silly to say since we don't know each other—but I was at your birthday party. At the Millers'?"

"Yes, of course, Betsy," I said. "I've been meaning to get together with you!"

"Me, too," she said, but her voice did not carry the polite enthusiasm of mine.

"Is there something I can do for you?" I asked.

"Well, actually I had a question. You're friends with Justine, right?"

"Well, *friends* is a strong word, Betsy," I said, thinking of the last conversation I had with Justine, the way she'd looked at me before she left.

"Did you go to the beach with her for the weekend recently?"

"Yes," I said. My heart was hammering in my chest so loudly I wondered if she could hear it. I did not like where this was headed. She was asking me about something I wasn't supposed to talk about.

"Well, I just wondered if anything strange happened while you were there."

"Strange?" I asked. Where would I begin?

"Yes. With Justine."

"Umm, no?" I lied.

"Can you hang on a minute?" she asked.

"Sure." I listened as she covered up the phone and spoke, her voice muffled by her hand. Was Tom in the background? Her children? My heart beat wildly, and I wondered where this was leading. Stupid weekend. What had she heard? I wished for the hundredth time I hadn't gone. I felt like I had wandered into a trap.

"Ariel?" she asked.

"Yes. I'm here." I sat motionless.

"Are you aware of Justine's relationship with my husband?" she asked.

"Umm, sort of? Just that they dated in high school." I felt a throbbing behind my eyes. Where was she going with this?

"Ariel," she said, "when you were out of town with Justine, Tom was out of town too. He said it was business. I had no idea that she was gone the same time or that there was anything to worry about. At the time I was still going on the assumption that we were going to make the best of the fact that Tom and I had become neighbors with his long lost love, and to figure out how to live with this … coincidence. I thought we could all be adult about it, what with Justine's happy marriage, not to mention my own."

I thought of how progressive it had all seemed.

"I think that Tom was in Myrtle Beach when you were." I heard the voice in the background again. "Okay, I guess I need to be completely honest. I *know* Tom was in Myrtle Beach when you were."

Like a movie reel in my head I saw Justine on the balcony talking on the phone with her back to me, taking forever to get ready the night we went out, standing in front of me at the club saying she was leaving, then disappearing into the crowd. I heard the creak of her bedsprings as she crawled in at the break of dawn. I closed my eyes to erase the images from my mind, but they wouldn't budge. In my head I knew that Betsy's phone call explained a lot, but in my heart I wanted another explanation to be true. "How do you know something's going on?" I asked, stalling. "Maybe this is all just a coincidence."

"There's lots of things. I know this sounds crazy, but I found something on our computer," she said. "He downloaded a Barry

Manilow song. Barry Manilow, Ariel. Would your husband download a Barry Manilow song of his own volition?"

I thought of our ride home, the Barry Manilow song she had tortured me with, and my blood ran cold.

"Wouldn't you want the truth? I mean, if you were in my shoes?" she went on. "I'm speaking to you from one wife to another. A wife who knows something's going on and just needs some help to prove it. The knowing but not knowing is driving me crazy."

I thought about the man next to me in the restaurant that night I had gone to dinner alone. The man who called his lover and then his wife. The two voices—two personalities—he used when he spoke to them. "Yes," I said, my voice weak, "I would want to know. But something's telling me knowing for sure isn't going to make you feel better."

"I just want the truth." She sighed. "I hope you have told me the truth."

My stomach sank to my feet, and I rested my forehead in my hand. I thought of Justine's face when she asked me not to say anything about the weekend. Surely she hadn't seen Tom. Surely there was another explanation for what was going on. She was going through a hard time. She had blown off steam. But was she committing adultery with our neighbor? Could the Justine I knew do that? It was unthinkable. There had to be an explanation beyond what Betsy was suggesting. Besides, I didn't even know this woman. She could be crazy, always accusing Tom's neighbors of being in love with him wherever they moved. I had to get more information before I ratted out my friend to a virtual stranger. "Yes," I said. "I have." Was I lying? "But if I find out anything that I think would be helpful to you, I will let you know," I offered, an olive branch to make up for the lie. She thanked me, and we hung up.

I immediately made another call.

Justine answered the phone just before voice mail picked up, as though she started to avoid me, then thought better of it. "I just got a phone call from Betsy Dean," I said.

"And?" Justine asked, her voice perky as ever. But I had learned something about Justine. The perkier her words, the less she meant them.

"She wanted to know what happened that weekend," I said.

"And what did you tell her?" I heard no panic in Justine's voice. I tried to take that as a good sign.

"That nothing happened, nothing out of the ordinary," I said dutifully, hoping my loyalty would bridge the gap that had opened up between us.

"Well, you know nothing happened so of course that's what you told her," she said.

"She said that Tom was there. In Myrtle Beach. Did you know that?"

She laughed. "Now how would I know Tom was there?"

"Well, I mean, he's helping you get a job and I thought maybe—"

"Maybe he went dancing at the same salsa club as us?" She laughed again. "You were there. Did you see him?"

"No, but—"

"But what? Oh, that's right. You weren't in the club the whole time, now were you?"

"Justine, I explained that." Heat rose up my neck, reddening my face. Yet I had nothing to be ashamed of.

"I know. And I accept your explanation. But you must admit it could look bad if someone got the wrong idea. Which is what's happening here. Listen, Betsy's a nice woman. You know I've tried to be her friend, and I genuinely like her. But this whole story sounds a bit paranoid, don't you think?"

I got up from the couch, allowing Justine's words to free me and fill me with hope like air in my lungs. "Yes, it was strange. I mean, how did she pick me to call? And how did she know about our weekend away?"

"This neighborhood's full of talk. That's what happens when gossipy types get involved. Always trying to stir up trouble where there isn't any. Look, I am sorry you got pulled into this. I really am." She paused, sighed. "Plus, she's neighbors with Erica, and I've heard they've gotten pretty chummy. Erica has been known, as I've said, to get in the middle of neighborhood drama. To stir the pot. I wouldn't be surprised if she was behind Betsy's paranoia."

"Well, I'm glad you told me the truth." It was more a question than a statement.

Justine paused. I heard her breathe in and out. "Of course," she said. "We're friends, right? Friends tell each other everything." She hung up before I could affirm that we were friends or comment on how much that meant to me. And yet, something in me still felt uneasy.

I drank a glass of water before scrolling on my caller ID to Betsy's number. She answered as soon as the phone rang, her voice breathy.

"Betsy?" I asked.

"Yes," she said. She spoke in a low voice. "Ariel?" she asked. I pictured her the night of my party, laughing and talking to neighbors I didn't know as Tom raised his glass to her.

"I just wanted you to know I talked to Justine and she assured me that she had no idea Tom was in Myrtle Beach. I just wanted to offer that as reassurance after our last conversation. I thought—you know—that you would want to know that."

She sighed. "Ariel, do you actually think she'd admit it to you if she did?"

"Yes," I said, nodding my head even though she couldn't see me.

She started whispering. "Listen, I can't talk right now. Tom's home. But I want you to know that I am going to try to believe both you and Justine. Just know that it's a bit hard. A wife just has an instinct about things like this," she said.

"I understand," I said.

"Do you?" she asked.

I started to answer but realized she was already gone.

CHAPTER 32

Ariel

The boys and I had our summer days at the pool down to a routine. We efficiently packed the things that had become second nature: sunscreen and water guns, towels and snacks. I carried the heavy bag, and Donovan pulled the new rolling cooler. They lined up like soldiers for their sunscreen, no words needed. They knew the drill. As they ran off to jump in the pool, I flopped down into the nearest lounge chair, pulling a novel from my bag. I had been reading the same novel all summer, it seemed. I wondered how other women had time to read.

A shadow loomed over me, and I looked up to find Erica standing beside me. "Can I sit here?" she asked, pointing to the chair beside me. I hadn't spoken to her since I took Heather's pictures, hadn't seen her since that day at the doctor's office.

"Sure," I said, shrugging. I wondered why I was being so apathetic toward this woman I actually liked. A voice echoed in my head: *Because Justine said so.*

She got settled on her towel and spritzed herself with suntan oil, smiling at me. "No SPF whatsoever. How's that for taking care of myself?"

"I usually forget to put anything on myself at all, so I don't have room to judge," I said with a half smile. "How'd you like Heather's pictures?" I asked, just to make conversation.

"They were great. She's so proud of them. Her friends, too. Did you get my thank-you note?"

I nodded, my mouth pressed into a grim line. I had read it and thrown it in the trash can hastily. "Thanks for that," I said.

We sat in silence for a while, our eyes closed to block the relentless rays of the July sun. Beads of sweat collected on my skin and ran like tears. I was about to jump in the pool to cool off when she spoke. "Listen, Ariel. I, uh, just wanted to let you know. That was me in the background when Betsy called you the other day."

"Oh?" I said, not opening my eyes. It was more of the confirmation I had been seeking that Justine was telling the truth.

"Betsy's my neighbor," she said. "We've become friends."

"That's great," I offered.

She paused. I opened my eyes and turned to face her.

"Betsy needs a friend right now," she said.

"I'm sure she does," I answered. "It's good she has you. Being new in the neighborhood and all."

"I was new here once. And I ran into some trouble myself not long after. I get what she's going through. It's very close to what I went through."

"Is that right?" I replied, cautioning myself against engaging in what could quickly become gossip with this woman. I liked her, but

I didn't trust her. I realized I trusted none of my new neighbors. That said a lot about this supposed dream neighborhood.

"Don't tell me you haven't heard my sad story?" she asked, leaning up on her elbow and looking at me intently. "Justine didn't gleefully fill you in?"

"No. Should she have?" I mentally arranged my features so they looked innocent.

She looked away, watched her daughter do a flip off the diving board and enter the water with a grace only afforded the young. She lay back and sighed. "I just thought—when—"

She closed her eyes as though the story would be easier to tell if she didn't have to make eye contact. I closed my eyes in solidarity. "When you didn't speak to me at the doctor's office that day, I thought it was because Justine had told you my story." Her laugh was bitter. "At least, her version of my story."

"She didn't say anything to me about you," I said. That wasn't true, but I didn't want to hurt Erica's feelings by repeating Justine's warning. And I didn't want to break Justine's confidence. I was getting exhausted just trying to keep up with who had told me what.

"I'm surprised she didn't warn you about me—say I was a bad seed or whatever it is she says about me."

I didn't say anything in response but waited for her to continue. "I was friends with her when I first moved here. She was nice to me, showed me the ropes, took me under her wing. All that stuff. She's a regular welcoming committee. So I wasn't surprised when she got to you first. Of course it helps that you live in her backyard."

"Yes, we share a gate so the kids can come and go. It's nice. The boys love their playset, and they have an open-door policy."

"My ex-husband helped build that playset," she said. "And after everything we went through, it's so hard for me to watch what's unfolding."

"You mean with Betsy and Tom?"

"Yes, Betsy and Tom. He's a lot like my ex. Of course, my ex was a pastor, if you can believe that."

I did not admit that I already knew that. A popular pastor, Justine had told me on one of our walks, with a growing congregation. "Really?" I said.

"A pastor who was just as weak as any other man who thinks with the wrong part of his anatomy. He ran around on me. And I took it for years. No one knew. And to this day, no one does. Everyone thinks I was this heartless shrew who wanted a divorce for no reason." Her words matched what Justine had said, only in a different way.

She leaned over on her chair and lowered her voice. I leaned closer to hear her. "He thinks I did it for him, but really I did it for her." She pointed at Heather, standing in line for another chance to dive off the board. "She has her daddy on a pedestal, and I wasn't going to be the one to knock him off. So I kept his secret, and in exchange he gave me the house and pretty much anything I wanted. He did quit being a pastor. I guess his conscience got the best of him." She paused. "He was the pastor for that big church that has the mothers' group you go to with Justine. I got ousted from there and, for the most part, from this neighborhood."

"It sounds very lonely," I said. My words fell short.

She lay back down. "It was hell. I became persona non grata around here."

"So why did you stay?"

"For Heather," she said. "She had her school and her friends and her home. I couldn't take that away from her after her daddy left. I had to make it work. Be a grown-up. I couldn't let what I wanted take away from what she needed."

"I'm sorry," I said. I tried to imagine what losing her marriage and her reputation all at the same time had done to her. That she still showed her face amazed me ... and earned my respect. She blinked at me, gauging whether I was sincere. "That must've been really hard on you," I added. "I don't know if I could've done it."

"Well, it's over now," she said.

"Is it?" I asked. I thought of Justine's warning to me and almost told her.

"For me it is. I've grown past it, become a stronger person because of it." She smiled. "I have my daughter and a beautiful home. There are some women in the world who would be very happy with what I have. I've learned to focus on that." She paused. "Plus, I see a bigger purpose for staying here now."

"What?" I asked. I wanted her to help me see the bigger purpose.

"I think I'm supposed to be here for Betsy, to help her figure all this out. I know all the signs, all the tricks. My ex gave me a crash course. It's the one thing I would consider myself an expert at." She gave me a wry smile, and I lay back down. "Tom's moving out." She turned to look at me with a look so serious my breath caught in my throat. "You can't tell anyone that."

"And you think he's cheating with ... someone?"

"Honey, I know he is. There's no *thinking* about it."

"But—"

"Look, I'm not asking you to figure it all out right now. But I am asking you to consider that there might be more here than meets the eye. You were with her; you know if she's different suddenly. You know if her behavior seems odd or if she did anything—*anything*—that didn't add up when you were away for the weekend. I know you want to protect her, but I just have to say that, in this situation, protecting her is the wrong thing to do. There are people—innocents—who are being hurt, and I just hope that you'll decide to do the right thing if you know anything or if you stumble upon anything."

I knew she didn't expect an answer, yet still I fumbled for one that would absolve Justine. I thought of how sincere—and sad—she had looked when she came over. She hadn't looked like a woman who was carrying on an illicit affair. No matter what, I didn't want to act too impulsively or spill my guts unnecessarily. If I kept silent, I could buy time for her to come to her senses and stop anything that might be going on. There was still time to derail this train. I closed my eyes, letting the sun warm me as I said a prayer to really see what was going on. And what I should do about it.

———

"Daddy's home!" Donovan called out as we pulled into the garage beside his car. This was a surprise. I couldn't remember the last time David got home before six. The boys scrambled out of the car and dashed inside to see their daddy, while I stayed outside and gathered wet towels and discarded pool toys from the seats. I felt him slip his arms around me from behind as I backed out of the van with my arms full.

"I got an earlier flight," he said.

"I see that," I replied, giggling as he nuzzled his face in my neck.

"I missed you," he said.

I heard the boys inside fighting and laughing at the same time. For a moment I stopped long enough to breathe it all in—the feeling of David's arms around me, the sound of his voice, the knowledge that we were all together and nothing was missing. No matter how often I let myself succumb to that sense of wanting more, for that moment I just let what I had be enough.

"I missed you too," I said. He moved his arms so I could turn around and take the things I was holding inside.

"You should make the boys do that," he said.

"They were excited to see you. I couldn't blame them."

"I thought we'd go out to dinner tonight. The boys want pizza. Does that sound good to you?"

"Not cooking sounds great to me." He could have suggested a greasy fast-food restaurant and I would've said yes.

"Maybe we could get a movie while we're out to watch when the boys go to bed?" he asked.

"That sounds about as close to perfect as I could ask for."

"It's a deal then." He started to walk away, toward the boys. "Oh," he said, turning back. "There was a message on the voice mail I saved for you. Justine."

I picked up the phone, wondering what she could want. I hadn't seen her in days.

Her voice on the message was chipper and bubbly. "Hey, Ariel," she said. "I am still applying for that job, but it looks like it'll be a few weeks before I know anything. I thought it might be a good idea for us to plan to do some freezer cooking. Let me know if you want to do it, and we can go grocery shopping together. I thought that might be fun! Okay, call me."

Ordinarily, I would've called her back as soon as I got her message, but instead I decided to let her wait. I wasn't going to run every time she called.

———

I closed my eyes and listened to the sounds of the boys laughing on the trampoline, exhausted after a long day of buying snacks and things for the upcoming Fourth of July festivities in the neighborhood. I let my body rest even as my ears stayed on duty. When the laughter changed to shrieks, I rallied long enough to get up and go see what was going on. It didn't sound like my boys' typical noises, but it didn't sound like anyone was hurt either. I stopped to peek out the window. My mouth fell open at the sight that greeted me.

Justine and her girls had joined the boys. Justine was jumping and bouncing the children up in the air, playing popcorn like she had scolded me for doing in the past. I bit back a smile and went outside. "What is going on out here?" I asked.

She stopped jumping and grinned broadly. It wasn't her normal smile. This smile was different. It reflected genuine happiness. "This is great exercise," she said, out of breath.

"I know," I said, returning the smile.

"We came over to find out when we're going to go grocery shopping. You never called me back about it." She turned to look at the kids. "Then we saw the boys out here and I thought, oh why not? What's the worst that can happen? Someone lose a tooth?"

Cameron laughed and flashed her toothless smile. "Jump again, Mom," she called out. It was a far cry from the scene I had witnessed the last time we were all gathered at my trampoline. I didn't know what had prompted Justine's behavior change, but I liked what I saw.

"Should I join you?" I asked. Silent Joe was playing music, as always. Bruce Springsteen sang about one step up and two steps back.

Justine waved me up, and the kids all cheered. "But, Mom," Donovan said. "That's more people than the rules allow."

I turned to smile at my friend. I didn't understand what was happening, but at that moment I didn't have to. "Well, then I guess you kids will have to get off. It's the adults' turn to have some fun," I said. The kids grumbled good-naturedly as they climbed down, giving Justine and me room to jump, room to fly.

CHAPTER 33

Justine

I was winded as I came in the house with the girls. Winded and happy. I couldn't remember the last time I had felt that kind of happiness—the kind that didn't come with any guilt attached. When the phone rang, I assumed it was Liza, calling because the due date for my piece in the newsletter had slipped my mind. I was trying to pay attention again to the things that used to matter in my life. I picked up the phone, prepared to make an excuse to Liza about Mark losing his job, to promise her I would get back on track. Instead I heard a pause just before a male voice asked for me. I should've hung up.

"This is her," I said. I decided that wasn't grammatically correct. Shouldn't I have said, "This is she"?

"Ma'am, my name is Steve, and I am calling on behalf of the collections department for Madison Furniture. Are you aware you've missed two payments on the furniture you purchased from them?"

"Ma'am?" he asked. "Can we make arrangements for payment? I am trying to collect on a debt you owe."

I stammered for an answer. "I—we—my husband … My husband lost his job, and we—"

"Ma'am, you made a promise to pay for this furniture. Perhaps there's a family member who could help you with the payments until then?"

I thought about my parents, the humiliation of calling them to ask for help. I was on a sinking ship, and I could either try to bail out water or just bail out. A simmering anger began to bubble just below my skin. But who was I angry at? Myself for living so close to the edge financially, for blindly trusting Mark to make things okay? Or him for losing his job? At the moment I couldn't decide. I just knew I had to get off the phone with this man who was pushing me to pay a bill we couldn't pay. We'd been slipping further and further into debt the more Mark didn't make quota, the less income he brought home. Losing the job was just the signature on the bankruptcy notice. We had been living in denial for months, fooling ourselves into thinking that we were safe if we stayed inside the bubble of our affluent neighborhood, not realizing that's the problem with bubbles: They shimmer and shine, but they burst easily.

"I'll talk to my husband, and we'll make arrangements," I said. "If you'll just give me a few days."

"Ma'am, you don't have a few days. If you don't pay, this is going to our legal department. I can call you back this afternoon. I hope you'll have made a plan by then. I suggest you do." He disconnected the call without saying good-bye or extending any basic courtesy to me. I wondered who would want a job like that? An angry person who enjoyed being rude all day? Or just a person who needed money so badly he was willing to do anything? Would Mark reach that point? Would I?

I stood there holding the phone for a minute, wondering what I could do, wondering what Mark could do. Should I make the effort to call my parents and borrow the money to catch us up? If I did, I was bailing water out of a boat with a gaping hole in the bottom. There was more where that came from—more bills we couldn't pay, more money we didn't have. The creditors were lining up: mortgage, car payments, credit cards. I didn't know much about our financial situation—I never wanted to know—but I did know it was bad and getting worse.

My friends at church would tell me to pray, to trust God, to read the Bible. But I couldn't do that. I was tired of pious answers from prideful people who would do nothing more than offer their pity, then gossip about me behind my back. *First she lost that part, then he lost his job....* I could see them shaking their heads, so secure in their own safety, unaware that the same wolves that had found us lurked in the shadows of their own landscaped lawns.

I threw the phone across the room. It hit the refrigerator and broke into two pieces, breaking just like I finally did inside. "Why?" I screamed at no one, but then realized I was screaming at God. "Why would You let this happen? I'm not even sure You're there." I sank to the floor and sobbed, my breath coming in heaving gasps. My hands were clenched in fists, and I stared at them, wondering what I could punch. I looked up to see Cameron and Caroline at the bottom of the stairs, clutching each other and staring at me with fear in their eyes. I could see my sister and me in the same pose a long,

long time ago, watching my mother cry because we were going to lose our house. I remembered the fear in my belly, the knowing that something was dreadfully wrong, and the powerlessness to stop it that made me feel so small and helpless.

I had vowed I would never let that happen to my daughters. I stood up and backed away from them, edging toward the door. I had to get away. I had to find a way to escape the fate that was upon us. When I had a plan, I would come back for them.

Grabbing the keys, I babbled out some nonsense and fled. It was only after I was in my car that I realized where I was going and who I was headed for: the one safe place in all of this, the one thing that made sense in my life anymore. I pictured his face, and a peace settled over me. I exhaled slowly, breathed in and breathed out as my heart rate slowed. I imagined falling into his arms, telling him all that was wrong. I imagined him telling me I was safe, telling me he would take care of me.

I rolled down the window of my car and let the warm air wash over me. I had tried to stay away. Even when he called to tell me that he'd moved out, that he wanted me, that the night we'd spent together had changed everything. Even then I'd resisted, told him he'd have to stop calling. I'd been strong only to find that none of it mattered. My commitment to Mark and the girls wasn't going to save my family. As I pressed on the accelerator, all I could think was that I didn't want to save my family anymore. Right or wrong, I just wanted to save myself.

CHAPTER 34

Ariel

Justine canceled a half hour before we were supposed to do our bulk grocery shopping. I hung up the phone and looked at David.

"What is it?" he asked. "You look upset."

I nodded. "She canceled." I walked over and flipped open my notebook. "I had this whole list drafted to use for tonight." I shook my head. "It took me over an hour to get this done," I moaned. David walked over and kneaded my shoulders.

"You can still go shopping," he said. "You don't have to have Justine."

"I know. I just wanted to do it together." I sounded pitiful and desperate and I knew it. What was wrong with me that I thought jumping on the trampoline was going to change everything that was wrong?

"Why? I mean, no offense, but it's grocery shopping, not a girls' night out."

"You're not supposed to get it. You're a guy."

"Are you that hard up for girl time?"

Girl time *with Justine,* I thought to myself. "Well, I do spend all my time with boys," I said. I stuck out my tongue at him.

"Hmm, do that again," he said and pulled me to him. I giggled and wrenched away.

"The boys are in the next room," I said.

"So?" he said, trying to grab me again as I darted playfully out of the way. "It's not like they're spying on us," he said.

It was David, then, who gave me the idea. And once I thought of it, I knew I couldn't let it go. I grabbed my camera, just in case it would come in handy.

———

I sat in David's car as it idled on the curb just ahead of Justine's house, nervously watching the rearview mirror for a sign of her van pulling out of her driveway. Call it woman's intuition or just a hunch, but I knew there was something up with her last-minute cancellation. At least, I hoped there was or I was going to feel really foolish coming home with no groceries and no explanation of what I had been doing while I was gone. I needed to come clean with David … and soon.

Sure enough, Justine's van backed out of her driveway on cue and she drove right past me, oblivious. I wondered if she would've even noticed if I had been in my van or if David's car had been an effective decoy. She was in her own world talking to someone on her cell phone as she zoomed past. I put the car in drive and followed her, feeling like a girl detective. I smiled to myself with the excitement of doing something so daring. I had no idea where she was headed; I just knew she wasn't with me like she was supposed to be. The thought seized me that she was going grocery shopping without me, and I wondered what I would do upon learning that. Would I finally let go of this friendship?

I used the tactics I had seen in all of the detective movies David dragged me to through the years. I stayed a few cars back and didn't make any sudden movements. From what I could see, she wasn't paying attention anyway. She was talking the whole time on her cell phone. I looked at the clock as we wove through traffic. I had hopes that I would still be able to get my grocery shopping done and get home without David suspecting anything.

We hadn't gone far when she turned into an apartment complex. I hung back a bit yet kept my eye on her as she steered her van into the parking lot, parked, and got out. I parked far enough away that she wouldn't see me and jumped out to follow her, taking the camera with me. I hadn't planned on following her on foot so I wasn't wearing stealth clothing. The truth was, I thought as I crept closer to the building I saw her enter, I hadn't planned on anything beyond tailing her. I hadn't thought past that one idea that seized me when David made the crack about the boys spying on us.

I tiptoed up the steps and peeked around the corner to get a glimpse of her knocking on a door. I knew who would open the door before I saw him with my own eyes. I watched through my viewfinder as he took her in his arms and kissed her. I watched her reward him with that same amazing smile, my camera clicking away, recording it all. And then they disappeared into the apartment and closed the door, leaving me sitting motionless on the staircase, trying to absorb the truth I'd been ignoring. I wished hopelessly that she had just gone grocery shopping without me.

I didn't know how long I had sat on the stairs. A man walked past me and mumbled something, knocking me out of my daze. I looked up to ask him what he'd said, but he'd already gone into his apartment. I knew I needed to get out of there. What if Justine and Tom came out of his apartment? Of course, where would they go that they wouldn't run the risk of being seen? They were trapped in that apartment with nowhere else to go. Was it worth it, I wondered? Did the joy of finally being together after all these years live up to the sneaking around they had to do?

Images of them flashed in my brain: that first moment at the pool, the night of my party, how he must have hovered just offstage that night at the beach. All telling moments I had been witness to, yet had not really seen. I felt sick as I thought about what they were doing behind that closed door. When I closed my eyes, I could see him taking her in his arms and their lips meeting over and over and over. I thought about Betsy asking me if I thought he had come down to the beach that weekend. I had dismissed the idea as ludicrous. And yet, there was a familiarity in the way he touched her, a possessiveness that could only grow out of prolonged and frequent exposure. I felt nauseous as I stood and made my way back to my car.

I didn't feel like a girl detective anymore. I felt like a middle-aged woman with a secret burning her up from inside out, holding the shards of a broken friendship that never quite was. I had wanted Justine to be perfect, but she was far from it. Everything was falling apart.

I didn't have to think about where I was going. It was as if the car knew where to go even before I knew. When I pulled into Erica's drive, I wondered if I should've called first. I sat for a moment and studied the house for signs of life and hoped that intruding on her at night would be okay, forgivable. I thought about her saying that we should help our neighbors. Wasn't that what I was doing?

I heard her unlocking a series of dead bolts before the door opened, the sign of a woman who lived alone. Would Betsy install dead bolts on her front door? Had she already? When she opened the door, Erica frowned at me for a moment. She skipped the pleasantries we had relied on in the past. "You never called or returned my calls," she said accusingly. The door was only halfway open, and her body blocked my entrance.

"I'm sorry," I said, my voice shaking.

"So why are you here?" she asked.

"Because now I know the truth," I said. "And if you let me in, I'll tell you the whole truth about Justine."

She opened the door wide and held out her hand to indicate I was welcome to walk in. I swallowed and entered her house. "You might as well come in," she said. "Because you don't know the whole truth about Justine."

"Do you remember that time she asked you to go out for a girls' night?" Erica asked, crossing her legs underneath her and leaning forward. "I saw you out by the entrance?"

"How'd you know about that?"

She lowered her eyes. "I just do."

"Yeah, I couldn't go," I said.

"She knew you wouldn't be able to, knew David was out of town," she said. "It was a cover with Mark. She still told him she was going out with you. It was the first night she and Tom saw each other. She's been using you as a cover to see him—that night, the weekend you went away, tonight. He always thinks you're with her."

"How do you know that?"

"Because she's done it before." She paused, leaned back against the chair. "With my husband."

"But your husband was her pastor!" I said.

She shook her head. "Justine wasn't even the only one. She was just the one who hurt the most, because I used to think we were friends."

"So that's why you don't like her," I said.

"It's more like that's why she doesn't like me. She knows I know the truth about her. She wanted me to just pack up and leave the neighborhood. I think she's always afraid I'm going to spread rumors about her. Instead I just let her do that to me."

"You knew that she talked about you like that?"

"Of course. You become the neighborhood pariah, you put two and two together." She shrugged. "But it was good for me."

"Good for you?"

"It taught me to let go, to stop trying so hard. In an odd way, Justine gave me the freedom to just be myself."

I thought about how different Erica was. How refreshing my conversations with her had always been. "So? Did it get this far with your husband?"

"No, he confessed before it became a full-blown affair. It was just flirtation, innuendo, a few looks that lingered too long. The guilt got to him. He resigned from his position as head pastor, and some guy at the church got him a good job. He went away quietly. I've tried to make sure Heather knows nothing, though lately I've suspected she knows more than she admits. As far as she knows—really as far as anyone knows—her dad stopped being a pastor because we got divorced. I've let her stay involved at the church … but I haven't gone back."

I thought about the whispering that went on about Erica behind her back, how the other women were afraid that divorce was catching, that she would steal their husbands, when the biggest predator of all was their own leader. "That's why you're helping Betsy so much," I said.

"I'm trying to collect real evidence Betsy can use when she goes to a lawyer." She paused and surveyed the room we were in, a living room I doubted she ever used. "My ex gave me whatever I wanted so I'd keep my mouth shut. Justine wanted him to protect her at all costs, and he was so entranced by her that he did. He thought he'd have to ply me with financial promises, but the truth is, I wasn't going to say anything for Heather's sake." She smiled with a glint in her eye. "But he didn't know that."

"I've got the proof you're looking for," I blurted out. "I took pictures of them just now."

"You did?" Erica asked. "Why?"

"I had a feeling. I always have. I just took awhile admitting it to myself. I didn't want to believe someone so … perfect … could do what she was doing. I guess I knew after the beach trip. I just thought that there was always time for second chances. For God to work," I offered.

"The thing about God is He doesn't force His way in. He works on people who are open to what He can do in their lives. Justine isn't, and she hasn't been for a long time."

"But she's a Christian. I saw the Scripture plaques in her house. And that display of crosses she has on her mantel. I saw the way the women at the mothers' group look up to her. I saw how she—"

"Acted," she said. "I'll give you that. She's a great actress. But this has been a long time coming. When Tom moved in, it was the straw that broke the camel's back, to use a cliché." She smiled at me with just the corners of her mouth turned up. "I think she's been really unhappy with Mark for a very long time, maybe always."

"But Mark's such a nice guy, and he clearly loves her so much. And she seems to love him. I can't understand her being unhappy. It just doesn't make sense. None of this does. Why would she throw all of this away?"

"The thing I've learned is marriage is a complicated thing that only the two people in it are really aware of. Those of us on the outside can think we know, but we just don't." She laughed and stood up. "You probably would've thought my husband was a nice guy too. You might've even been one of those people who believed he was a great guy and I destroyed the marriage for nothing." She walked into the kitchen, and I followed her even though she had not asked me to. I watched as she filled a glass of water for each of us. I took mine gratefully and drained nearly the whole thing.

"I wouldn't, you know," I said. "Have taken his side. Or thought bad about you."

Erica tipped her glass to me. "Ariel, no offense, but you already did."

"But I—" I protested.

She drank from her own glass and smiled at me over the rim. "I forgive you," she said and winked. "Just don't do it again."

"I won't," I said. And then, because it felt right, I clinked my glass with hers, even though mine was nearly empty. I knew that didn't matter to her.

CHAPTER 35

Ariel

When I got home, David was asleep in our bed, still holding the book he had been reading. As I attempted to pull it from his hands, he woke up and looked at me, confused.

"Shhh," I soothed him, "I just got home. Go back to sleep."

He sat up and squinted at me as I turned on my bedside lamp. "Where were you?" he asked. There was no accusation in his tone, I noticed, just concern.

"I stopped off at Erica's after—" After what? After I followed our neighbor—my friend—to her lover's apartment? How did I explain where I'd been? I sat down beside him on the bed facing him. "Do you really want to hear this?"

He nodded, his eyebrows still knitted together.

I took a deep breath. "Are you sure? I mean, we could talk about it in the morning. It's late," I offered.

"In the morning I leave for Tampa," he reminded me. I nodded.

I would love to go to Florida, I thought. To flee all of this and hang out on the beach.

"Okay, so I'll tell you now," I said. "I mean, if you're sure—"

"Just tell me already," he said, smiling.

I paused, frowning at the order of the words, searching for a way to tell what I'd become so used to withholding. "Do you remember Tom Dean? The new neighbor we met at the pool at the summer-kickoff party?"

He nodded.

"Well, it turns out he's Justine's long lost love from when they were kids." I raised my eyebrows as if to say, "What are the odds?" "So she and I went on that weekend together, right?"

He nodded again, his eyes still sleepy.

"And there was something I didn't tell you. Because she asked me not to and—well—I didn't. But now I need to tell you. That night we went to a club and danced. It was this cheesy salsa-dancing club, and even now I'm not sure why we went. Remember I texted you from there?" He nodded, still blinking away the sleep from his eyes.

"She was acting so weird the whole time. I wrote it off as just a reaction to Mark losing his job and her being stressed about it. She told me on the way home that she was going to have to go back to work. I could tell it wasn't what she wanted, so I knew she was upset and maybe just a little bit mad at Mark for putting her into that position. So I totally sympathized with her feelings, you know?"

"So you kept a secret from me for her?"

I nodded and dropped my eyes. "I'm sorry. It felt wrong and I knew I shouldn't. I wanted to tell you the whole thing as soon as I got home."

"I would never keep a secret from you for anyone," he said, looking wounded.

"I know. Please forgive me."

"Finish your story," he said.

"Well, so what happened was we were at this club and it was really hot and crowded and just cheesy. I wanted to get some fresh air and this guy bought me a drink and I sat with him outside and drank it." Was it really as innocent as I was describing? I looked him in the eyes. "And I shouldn't have done that, but I promise it really was harmless." I thought of the look Brian gave me as I rode away in the cab. Was it really harmless?

"Are you still in touch with him?" he asked.

"No. I promise, it was nothing like that." I thought of his card tucked into the money but left that part out.

His hand found mine in the bed, and he squeezed it. "Please don't ever do something like that again."

"I won't," I said. "It made me feel terrible. Icky. I don't belong in that world."

He smiled. "Good."

I smiled back and scooted closer to him. "So while I was out there on the patio, Justine comes and finds me and says that she's leaving with some people from the club to go on to another club. And then she just left me." I paused, wondering if I should tell him about Brian paying my cab fare home. I decided to tell the truth. "So when I realized I didn't have enough cash to get a cab home, the guy paid for it."

"And he definitely wasn't in that cab with you?" David asked, his voice sounding anxious, even doubtful. My heart began to pound with the implication. I realized what it was I had done as I sat there with Brian that night. I had flirted with temptation, daring it to rub off on me, rationalizing that it wouldn't leave a permanent stain—a Crayola to a Sharpie. Was I any different from Justine? What if David had just lost his job and I was scared about our future? What if Brian had been someone I used to love ... someone I always wondered about? Would I have let him get in that cab with me?

"No," I said in answer to David's question, but also to my own. I thought of the flicker of wanting I felt in that moment before the cab pulled away from the curb. I saw Justine fall into Tom's arms in the hallway all over again. I pushed aside the images that filled my mind and focused on David, continuing with the story.

"I left and went back to the condo totally alone. But Justine didn't come in till dawn. And she begged me not to tell anyone. So I didn't. Until tonight. When she canceled on me tonight, I decided to follow her." I traced my finger around the pattern on our bedspread and tried to corral my erratic thoughts. "I couldn't have even told you why exactly I was following her, except that some part of me just knew. I guess I had to see it with my own eyes or I would've never believed it." I looked at him. "I found out that Tom left his wife. And there's suspicion that he and Justine are having an affair. That he was there in Myrtle Beach that night."

"So you followed her to see if she'd go to him?" David asked.

"Actually I told myself I was following her to see if she went grocery shopping without me. I've still tried to make all of this be about our friendship, about why she and I couldn't quite get it right no matter how hard I tried to be a good friend to her."

"And what did you find out instead?"

I shook my head and looked at him. A tear rolled unbidden down my cheek. "That she's not thinking about me at all. I've just been a means to an end, an opportunity to enable her to do what she wanted. Our friendship, it turns out, never really existed. She was just using me." I hadn't realized any of that until I said it aloud to David. But as the words left my mouth, I knew they were true.

He pulled me to him, stroking my hair. A single tear slipped from my eye and hit his T-shirt, leaving a small wet circle as proof of its existence. "So tonight I followed her to his apartment and watched as she kissed him in the hallway and went inside. Then I sat there for a really long time and figured out what to do next."

My voice was muffled from talking into his T-shirt. I sat up. "So I went to Erica's—she's a neighbor of Tom and Betsy's and she's been helping Betsy. And I told her everything so she could help me figure out what to do."

"And what did she tell you to do?"

"To come home and tell you, which I'm doing. And to tell Betsy. She doesn't want to be the one to tell her since she didn't see it for herself. She said it would be better coming from me." I flopped down beside him on my pillow and stared at the ceiling. "So now I'm faced with a dilemma."

"Why?" he asked.

"Why what?"

"Why is it a dilemma?"

I raised up on my elbow and turned to face him. "Because I am betraying Justine. And it feels like I'm giving up on her. I know that once I do this, everything's going to move very quickly. And I just wish it wasn't up to me to blow the whistle."

"What would you want Betsy to do if she knew something like that about me?"

"Well, I would want to know, of course. I mean, I guess I would. Does any wife want to know something like that about her husband?"

"You said she already knows, she just needs proof. You can give her what she needs. Like it or not, you need to do the right thing and tell her what you know."

"But I wouldn't know if I hadn't followed her. And I still don't know the extent of what happened at the beach."

"What's your gut telling you?"

I stuck out my tongue at him. "That something happened between them. And it wasn't good." I rested my head on my arm.

"Look, I know you liked the idea of being Justine's friend. She challenged you to be a certain kind of person—someone you believed you should be. And I know you wish that nothing would've changed. But the reality is, something did." He cupped my chin with his hand, lifting my eyes to meet his. "You can do what's right. Don't be afraid of that."

He yawned and slid down on the bed, closing his eyes. "I've got to get some sleep. Early morning tomorrow." He reached over and patted my head like a child. "I have faith in you, Ariel. You've just got to have faith in yourself. I think that's what this is all about. I think that's what you need to learn. You've got a lot in here," he said, pointing at my heart. "Trust that."

I lay silently beside him, letting his words sink in. Within minutes, he was snoring. I envied his ability to slip into unconsciousness so easily. My mind raced and my eyes darted around the room. I clicked the bedside lamp off and slipped from the bed, padding out into the hall to check on the boys. One by one I kissed their sleeping faces, studying the curves of their dark, glossy eyelashes, the traces of babyhood still left in their chubby cheeks, their pursed lips, a sign they were just as intense in their dreams as they were in daily life.

I lingered in the dark, the soft light from the hall making them seem ethereal, angelic. I hardly ever paused long enough to see them this way—too intent on getting them to sleep so I could have my own time. That night I didn't want any more of my own time; I wanted more of theirs. In their world there was no adultery, no betrayal. I wished all that awaited me when I woke up was cereal and cartoons and wringing the last few drops of summer out of the day. I returned to my room thinking of what awaited me instead—a phone call I didn't want to make but had to. I fell asleep praying for the strength to do what was right and for God to guard me from situations that could land me in the same situation Justine had gotten herself into. I was learning we all need protection from ourselves.

Justine was at my door at seven a.m., looking chipper and ready for a walk as though nothing had happened, as though we still walked all the time and the gap between us didn't exist, as though I had not stood and watched her kiss Tom just the night before and the proof wasn't in my camera. I wanted to close the door in her face, tell her I was just too tired to keep up this charade and to please find someone else to confuse. Instead I forced myself to return her smile and let her into my kitchen just the same as I had all summer long. "I thought we could walk," she said, a little too falsely.

I picked up my coffee and took a sip, staring at her. "I'm not really in the mood to walk," I told her. I prayed silently, asking God to help me stand up to the woman whose approval I used to want more than anyone's—even His.

"Oh, okay," she said, her voice lowered. "Is everything okay?" she asked.

I shook my head, surprising myself that this was coming out the way it was. I had intended to tell Betsy, not Justine. "I know," I said. "About Tom. And you."

She waved her hand, dismissing my admission. "You're just listening to gossip," she said. "People's minds are running away with them. Just because Tom and I were involved once doesn't mean we're involved again. He's helping me get a job, that's all. My husband lost his job, and I have to do what I can. I've poured out my heart to you." Her eyes were wide, and there was no trace of the smile I was used to.

"I followed you last night," I blurted out. "I saw you. I saw him. I—I had to see for myself."

"What?" she shrieked.

The boys came running into the room, alarm on their faces. "It's okay, boys," I said. "You can go back to watching cartoons." I shooed them out and turned back to Justine. "I thought," I said, sounding pitiful, "that you were going grocery shopping without me. I thought that you just didn't want to be with me. I was worried about our friendship, which just seems so stupid now, considering."

She snorted. "What friendship? If you don't trust me any more than that, then what good is our *supposed* friendship?"

"Look, I've known something was up for a while now—since before that weekend at the beach. So when you canceled last night, I just had to know if you were lying to me. I knew you were lying; I was just wrong about what." I raised my eyebrows at her.

Her lower lip trembled, and she looked at me as tears filled her eyes. "So what do you want?" she asked.

"Want?" I laughed. "Want? I want a friend, a good neighbor. I want to borrow sugar from you and learn about organization and trade recipes and talk over the back fence. But that's not what I get. So now I just want honesty. I want you to be honest with Mark, and with Betsy. I want to move past this and get on with my life, and I want you to figure out what it is you want. Because apparently you don't know."

Tears ran down her face, and she didn't even bother to wipe them off. They hit the kitchen floor like little drops of rain. "I do know what I want," she said. "That's where you're wrong." She sniffed and walked over to my paper-towel dispenser, helping herself to one.

She dabbed at her eyes. "I want Tom," she said. She closed her eyes and sighed. "I don't think I've ever said that out loud. To anyone."

I shook my head. "Tom's not your husband," I said. "You've got kids. You've got a life. You made vows."

She wadded the paper towel up and glared at me. "Don't tell me about vows. Don't tell me what I should do. You in your picture-perfect world. 'Teach me how to organize. Teach me how to bake bread. Teach me how to plan meals.' As if that will make you happier, better. News flash: It doesn't." She snorted. "I'm living proof. I ran around making my life perfect, and I was still miserable. Tom happened to me for a reason. I realized I've been waiting for him all my life."

I ignored her romantic babblings. "Justine, I hope you'll do the right thing. You still have time before things go any further to do the right thing. It might take some work, but you and Mark could work through this. Mark loves you; he'll—"

"You don't know the first thing about Mark's feelings. You don't know the first thing about what goes on in our marriage, behind closed doors. You have no idea how miserable I was. For years." She pressed the damp piece of paper towel to her eyes. She looked at me, tears welling. "Maybe I did have perfection—at least your version of it. But I always wanted more than what I had." She shrugged, looked around. "I think we all have a little bit of Eve in us. She had perfection and everything she could ever want and still she reached for more."

"But I believe any marriage can be repaired," I said quietly. "Even yours. Even now."

She shook her head sadly. "I'm afraid it's already gone too far. Tom's left Betsy."

"I know," I said. I watched as shock registered on her face. "But you're still living with Mark. You could put the brakes on, work on your marriage—"

"You're living in a dream world, Ariel," she said. "Look, don't take me for a heartless woman. I didn't get up one day and decide to ruin my family. Yes, I was sad and things weren't good. And then one day out of the blue I look up and there's this person standing in front of me. The one person I always wondered about. And it turns out he's not happy either. You can't deny there's something to it."

"Whatever that something is, it's nothing good. I can assure you of that," I said. Tears filled my own eyes as I let myself feel the loss, not of what we had, but of what we now, certainly, would never have.

"But there's something between Tom and me that I've never felt before. Ever. With anyone. I can't deny that. I never meant for any of this to happen. And I am sorry," she said. "But I have to take this chance I've been given. A chance at real happiness."

"Real happiness is over there," I said, pointing to her house through my kitchen window, the house I had gotten used to watching day in and day out. "Real happiness is Cameron and Caroline. Real happiness is the way Mark talked about how you two met. You still have a chance at real happiness. You can't ignore that."

"Do you remember when Tom was talking at your party? About those letters we traded all those years?" she asked.

I nodded.

"Did you know I've still got every single one he ever sent me? I've kept them all these years. I would get them out and reminisce, wonder what would've happened if he had come to visit like we planned. I had just reread them two weeks before he showed up at the pool. It felt like a miracle, like I had conjured him up. I couldn't even believe it was really happening. The next day I felt like I had dreamed it." She paused, looking in the direction of her house, yet not really seeing it. "I am not willing to let that dream go. Not yet. For once I am doing something for me. Just me."

She moved toward the door and placed her hand on the knob. "I don't expect you to understand."

"I don't," I said. "I really don't. You're sacrificing too much. And you don't have to."

"Like I said, it's gone too far now." She smiled the same sad smile. "All I can do is ride this out and hope the dust settles soon."

"I feel sorry for you," I said. "You're going to miss it. All of it. Everything you've worked to build, gone. And for what?" I waited for her to give an answer, picking at a hangnail, the pain of pulling on it distracting me from the answer she wasn't giving me. She wouldn't look at me. "I can't keep quiet about what I know," I finally said. "So either you tell them or I will."

She raised her eyes to glare at me. "You do what you have to," she said, the chill in her voice unmistakable. "Good-bye, Ariel." I stood for a long time, just staring at the door even though she was gone.

That afternoon I took a glass of lemonade—made from powder, not fresh-squeezed, a small act of rebellion toward Justine—out to the deck and sat with a magazine on my lap while the boys played. I did a good job of looking busy and occupied even though I never read a single article. Every so often I would look up to applaud something the boys did, but otherwise my mind was focused solely on Justine and our conversation. I thought of her sitting with those letters, allowing herself to dwell on Tom even as she appeared to be happily married to Mark. Did the thoughts she was having cause the problems in her marriage? Which came first, the thoughts or the problems? Round and round the two went in my head as I tried to make sense out of what she had said, to rectify the two Justines in my head—the one I spoke to hours earlier, and the one I thought I knew.

I glanced around the yard, making a note in my head to remind David to treat the yard for weeds as fall approached. I was hypersensitive about weeds after a perfectly innocuous purple flower had sprouted up in our old yard years ago. The next week there were even more purple flowers. The boys had brought me a few, clutched in their chubby fists, proud of their gift. I dutifully put them in water, exclaiming over their beauty. Very quickly the pretty purple flowers choked out the grass and took over our yard. David and I got a crash course in weeds that can take over a yard, and I became hypervigilant about treating for weeds before they became a problem. One harmless purple flower became a force to be reckoned with—out of control before we realized the harm that lurked just under the surface. I couldn't remember the name of the weed, but what did it really matter? A weed was a weed, meant to be plucked up by the roots and destroyed before it was too late.

I walked into the house and retrieved my notebook from its home on the built-in desk. I scribbled down a note to myself about treating for weeds. Idly I flipped beyond my to-do section, unaware of what I was looking for except a connection to the Justine I once knew, a clue as to how I could stop what was happening. I flipped past the recipes for homemade cleaning products and lists of menus, my eye falling on the notes I took that first day at the mothers' group meeting. I read through what she had said as if deciphering a code. In the middle of my notes was the comment I had written in frustration: "She makes it look easy." I stared at the words, thinking of how false they were, how wrong I was. I was swindled by her, taken in by the act she had put on for us all. Was everyone, or was I especially vulnerable because I wanted to believe that perfection was obtainable? That if I just did x, y, and z I would get the hoped-for outcome?

The words swam in front of me as my eyes lost focus. I blinked and looked again. "She makes it look easy" spelled SMILE. I looked away from the page, in the direction of her house, as I recalled that first day we met, how her smile had captivated me, drawn me in. She had made me believe that her smile was real, that I could trust her to be as brilliant and warm as her smile told me she was. She covered everything with that smile, yet nothing about her was real. I had emulated a mirage, cobbled together a friendship out of bits of kindness and scraps of goodwill. It was time to let the mirage go. I closed the notebook and rose from my seat, my mouth set in a determined line. I had a phone call to make. It was long past time.

CHAPTER 36

Ariel

Betsy answered the phone on the first ring. "Yes?" she asked, her voice breathy and low. She sounded uncertain, as if taking my call was a bad idea.

"Hey," I said. "It's Ariel."

"I know who it is," she said. "Caller ID."

"Right," I said. "I just—I—"

"Ariel, do you have something to tell me?" she asked, impatience edging her voice.

"Yes, did Erica talk to you?"

"She just said you might have some new information."

"Yeah … I do." I looked outside at the boys to make sure they were staying off the playset. I didn't need a run-in with any of the Millers right now. I sighed. I had to tell her, yet I didn't want to. Would any woman want to hear what I was about to say? "I followed Justine last night," I blurted out, going for the quick and painless method, like ripping off a Band-Aid.

"I see," she said, though I knew she did not. How could she see? I knew and I still couldn't.

"She went to Tom's new apartment. I—" I hedged on how much information to supply her with but plowed forward with the truth. "I saw them kiss in the hall before they went inside."

She was very quiet, but I could still hear her breathing.

"There's more," I said. "Do you want to hear it?"

"Yes," she said. Though she didn't sound like she wanted to hear it.

I swallowed and took a deep breath. "Do you remember when you called me about the beach weekend, and I told you that I didn't think anything went on?"

"Mmm-hmm," she said.

"Well, I've sort of rethought that since then. There was a night when she went out without me." I watched as the boys went through the gate and joined Cameron and Caroline on the playset just like any other day. "I have no idea where she went, and she didn't come home till dawn." I sat silently, wondering if she was even still on the line. "Are you there?" I asked with caution.

"I'm sorry," she said. "I'm just trying to understand all of this."

"Me, too," I said.

"Ariel, forgive me for saying this," she said, "but you're trying to understand a friendship not working out. I'm trying to understand a marriage not working out. It's two different things."

I stood there, stung by her words. And yet, she was right. "I'm sorry," I said. "I didn't want to tell you any of this, but I tried to put myself in your place and I figured I would want to know, I mean, as hard as it is."

"I really hope you're never in my place." She sighed. "I wouldn't wish this on my worst enemy."

I said good-bye and sat down heavily, switching on my computer with a resolute sigh. I watched as the photos I had downloaded came up in little thumbnails across my screen. The photos started out so innocently: Justine and me on our beach trip mugging for the camera, floating on rafts, trying on dresses. I wanted the photos to end there, for that to be the end of the story. I remembered at the time I thought it was just the beginning of ours. Mechanically I transferred the incriminating photos to a file. I looked at the photos of Justine and me together one last time before I dragged them all to the recycle bin. There was no point in saving them now.

CHAPTER 37

~~~

Justine

I walked through the house, saying my quiet good-byes, doing my best to block the memories that lurked in every nook and cranny. Here was the place I used to sit Caroline in her high chair to have her snack. Here was the perfect spot for our Christmas tree, which we always decorated together. Here was where I stepped on the piece of glass I had to have removed from my foot. Mark called me Hopalong as I limped around afterward. He offered to carry me up the stairs if I needed him to. Here was the piece of string I stretched across the wall to serve as an art gallery for all the girls' school creations, a place that always looked sunny and happy in our house with all their cheerful drawings lined up. Would Mark remember to hang their pictures without me here to do it? What would happen to their crayoned drawings of this house with the four of us out front smiling? Would those stop altogether? Would they draw only three people now?

I sat down at my place at the kitchen table for the last time, my arms hanging uselessly by my side. Tom was waiting for me at his apartment. He wanted to take me out to dinner to celebrate finally being together. But how did you celebrate something like this? From the beginning there had been no happy answer, no workable solution. No matter how I approached it, someone's heart was going to be broken: mine, Mark's, Tom's, Betsy's, all of our children's. Something had pulled us along until we were caught up in it and too far gone to get back to where we had started. As of today my children were without a mother in the home. As of today Mark was losing a wife. As of today Betsy would know for sure that Tom wasn't just renting that apartment to sort things out like he had told her. With me living there, there would be no question as to our intentions. As soon as we could, we would be married.

And I would finally have what I wanted. Only wanting it and having it turned out to be two very different things.

I rose from the table and picked up the last bag. My parents had taken the girls so they didn't have to see me pack and leave. I could tell by my mother's steadfast refusal to look directly at me that she was angry with me. And yet she hadn't said so yet. Later, when the dust had settled, I would hear from her. In the meantime, I could pretend I had her support.

I gave the house one last glance, thinking of how—just one year ago—I believed I was as happy as I could be. For just a moment I let myself picture the way things were. Laura was sitting beside me at the table sipping coffee that was light on coffee and heavy on flavored creamer, just the way she liked it. She had Mopsy on her lap. The girls were in the den playing, the happy music from their toys providing the soundtrack to our days. When I looked over and smiled, they smiled back. Dinner was in the oven, and soon Mark would be home. Then, I had lived completely in the moment, rarely letting myself think about what I didn't have, focusing instead on what I did. It was, in hindsight, a good way to live, a way I could never get back to. The gap between then and now had become too wide to cross. So I stood at a distance and watched.

CHAPTER 38

⌣

Ariel

I walked across the neighborhood park, my purse swinging from my shoulder. Normally I came with the boys so they could swing. From my perch on the bench I would watch them point their toes to the sky as they swung higher and higher, then jumped, my heart hurtling down toward the ground with them, suspended until the moment I knew they were okay. The entire journey of parenthood captured in a single moment.

I saw a figure on the bench and waved. She lifted her hand in response. "Glad you could meet me," Betsy said.

I sat down beside her and handed her the photos, already printed off per her request, and a Zip drive with the files on it. "Erica said you wanted these." I felt like we were playing parts in a spy movie, or at least an episode of *Desperate Housewives*. She took the pictures and, without looking at them, shoved them in a tote bag at her feet. The bag, I noticed, read "A happy family is but an earlier heaven." My heart clenched.

"How are you not falling apart?" I asked. "I mean, you're dressed, you're here." I stole a glance at her. "You're wearing makeup." We both kept our eyes trained on the empty swings. "I'd be in a fetal position on the floor somewhere," I added.

She didn't speak for a bit. I waited to hear what she would say. "He's done this before. I guess you didn't know that."

"What?" I tried to find a place in my reality to put this latest revelation but couldn't. It seemed nothing about Tom or Justine was as simple as they wanted it to seem.

"Where we lived before. It was one of the reasons we left. We stayed for about a year after, but ... well, the gossip, the damage. It was done."

"Was it someone he knew before? Like this?"

She shook her head, and I stole another glance at her. She looked worn, tired. But she didn't look sad. Resolution hung on her shoulders like a cloak. "It was someone we knew at church. Tom was a deacon." She laughed bitterly. "She was on some committee with him. He said she 'touched him in a place that no one ever had.' Her marriage broke up, but I—"

A few seconds of silence passed. I watched the slight breeze move the swings, as though phantom children were on them. "I moved here with him, let him talk me into starting over, as if we could outrun the problems." She looked at me for the first time, and I noticed how pretty her eyes were, and how kind. "You can convince yourself of pretty much anything when you're trying to save your family."

I nodded. "I would've done the same," I said. "I imagine you want to believe the best about the man you love."

"You do. You also want to believe the best about yourself. You want to believe that you couldn't have been that bad a judge of character. That you could've missed the things in his soul that would lead him to do this. It's scary." A dog ran through the park, and I thought of Lucky, who never escaped anymore, and how Justine had found him the day we met. "It's actually a comfort, knowing that he's done this before. That he'll just keep doing it again and again. That she's nothing special."

I thought about the look I saw Justine and Tom give each other in the hallway of his apartment, the look that—when Betsy chose to look at the pictures—she would see for herself. I found it hard to believe that Justine was nothing special to Tom. But I said nothing.

"When all that happened with Tom before, I got to a really good place with God. I had to lean on Him to get through it. Because it happened at church, I had to really evaluate what I believed and where my belief was based—in people or in Him. I had equated church to social connections, to expectation, to this part of my life that I gave very little thought to. It was just what you did. God was something you were expected to pay lip service to if you were a good person.

"And then one day I found out that everything I'd ever held dear, that all of it was hanging by this very thin thread that could break at any minute. If I lost Tom, I could lose my home, the family I loved. Where would that leave me? Who would I be? I had to stop paying lip service to God and really go to Him daily, ask Him for the strength to get through it." She smiled without showing any teeth. "And you know what?"

I shook my head. She was tapping into every fear I'd ever had.

"It turned out He was enough. If I lose everything—which I'm getting ready to, it would seem—I will still have Him, and He will be enough. He will take care of me. He will see me through. And even more than that, He will make good come out of it. I can't see it right now, but He's been faithful in the past, and He will be again." She paused. "I just needed to tell you that because I know how sad you feel about all of this and how involved you've been. I don't want you to feel responsible or to think that you should've done something different. I want you to know that I am going to be okay. My Daddy's going to take care of me."

A tear ran down my cheek, and I reached up to wipe it away. "That must be a really good feeling," I whispered.

She put her hand over the top of mine. "God loves you very much. Let Him be enough for you. Don't be afraid of the future, and stop trying to control it. There's so much waiting for you out there. For both of us." She squeezed my hand. "I can't wait to see where we all end up. God's got it under control. That much I know. And that brings me great peace. I want you to find that same peace. I'll help you as much as I can."

"I could use some peace," I said with a sigh.

She laughed. "And hey, maybe you have a future in private investigation. Erica says the pictures are good." She rose from the bench and swung the tote bag over her shoulder. She surprised me by pulling me into a hug.

"So," I said, "Erica says you're still going to sing in the Patriotic Pageant."

She shrugged. "It's my part. Why shouldn't I?"

"You go, girl." I held up my hand, and she gave me a high five.

"Are you going to come?" she asked.

"I wouldn't miss it. I'll be the one cheering for you the loudest."

She winked at me, and I sat back down on the bench to watch her walk away. I had wanted to be friends with Justine so I could learn how to control my domain and also control my future. Then I had wanted to catch Justine so I could stop her from making an irreversible mistake. In the end, neither mattered. People did what they wanted to do and life spun out of control no matter how much I tried to rein it all in. Betsy found peace in spite of that. It was time for me to do so as well. I had to let God be enough—not David, not the boys, not my house, and not Justine. Just Him. Alone in the empty park, I whispered a prayer asking Him to be enough and to help me just let go. I pictured myself falling, falling, falling and His arms open, always waiting to catch me.

⁓

I slid into the pew next to Erica and Heather, the boys and David following behind me quietly to fill in the remaining empty seats in our row. Erica nudged me and smiled. Heather leaned across me and waved at the boys, who smiled shyly at her. As the first orchestra strains sounded, I whispered to Erica, "Was Betsy nervous about this?"

Her eyes misted over. "Nah," she said. "She knew we'd be here. Sometimes that's all it takes."

I turned my eyes to the stage to watch as the choir came out to fill the risers, flanked by a hundred children dressed in red, white, and blue. I leaned over to Erica and whispered, "I'm proud of you for coming here tonight. For being here for her."

She smiled at me. "That's what friends do," she said.

I squeezed her hand and found Betsy in the choir, looking scared but happy. She wiggled her fingers at me, and I gave her a thumbs-up. There was a pause before the choir started to sing, and I sat in expectation, waiting to celebrate our freedom.

... a little more ...

When a delightful concert comes to an end,

the orchestra might offer an encore.

When a fine meal comes to an end,

it's always nice to savor a bit of dessert.

When a great story comes to an end,

we think you may want to linger.

And so, we offer ...

AfterWords—just a little something more after you

have finished a David C Cook novel.

We invite you to stay awhile in the story.

Thanks for reading!

Turn the page for ...

- **Author Interview**
- **Discussion Questions**
- **Recipes**
- **Excerpt from *The Mailbox***

AUTHOR INTERVIEW

Q: *This is your second novel. How is it different from your first novel?*

A: *She Makes It Look Easy* is an entirely different novel from *The Mailbox,* which was light and breezy and fun—a great beach read. This novel is more serious in nature, and while it takes place in the summer and could certainly be read by the pool, the similarities pretty much end there. This novel required me to dig deeper into the writing—the craft. I couldn't rest on the unique premise or the fun "are they going to end up together?" plot. This time I had to work harder to develop the characters, to dig into their motivations and complexities. It required more of me as a writer.

Q: *What did you like about writing this novel?*

A: Though I resisted it at first, I ultimately enjoyed digging into the character of Justine, juxtaposing her and Ariel. I found that when I was writing Ariel, I couldn't wait to get back to Justine. At first she felt dangerous, but as time went on and I dug into what made her tick, I just felt sorry for her. It was good for me to get inside her head and discover my own sympathy for her. I didn't like the choices she was making, but I really did like her and want more for her—even if she ended up not choosing more for herself. I can only guess that's what God feels like when He sees us making the wrong choices.

Q: Is this novel based on a true story?

A: This novel is based on something that happened in my own community, something we watched happen right before our eyes but dismissed because we trusted the people involved. We thought they were immune, and we wanted to believe the best about them, similar to what Ariel does in the story. I never forgot the experience and wanted to revisit it through this book. Of course as with any fiction, I doctored it up a lot so what was true is now so buried under my own creation it doesn't look at all like the situation I witnessed. But some of the scenes were inspired by things I saw—and the rest was easy enough to imagine.

Also, a lot of the scenes with Ariel's boys were shared by my friends who are the mothers of all boys. They served as my creative consultants: the real Ariel and my friend Tamery. It was Ariel who told me boys will do things in packs they'd never do on their own, and that quote made it into the book. Some of the kid stories are from my real life too. You can't make some of this stuff up!

Q: Is Essex Falls based on a real neighborhood?

A: Not really. So many of those master-planned communities have sprung up in the suburbs that it was easy enough to hodgepodge the different ones I've seen and create Essex Falls. My family and I do not live in a neighborhood like Essex Falls primarily because my husband does not want to live so close to his neighbors and be so involved in each other's business, which is what you see happening in the story. However, our next-door neighbor has been known to play music on his screened-in porch, which is what inspired Silent Joe.

Q: *Have you found your stride as a writer after two novels?*

A: I have found that writing one thousand words a day is my sweet spot. If I write one thousand words every day for eighty to ninety days (about three months), I've finished a draft. Getting into the habit of consistently writing every day has been like exercising every day: My writing muscles have gotten stronger, so to speak. I try to stick to writing one thousand words a day no matter what.

Q: *What's next for you?*

A: I'd love to write more love stories like *The Mailbox,* and I have some ideas for stories along those lines. Plus, I am playing with a Christmas novel that I hope one day you'll see in print. Most of all I just intend to keep on writing.

DISCUSSION QUESTIONS

1. When Ariel moved in, she was immediately impressed with Justine. Why do you think she was?

2. At what point did you know all was not right with Justine?

3. How was Justine's life-management notebook helpful or not helpful to Ariel? Why do you think Justine loved it so much?

4. If you were in Justine's place where someone you once deeply cared for was suddenly back in your life, what would you do? Do you think the affair could have been prevented?

5. Was Ariel wrong for going out on the patio with the guy at the salsa club? Why do you think she did that?

6. What does this book teach us about women like Erica? Has it caused you to rethink someone you assumed you know all about?

7. How was Mark culpable in his marriage's unraveling? Were he and Justine in trouble before Tom came on the scene? What can we learn from this?

8. Was Justine's leaving inevitable? What was her alternative?

9. How did you feel about the ending? Would you have chosen for Justine to make things work, or do you feel it was more realistic to let things happen as they did? Have you ever known someone whose story ended differently than you would have liked for it to?

10. Ultimately what did Ariel learn about Justine? Betsy? Erica? Herself?

RECISPES

Blueberry Lemon Tea Bread

1/2 cup margarine or butter, softened

1 1/3 cups sugar (divided)

2 cups all-purpose flour

2 tsp. baking powder

1/2 tsp. salt

2 large eggs

1/2 cup milk

1 1/2 cups blueberries

1/4 cup fresh-squeezed lemon juice

Preheat oven to 350 degrees. Grease and flour 9 x 5 loaf pan.

In large bowl, with mixer at low speed, beat margarine and 1 cup of the sugar just until blended. Increase speed to medium, and beat until light and fluffy, about 5 minutes.

In medium bowl, combine flour, baking powder, and salt.

Reduce speed to low, add eggs one at a time, beating after each addition until well blended, scraping bowl with rubber spatula. Alternate adding flour mixture with milk, mixing just until blended. Gently fold in blueberries. Spoon batter into loaf pan.

Bake loaf for 1 hour and 5 minutes or until tester inserted in center comes out clean. Cool loaf pan on wire rack for 10 minutes, then remove from pan.

With skewer, prick top and sides of warm loaf in many places. In small bowl, mix lemon juice and remaining 1/3 cup sugar. With pastry brush, brush top and sides of warm loaf with lemon glaze. Cool cake on wire rack.

Justine's Marinade

1/2 cup white wine

3/4 cup olive oil

3 Tbs. soy sauce

1 Tbs. Worcestershire sauce

1 Tbs. Dijon mustard

1 tsp. honey

Sea salt

Pepper

Place all ingredients in gallon-size plastic bag and add chicken pieces. Marinate for at least 4 hours, but the longer the better. Grill.

Easy Homemade Yeast Rolls

1 pkg. dry yeast

2 cups very warm water

1/4 cup sugar

3/4 cup vegetable oil

1 egg, beaten

4 cups sifted flour

2 Tbs. baking powder

2 tsp. salt

Dissolve yeast in water. Add sugar, vegetable oil, egg, flour, baking powder, and salt to yeast. Stir together. Store in refrigerator for up to 1 week. To bake: Spoon into greased muffin tins. Bake at 425 degrees for 10 minutes.

Homemade Play Dough

1 cup flour

1/2 cup salt

3 Tbs. vegetable oil

1/3 cup water

Food coloring

Pour 1 cup flour, 1/2 cup salt, and 3 tablespoons of vegetable oil into a medium bowl and stir with a wooden spoon. Add 1/3 cup water tinted with 17 drops of desired shade of food coloring. Knead dough with hands until it feels smooth. If the dough is crumbly, add more oil; if it's sticky, add more flour. The dough can be stored in an airtight container in the refrigerator for several weeks. You can also add scented oils (peppermint, almond, etc.) to the dough.

Also from David C Cook

THE MAILBOX

—A NOVEL—

MARYBETH WHALEN

transforming lives together

THE MAILBOX
Published by David C. Cook
4050 Lee Vance View
Colorado Springs, CO 80918 U.S.A.

David C. Cook Distribution Canada
55 Woodslee Avenue, Paris, Ontario, Canada N3L 3E5

David C. Cook U.K., Kingsway Communications
Eastbourne, East Sussex BN23 6NT, England

David C. Cook and the graphic circle C logo
are registered trademarks of Cook Communications Ministries.

The Web site addresses recommended throughout this book are offered as a
resource to you. These Web sites are not intended in any way to be or imply an
endorsement on the part of David C. Cook, nor do we vouch for their content.

This story is a work of fiction. All characters and events are the product of the author's
imagination. Any resemblance to any person, living or dead, is coincidental.

All Scripture quotations are taken from the *Holy Bible, New International
Version*®. *NIV*®. Copyright © 1973, 1978, 1984 by International Bible
Society. Used by permission of Zondervan. All rights reserved.

Don Henley's "Boys of Summer," *Building the Perfect
Beast* © 1984 The David Geffen Company.

LCCN 2010923222
ISBN 978-0-7814-0369-6
eISBN 978-1-4347-0217-3

© 2010 Marybeth Whalen

The Team: Terry Behimer, Nicci Jordan Hubert,
Sarah Schultz, Jack Campbell, and Karen Athen
Cover Design: Amy Kiechlin
Front Cover Photo: iStockphoto.com
Back Cover Photo: Peter Doran, www.peterdoranphotography.com

Do you ever wonder, where did the summer go?

The Blue Nile, "Broken Loves"

The Kindred Spirit Mailbox
Sunset Beach, NC
Summer 2003

The Kindred Spirit waited from a safe distance for the man to leave the mailbox before she approached in the amber light of the late July evening. Because they knew each other, she would normally have spoken to him. But not here, lest he suspect her purpose. She watched until he drifted out of sight before she limped toward the mailbox tucked into the dunes, her knee aching dully. The doctor wanted to replace her knee but the recuperation would keep her from coming to the mailbox. There would have been no one to tend it in her absence, so she told the doctor the surgery would have to wait.

The sun had nearly set, as she removed her turtle-watcher visor and stowed it in her bag. No one saw her take out the notebooks and various pieces of loose-leaf paper, all dampened by the sea's spray and more than a few tears. She planned it this way, making the trek out to the mailbox only when she could come and go unnoticed, keeping her identity a mystery. She replaced the filled notebooks with blank ones, their pages crisp and smooth. She added a few new pens and took out the ones that had gone dry. Finally, she laid some extra loose-leaf paper on top of the new notebooks, smoothing it out with satisfaction, anticipating the words that would fill the pages by the time she returned.

She turned away from the mailbox and looked out at the sea. She breathed in the scent of the ocean, watched two seagulls chase each other in midair, then turned to walk slowly back down the beach, the weight of the notebooks she had stowed in her tote bag causing her shoulder to stoop slightly. She looked like the crazy old woman she had become, hunched over and limping, her hair askew without her visor, coming and going in secret from a rusty old mailbox that had started out as a mystery and become part of coastal folklore.

For years she had made this journey, taking her duty as keeper of the mailbox as seriously as a pastor takes his time in the pulpit. The Kindred Spirit played an important, albeit anonymous, role in their community. Every time she collected the notebooks, she remembered what the previous Kindred Spirit told her as she was dying of cancer—too weak to make the journey to the mailbox anymore—and asked her to step in. "This isn't just some forgotten mailbox on a desolate stretch of beach. This is a place where dreams are shared, tears are shed, and lives are changed." She remembered nodding soberly, grasping her responsibility to not only tend the mailbox but also to keep her own identity a secret. In her bag she carried the words of many strangers, scribbled in moments of grief or hope or joy, with the belief that the Kindred Spirit would guard their words, gathering them like pennies from a wishing well, protecting them like the treasures they were.

When she got home, she would make a pot of tea and sit down with the letters, reading through them deep into the night and praying for those who had written the words before she packed them away with the others, her own little ritual.

As she made her way home, she thought about the man she saw at the mailbox, wondering why he had been there, what story he had to tell. She had known him his whole life, yet didn't know why he came to the mailbox. That part, she suspected, was private. She knew that—like everyone who visited the mailbox—a matter of the heart had sent him there.

Chapter 1

Sunset Beach, NC
Summer 1985

Campbell held back a teasing smile as he led Lindsey across the warm sand toward the mailbox. Leaning her head on Campbell's shoulder, her steps slowed. She looked up at him, observing the mischievous curling at the corners of his mouth. "There really is no mailbox, is there?" she said, playfully offended. "If you wanted to get me alone on a deserted stretch of beach, all you had to do was ask." She elbowed him in the side.

A grin spread across his flawless face. "You caught me." He threw his hands up in the air in surrender.

"I gotta stop for a sec," Lindsey said and bent at the waist, stretching the backs of her aching legs. She stood up and put her hands on her hips, narrowing her eyes at him. "So, *have* you actually been to the mailbox? Maybe the other kids at the pier were just pulling your leg."

Campbell nodded his head. "I promise I've been there before.

It'll be worth it. You'll see." He pressed his forehead to hers and looked intently into her eyes before continuing down the beach.

"If you say so …" she said, following him. He slipped his arm around her bare tanned shoulder and squeezed it, pulling her closer to him. Lindsey looked ahead of them at the vast expanse of raw coastline. She could make out a jetty of rocks in the distance that jutted into the ocean like a finish line.

As they walked, she looked down at the pairs of footprints they left in the sand. She knew that soon the tide would wash them away, and she realized that just like those footprints, the time she had left with Campbell would soon vanish. A refrain ran through her mind: *Enjoy the time you have left.* She planned to remember every moment of this walk so she could replay it later, when she was back at home, without him. Memories would be her most precious commodity. How else would she feel him near her?

"I don't know how we're going to make this work," she said as they walked. "I mean, how are we going to stay close when we're so far away from each other?"

He pressed his lips into a line and ran a hand through his hair. "We just will," he said. He exhaled loudly, a punctuation.

"But how?" she asked, wishing she didn't sound so desperate.

He smiled. "We'll write. And we'll call. I'll pay for the long-distance bills. My parents already said I could." He paused. "And we'll count the days until next summer. Your aunt and uncle already said you could come back and stay for most of the summer. And you know your mom will let you."

"Yeah, she'll be glad to get rid of me for sure." She pushed images of home from her mind: the menthol odor of her mother's cigarettes, their closet-sized apartment with parchment walls you could hear the neighbors through, her mom's embarrassing "delicates" dangling from the shower rod in the tiny bathroom they shared. She wished that her aunt and uncle didn't have to leave the beach house after the summer was over and that she could just stay with them forever.

The beach house had become her favorite place in the world. At the beach house, she felt like a part of a real family with her aunt and uncle and cousins. This summer had been an escape from the reality of her life at home. And it had been a chance to discover true love. But tomorrow, her aunt and uncle would leave for their home and send her back to her mother.

"I don't want to leave!" she suddenly yelled into the open air, causing a few startled birds to take flight.

Campbell didn't flinch when she yelled. She bit her lip and closed her eyes as he pulled her to him and hugged her.

"Shhh," he said. "I don't want you to leave either." He cupped her chin with his hand. "If I could reverse time for you, I would. And we would go back and do this whole summer over."

She nodded and wished for the hundredth time that she could stand on the beach with Campbell forever, listening to the hypnotic sound of his voice, so much deeper and more mature than the boys at school. She thought about the pictures they had taken earlier that day, a last-ditch effort to have something of him to take with her. But it was a pitiful substitute, a cheap counterfeit for the real thing.

Campbell pointed ahead of them. "Come on," he said and tugged on her hand. "I think I see it." He grinned like a little boy. They crested the dune and there, without pomp or circumstance, just as he had promised, stood an ordinary mailbox with gold letters spelling out "Kindred Spirit."

"I told you it was here!" he said as they waded through the deep sand. "The mailbox has been here a couple of years," he said, his tone changing to something close to reverence as he laid his hand on top of it. "No one knows who started it or why, but word has traveled and now people come all the way out here to leave letters for the Kindred Spirit—the mystery person who reads them. People come from all over the world."

"So does anybody know who gets the letters?" Lindsey asked. She ran her fingers over the gold, peeling letter decals. The bottom half of the *n* and *e* were missing.

"I don't think so. But that's part of what draws people here—they come here because this place is private, special." He looked down at his bare feet, digging his toes into the sand. "So … I wanted to bring you here. So it could be our special place too." He looked over at her out of the corner of his eye. "I hope you don't think that's lame."

She put her arms around him and looked into his eyes. "Not lame at all," she said.

As he kissed her, she willed her mind to record it all: the roar of the waves and the cry of the seagulls, the powdery softness of the warm sand under her feet, the briny smell of the ocean mixed with the scent of Campbell's sun-kissed skin. Later, when she was back at home in Raleigh, North Carolina, she would come right back to this moment. Again and again. Especially when her mother sent her to her room with the paper-thin walls while she entertained her newest boyfriend.

after words

Lindsey opened the mailbox, the hinges creaking as she did. She looked to him, almost for approval. "Look inside," he invited her.

She saw some loose paper as well as spiral-bound notebooks, the kind she bought at the drugstore for school. The pages were crinkly from the sea air and water. There were pens in the mailbox too, some with their caps missing.

Campbell pointed. "You should write a letter," he said. "Take a pen and some paper and just sit down and write what you are feeling." He shrugged. "It seemed like something you would really get into."

How well he had come to know her in such a short time. "Okay," she said. "I love it." She reached inside and pulled out a purple notebook, flipping it open to read a random page. Someone had written about a wonderful family vacation spent at Sunset and the special time she had spent with her daughter.

She closed the notebook. Maybe this wasn't such a good idea. She couldn't imagine her own mother ever wanting to spend time with her, much less being so grateful about it. Reading the notebook made her feel worse, not better. She didn't need reminding about what she didn't have waiting for her back home.

Campbell moved in closer. "What is it?" he said, his body lining up perfectly with hers as he pulled her close.

She laid the notebook back inside the mailbox. "I just don't want to go home," she said. "I wish my uncle didn't have to return to his stupid job. How can I go back to … her? She doesn't want me there any more than I want to be there." This time she didn't fight the tears that had been threatening all day.

Campbell pulled her down to sit beside him in the sand and said nothing as she cried, rocking her slightly in his arms.

With her head buried in his shoulder, her words came out muffled. "You are so lucky you live here."

He nodded. "Yeah, I guess I am." He said nothing for a while. "But you have to know that this place won't be the same for me without you in it."

She looked up at him, her eyes red from crying. "So you're saying I've ruined it for you?"

He laughed, and she recorded the sound of his laugh in her memory too. "Well, if you want to put it that way, then, yes."

"Well, that just makes me feel worse!" She laid her head on his shoulder and concentrated on the nearness of him, inhaled the sea scent of his skin and the smell of earth that clung to him from working outside with his dad.

"Everywhere I go from now on I will have the memory of you with me. Of me and you together. The Island Market, the beach, the arcade, the deck on my house, the pier ..." He raised his eyebrows as he remembered the place where he first kissed her. "And now here. It will always remind me of you."

"And I am going home to a place without a trace of you in it. I don't know which is worse, constant reminders or no reminders at all." She laced her narrow fingers through his.

"So are you glad we met?" She sounded pitiful, but she had to hear his answer.

"I would still have wanted to meet you," he said. "Even though it's going to break my heart to watch you go. What we have is worth it." He kissed her, his hands reaching up to stroke her hair. She heard his words echoing in her mind: *worth it, worth it, worth it*. She knew that they were young, that they had their whole lives ahead of them, at least that's what her aunt and uncle had told her. But she also knew that what she had with Campbell was beyond age.

Campbell stood up and pulled her to her feet, attempting to keep kissing her as he did. She giggled as the pull of gravity parted them. He pointed her toward the mailbox. "Now, go write it all down for the Kindred Spirit. Write everything you feel about us and how unfair it is that we have to be apart." He squinted his eyes at her. "And I promise not to read over your shoulder."

She poked him. "You can read it if you want. I have no secrets from you."

He shook his head. "No, no. This is your deal. Your private world—just between you and the Kindred Spirit. And next year," he said, smiling down at her, "I promise to bring you back here, and you can write about the amazing summer we're going to have."

"And what about the summer after that?" she asked, teasing him.

"That summer too." He kissed her. "And the next." He kissed her again. "And the next." He kissed her again, smiling down at her through his kisses. "Get the point?

"This will be our special place," he said as they stood together in front of the mailbox.

"Always?" she asked.

"Always," he said.